The Way You Want to Be Loved

'Literature from India's Northeast—a self-sufficient region with a mélange of languages, cultures, and peoples—has remained relatively obscure to the wider world until recently. In the last two or so decades, a number of outstanding writers and translators [have dispelled] its obscure position and challeng[ed] the way Indian literature is read globally. One prominent name associated with this dynamic wave of storytelling is Aruni Kashyap . . . Tales of insurgency and violence, of myth and history, of sexuality and demography, of diasporic and local frontiers make his [Kashyap's] new collection of ten short stories simply an enthralling experience.'

—Split Lip Magazine

'One of India's rising literary voices.'

—The Florida Review

'These powerful stories shorten the distance between South Asia and America, which are, refreshingly, not positioned as opposite pulls but as companion landscapes where dream, desire, and defiance thrive. With a cast of characters who are emotionally intelligent yet still flawed, imperfect, yet still endearing, Aruni Kashyap eschews the predictable narratives and brings us unique takes on leaving home, loving family, and longing for passion. Daring and surprising, *The Way You Want to Be Loved* is the must-read of our times.'

—Rigoberto González,
author of *To the Boy Who Was Night*

'This masterful collection mixes Chekovian realism with Borgesian magic to create a new and vital literary voice for our times. With wit, intelligence, and humor, Kashyap's stories grapple with the tangled predicament of anyone who has ever felt themselves an outsider: in a new country, in the labyrinth of academia, or within one's own family. These stories range the world from the mountains of the Himalayas to the cold plains of the American Midwest, and I would happily follow Kashyap's writing anywhere.'

—NATHAN OATES,
AUTHOR OF *A FLAW IN THE DESIGN*

'An impassioned reflection on displacement, dispersal, and life in the diaspora.'

—WASAFIRI MAGAZINE

'A new voice in the burgeoning oeuvre of anglophone fiction from northeast India. Kashyap's collection of short stories continues the exploration of the impact of political violence on everyday life in the northeast Indian state of Assam that characterized *The House*, while simultaneously charting new territory.'

—WORLD LITERATURE TODAY

'In *The Way You Want to Be Loved*, Kashyap precisely embarks on a journey to undo the single-story surrounding his homeland. He makes no effort to play safe by catering to the mainland's expectations from a writer coming from India's Northeast. With the first story itself Kashyap plunges headlong into murky waters without losing sight of his goal—to narrate the tales of displaced individuals desperately negotiating home.'

—HUFFPOST

'In their very existence, Kashyap's stories are defiant, challenging the mainstream intelligentsia's authority: Why must the voice of the subaltern fit the narratives constructed by those that are not? *The Way You Want to Be Loved* is a book we did not know we needed, and for precisely that reason, a book that must be read.'

—THE HINDU BUSINESS LINE

'To open author Aruni Kashyap's book *The Way You Want to Be Loved* is to find your way into a wonderland of long short stories. . . . Watch out for this voice from a lesser-known corner of our country.'

—THE NEW INDIAN EXPRESS

'When an author writes from a restive part of India—say, Kashmir or, in the present case, Assam—readers often expect him to focus on questions of violence or identity. This can unwittingly infringe on the author's right to express himself freely and relegate his own experiences to a secondary position. In *The Way You Want to Be Loved*, Aruni Kashyap not only addresses this issue, but also challenges it through remarkable short stories, while exploring the ideas of linguistic and ethnic stereotypes and sexuality.'

—THE TELEGRAPH

'In a cool, dispassionate tone that mines intimate, sometimes incidental situations, Kashyap's stories are quietly affecting, often sparkling with valuable insight. . . . Kashyap explores love and sex, desire and myth, violence and conflict, at an easy, page-turning pace. It reminded me very much of Chimamanda Ngozi Adichie's unforgettable collection of stories, *The Thing Around Your Neck*, which drew out quietly devastating moments in the lives of Nigerian men and women, many of them living away from their homeland in America, caught in an unending abyss between two disparate worlds.'

—THE ASIAN AGE

'The stories that make up Aruni Kashyap's unflinching new collection, *The Way You Want to Be Loved*, roam between the turbulent villages of Assam and the frigid placidity of the American Midwest and explore the complexities of identity and isolation, violence and resilience amidst diverse backdrops. In these wide-ranging stories, folklore and sorcery are interlaced with spikey meditations on race and belonging. The connective tissue is found in the centering of characters who intentionally and unintentionally don't fit the norm, who push against the urge to generalise—and the urge to dismiss.'

—HELTER SKELTER

'There is this sense of "translation" throughout Kashyap's [short]-story collection. Every character is an outsider to the world around them: a homosexual man in his village in Assam, an Assamese in New Delhi, an Assamese in America, an inter-racial couple in the home of a conservative American family, and so on. The stories present characters that exist without that perfect jigsaw fit, of a world where we are always left with a sense of unfinished, of new questions to answer even after the story is long finished.'

—THE CHAKKAR: AN INDIAN ARTS REVIEW

'An intense page-turner.'

—MENSXP

'The award-winning US-based Assamese writer has delivered a collection of immersive short stories, which address themes including repression, fundamentalism, and the violation of human rights. The book also asks important questions about environment and territorial sovereignty, along with giving urgent insights into an often silenced and marginalized culture.'

—EASTERN EYE UK

'Through the short stories in *The Way You Want to Be Loved*, Kashyap points to a binding element in the midst of our differing perceptions of home. It is, as he seems to say, the necessity to be more tolerant and accepting, to lend an ear, to be kind, and to empathise, whether with yourself, your family, friends, or even a stranger. He points to how our different perceptions of home need not threaten our identity—there is no need to resort to violence to assert and establish our identity over anyone else's. For Kashyap, all our different homes can be brought together to form a happy society through kindness and acceptance. And it is through this that the wandering person finds a home in a heart.'

—THE CURIOUS READER

The Way You Want To Be Loved

The Way You Want To Be Loved

Stories

ARUNI KASHYAP

Published by Gaudy Boy LLC,
an imprint of Singapore Unbound
www.singaporeunbound.org/gaudyboy
New York

For more information on ordering books, contact jkoh@singaporeunbound.org.

ISBN: 978-1-958652-08-4
eISBN: 978-1-958652-09-1

Library of Congress Control Number: 2024934822

Cover design by Flora Chan
Interior design by Jennifer Houle

For
S. A.

CONTENTS

SKYLARK GIRL

From this distance, the students sounded like birds chirping. They looked carefree, but they had been busy earlier that day, sprinting across the campus for classes and lectures well into the evening. Often, their clothes were crumpled, and the men had weeklong stubbles. Yet, their eyes were still bright, and their young faces glistened. In the evening, a light breeze cooled the campus. Students flocked to the local dhaba or the Chinese takeaway for a quick cup of tea, a snack, a late lunch. The trees on the perimeter of the university's fifty acres were no more than six feet tall, announcing that they were planted less than a year ago, that the university was new and was trying to make its presence felt through conferences such as the one Sanjib was here to attend. Last night, when he had arrived, driven by a university-employed driver in a Toyota Innova, it was midnight, but many students were still roaming the grounds. As he took charge of his room at the guesthouse, Sanjib missed his undergraduate days. He couldn't believe that was almost fifteen years ago.

It was around eleven now. He had spent the day attending panels on Indian literature, Dalit literature, literature from Northeast India. And now he was unable to sleep. The well-lit campus provided no privacy, even at night. He found a concrete bench to sit on, right under a tall lamp. They run on solar power, the chief organiser of the conference, a middle-aged man in a black kurta, had told them during the Northeast-themed lunch— Naga and Assamese dishes. Sitting on that concrete bench, Sanjib read aloud the story he had selected for his session the next afternoon. It felt odd, but he had to read the English translation rather than his own Assamese writing. His English had a thick accent. He halted. How would he tackle questions from the audience? As an undergraduate, he had studied chemistry, but by the time he took his final-year exams, Sanjib had had enough of farty smells in labs. He decided to enrol in a master's programme in Assamese literature. It was a new lease on life: he started writing again and gathered a loyal list of readers for the poems and stories that were published on the department's wall magazine. By the end of his first year, he had not only made it to several mainstream print magazines, but was also elected as the university's magazine editor. It was the most amazing thing that had ever happened to him.

But his mother disagreed. She thought *this* was the most amazing thing to happen to him—this invitation to read at an international conference. For his mother, Delhi was very far. Delhi meant the army that 'committed atrocities' on the villagers in the nineties. Delhi was for rich people. Its universities were first class. Delhi was the stepmother who treated the people of Assam poorly. That one of those places in Delhi had recognised her son's calibre and invited him to participate in this all-expenses-paid conference was his life's greatest achievement, she felt.

To confirm his participation, he had to email them a draft of one of his stories, translated into English. He cycled six miles in search of a shop with a computer plugged to an internet connection, because even though there were nearly five major mobile phone companies competing for attention with free data and unlimited talk time, none of them worked properly in his village. At first, he requested a friend's mother, a professor at the local college, for help with the translation, but she was too scared to agree. She said that after teaching Keats and Eliot and Shakespeare for twenty-five years in Assamese to students of English honours who didn't understand English, she didn't have the confidence to translate his story into English. This was a big thing, a matter of great prestige for the town, so she would connect him with someone at the Cotton College State University, who would be happy to translate it. The four best stories from the conference would be published in an international anthology, which would be an incentive for this ambitious young colleague of hers.

Three weeks after he received the letter, Sanjib travelled to Guwahati, four hours away, with his mother's blessings. During the trip, he wondered who had nominated him for the conference. He had in mind a few possible suspects but wasn't sure he wanted to think about it. All he had been told was that nomination letters were sought from experts and editors and that several literary critics had recommended his powerful stories. And now, here he was, sitting on a concrete bench at midnight, practising to read a whole story in a language in which he had never spoken a full sentence.

//////////////////

Three weeks before Tejimola's birth, her mother, Numoli, had eaten so many ripe orange peaches and swallowed so many slippery seeds that she was reminded of her childhood fear. She had strange dreams of becoming a large-trunked tamarind, a lanky and weak papaya, a mango tree where ghosts resided. All night, she twitched on her bed. In the morning, when she told her husband, the wandering businessman Dhaniram Saud, he chided her. He said her fears were baseless. But Numoli disagreed: the dreams were from the morning, and she was facing east then, and she had woken up drenched in sweat. She gave him his cup of tea, made from the dried bark of a mature arjun tree. Aghuni, the tall and large-eyed midwife who would help with the delivery in three weeks' time, was sitting in the backyard. Later, she told Numoli there was nothing to be afraid of. It wasn't a childhood fear that was haunting her; her dreams were anticipating the unborn baby. The lush, leafy mango tree that she had transformed into in her dreams, standing all alone in a chrome-yellow harvested paddy field, signalled a healthy baby, she said.

Never before had Aghuni been wrong in her interpretation of dreams, but this time she was. Numoli died giving birth to Tejimola. While cutting the umbilical cord, Aghuni saw tiny light-green buds on Numoli, which confused and scared her so much that she removed them hurriedly. But Numoli was also bleeding and gasping for breath, and Aghuni didn't know what to do to help her. By the time she had bathed the baby, those buds had started to mature into leaves. She plucked them one by one, like plucking fine feathers off the body of a pigeon being prepared for cooking. Soon, Numoli's eyelids were covered with parrot-green peach leaves. Aghuni plucked each one. Bud by bud, leaf by leaf. She scrubbed the baby's skin with powdered lentils only after she had removed all the leaves from the mother's body. Aghuni tried hard to make Numoli look like a normal corpse. She informed Dhaniram Saud about the birth of his daughter. There was no one else in the labour room.

That night, Aghuni told Dhaniram Saud that she would like to stay until the baby girl could take care of herself and was married off to a good boy who would be able to keep her by working in the rice fields or in the newly founded tea gardens of the British, although those were swarming with workers who spoke a strange language from elsewhere. She loved the baby's dead mother like a sister, she said. Aghuni didn't speak to him of her real fears. She was worried the baby would start sprouting leaves and die, like her mother did. Though she didn't know how she'd prevent it, or how she'd save the girl, Aghuni wanted to linger.

Saud built her a small but strong hut in his backyard. Aghuni had no relatives to return to, so she accepted that hut as her own. But she used it only to keep her clothes and belongings and the ornaments her mother-in-law had given her on her deathbed. Her days were spent beside the baby's cradle and, later, her bed.

They had named the baby Tejimola, but everyone affectionately called her 'Teji'. By the time Saud married a second time, because the village elders pressed him to remarry so that the girl had a mother's caring hands around her, Aghuni had plucked different kinds of leaves off Teji's skin. She used varied pastes, such as that of black-eyed beans or fresh turmeric. She didn't want to repeat her first haphazard, methodless plucking. She thought it was the reason Numoli had died, for which she still blamed herself. As a result of Aghuni's regular ministrations, which she masked as 'skin care' so that the stepmother, Romola, wouldn't know what was going on, Tejimola had the most glowing skin in the whole village. She was dark-skinned, like mature eels and catfishes, and shone even on moonless nights or at dusk when the day and night met for a while to chat. She also had the most beautiful oval eyes, like slim fishes, with long, thick eyelashes, and only Aghuni worried that they could turn into the vines of a bottle gourd. The worry probably killed her. Two weeks before the red-necked leaf-green parrot sang to a middle-aged Saud, who was packing his bags for a trip around the world to sell his wonderful handicrafts and silk clothes, Aghuni passed away in her sleep.

The parrot sang:

When you see me, you frown,
Into a lady your daughter has grown,
When will you get her
a groom from the town?

Its shrill voice and accusatory tone reminded Saud of his second wife, Romola, who was the most quarrelsome woman in the village and treated Tejimola like a slave. He looked at the bird, sighed, and assured him that, as soon as the steamer reached the chest of the Brahmaputra river, he would begin the search for a handsome groom for his only daughter.

As was the case whenever Saud travelled, the night his boat floated towards the Bay of Bengal, Romola cooked delicious dishes for her three sons but gave Teji only leftover rice with salt, made her sleep on the floor on a bamboo mat, and forced her to do the dishes, wash clothes, and even tether the cows when they returned home, a man's job.

Tejimola was not saddened by this, for she loved the only person she could call 'Ma'. The night Saud left, a small green bud sprouted on her finger. She used sandalwood paste to remove it as soon as she could.

///////////////

Sanjib had never thought himself a handsome man. During those postgraduate days in Gauhati University, it was Riti who had made him feel that way. She had accosted him after an open-mike on campus and asked if he would share his mobile number and go out for coffee with her. When he said he didn't like coffee, she called him every day for weeks inviting him to have tea, Thums Up, Coca-Cola, Citra, cane juice, until he agreed. 'Tea,' he said. 'I will have tea with you.' During what they would later call their first date, he was surprised that someone so attractive and interesting was drawn to him. They dated for two years, and everything seemed just right. But he knew he had made a mistake when she took him home for the first time—a huge two-level building in one of the most expensive parts of the city. Their living room had an artificial stream and an aquarium that covered the length of the wall, and the tables had expensive wooden and bronze statues.

The marble floor was so clean that he felt his cheap two-hundred-rupee chappals were permanently tainting it.

Later he told her, you know there is no future to this relationship. Don't you know my father is a farmer? He doesn't even own land. Some years, he doesn't get to sharecrop because the Bangladeshi immigrants do it at cheaper rates. And your parents own one of the largest construction companies in Northeast India. Must every relationship have a future, she asked, voice quivering. He paused. They were sitting on a wooden bench in the university campus. It was April. Final exams were at least a month away. She was planning to go abroad for her doctoral studies. Or MPhil. He didn't know. She had never discussed it with him. The krishnachura tree was in full bloom, its flowers reaching towards the blue spring skies like flames feeding on a large heap of straw. He asked, what is the point then? I don't want to be anyone's 'timepass'. Later, she had texted him, he was never a timepass; what a horrible way to brand their relationship. There was meaning in it. And unlike him, she saw a future for them. He read her text. He thought about the marble floor and his tattered chappals that had been stitched and repaired by the village cobbler. He replied that she was able to see that future because she was on higher ground. He still had a lot to build. A ladder, a staircase—god knows what else—to reach her level. The marble floor and those tattered slippers. Such a mismatch.

At the conference luncheon—where the panellists were supposed to meet and bond with the moderator and plan the discussion—he felt like a misfit. The food laid on the table was colourful and looked delicious and fresh, with a lot of vegetables, but he didn't know what to pick. The labels didn't mean anything to him: paella, tortillas, fajitas, quesadilla, guacamole. For a second, he wanted to fish out his phone to Google those words, but he was shy. They had said lunch was going to be Mexican, and he was looking forward to it, but he didn't know the names would be in Spanish, too.

He filled his plate with rice, beans, and vegetables, though he knew it was not quite right—something should be mixed with something, and he was doing it all wrong. Embarrassed, he sat in one corner. The rest of the panellists joined him after reading his nametag. Their hellos were cheerful enough, but he was relieved to meet John, the Naga writer. John knew Nagamese, and Sanjib spoke it fluently. Sanjib hoped he could be friends with John and hang around him. For a moment, he forgot his regret at having accepted the invitation. What would happen if his story was accepted in some journal that he had never seen? He didn't know. He was a school-teacher who didn't even get his salary regularly.

He felt he was back in Riti's house—a large aquarium, marble floors, his tattered slippers. The moderator was a tall, well-built Punjabi man who introduced himself as an editor. He said his publishing house took a lot of pride in publishing writers from the Northeast. Most of the writers present there, the Arunachali man, the Mizo woman, the Khasi girl, and the Nepali writer from Sikkim, seemed to know the editor already. They laughed like long-time friends and occasionally referred to other writing conferences they had been to together. Sanjib realised he was the only one among them who didn't write in English. He felt like he shouldn't be there; like that classmate who came to school with long nails and smelly clothes and got bullied by everyone. So, he tried to focus on his food instead. The rice was lime flavoured. The vegetables were crunchy. The green paste was amazing.

The editor said they must show the world what a real Northeastern story was. I am like a crusader for stories from the Northeast, he told Sanjib. So nice to meet you, young man. I am really looking forward to your reading and finally finding out what you have written. Sanjib thanked him but was also surprised that the editor hadn't read his story yet. He would be the one nominating stories for the international anthology, John had said.

What's his name, Sanjib asked.

John was surprised. He raised his voice, 'Toi na jani?'

Sanjib said he didn't. Impress him, John whispered, stabbing a piece of chicken with his fork. If you impress him, you may even get a book contract.

I see, Sanjib responded, and thought about his mother. How proud she would be.

///////////////

Tejimola was surprised at her stepmother's generosity. She had asked for a good cotton dress from her dead mother's shelf to wear to her best friend's wedding. Instead, Romola brought out an expensive golden muga-silk dress from Sualkuchi. Tejimola hesitated. But Romola smiled warmly and said, 'Ah, you don't have to wear those old designs. And you should start wearing a full-sleeved jakit-blouse, too. That is one convenient thing the British people brought with them—instead of wrapping the reeha, now you can wear a blouse under your dress. Here, I have a matching blouse.'

Tejimola hesitated still. 'Ma, are you sure?'

'Ah, I am growing old, my dear Teji! If the grown-up girl of the house doesn't wear my clothes, who will? Haven't you seen your brothers? God knows what kind of women they will bring home when they grow up. If this old lady gets a corner to rest in and two meals a day after they bring home women to share their beds, I will consider it enough. But then, who would wear my beautiful clothes? You must deck up for your best friend's wedding. Will you be able to go alone?'

'Yes, I can go alone.' She looked at the mekhela-sador hesitantly and added, 'It is a beautiful set.'

But Romola had plans. Sinister plans. While packing the dress in a jute satchel, she had placed a smouldering wood and a small brown-skinned rat in the folds.

The path to Tejimola's best friend's house was windy. It was the month of Phagun, and blood-red silk cotton flowers spread a carpet on the road. The long, slim petals looked like a sex worker's nails. Teji felt something moving in her jute satchel. She wanted to open it and check. But she was scared because her stepmother had warned her not to look inside before reaching the wedding. Romola had said that the clothes would become dirty because it was so windy and dusty. Teji knew her anger. She had been overwhelmed at the sudden display of love and didn't want to disappoint her. She walked faster, resolving to check what was wrong only after reaching her friend's place, where she would take a bath and change. She didn't see the occasional wisps of smoke coming from the jute satchel because she had tucked it between her arms and pressed it to her body.

When she finally unwrapped the dress, Teji was horrified at seeing it partially burnt and rat-chewed. She sat in a corner of the changing room and wept. Her stepmother would kill her. The dress was a wedding gift from an old aunt.

Sokhi, her best friend, tried to console her. 'Come on, Teji, you are not responsible for this.'

'But how do I explain it, Sokhi?'

'You don't have to explain anything—just tell her the truth.'

Someone called out to Sokhi from the other room. It was time she bathed. The smell of flowers and different kinds of lentil paste that would be applied on her body during the ritual bath dispersed the sullenness of the room. Sokhi opened a wooden box and took out a new pat-silk set that she had received as a gift and gave it to Tejimola. But Teji couldn't enjoy the wedding. A fear pulled at the tender strings of her heart like the sorrowful tone of a buffalo-horn aerophone.

She was sad. The teller of wonderful stories, her best friend, with whom she had shared the news of her first period and first loves, was going away. She wondered when they would meet again and hoped to marry someone who lived in her best friend's new village. But the fears didn't subside; like monsoon rivers, they overflowed, since she did not have answers for the burnt silk dress. When the women sang the parting song, and Sokhi went to hug each person she was close to, Teji couldn't stop crying.

> *O Lucky Daughter of the house!*
> *With betel nuts in your hands,*
> *Go say goodbye to your mother.*

> *With silk clothes in your hands,*
> *Go touch the feet of your father.*
> *With worn-out toys in your hands,*
> *Go kiss the forehead of your little brother.*
> *With gold ornaments in your hands,*
> *Go clasp the palms of your elder brother.*

> *With mischief twinkling in your eyes,*
> *Go hug your closest girlfriends,*
> *Whom you will never meet again—*
> *Remember: a girl's life is just a*
> *String of ephemeral images*
> *Formed by meeting nimbus clouds.*

> *Before leaving the courtyard of this house,*
> *At least turn back once, if you*
> *Don't want the pots and pans of this house*
> *To follow you down the dusty road.*

> *O Lucky Daughter of the house!*
> *O Lucky Daughter of the house!*

Teji's stepmother didn't believe her. She caught hold of Teji by her long, silky hair and slapped her. As punishment, she put the girl to grinding rice. Tejimola pleaded, said that she would do all her stepmother wanted, but Romola had planned Tejimola's death for a long time, and this was a golden opportunity. Saud wasn't around. At first, she smashed the girl's right hand with the grinder. When she cried, 'Ma, you crushed my right hand,' Romola said, 'Use your left,' which she crushed in no time. And then she forced her to use her feet. When she cried, 'Ma, you smashed both my feet, please let me go,' Romola asked her to use her head. She cracked her skull, too, with the stave.

Romola buried Tejimola in the backyard. All these years, her flesh and blood had been waiting. As soon as Romola turned her back, the girl's flesh started to germinate and gradually turned into a gourd-bearing creeper. The soil sucked up her blood, drawing nourishment. The leaves, twigs, and the roots protected her soul, kept it intact.

In the lonely backyard, during windy afternoons, the plant would sing songs, and the fresh smell of gourds would spread. It was normal for songs to float in the slow, windy afternoons thickened by the sounds of cooing doves. The creeper's songs were soft. Anyone near enough to hear it would believe a woman was singing someplace faraway.

///////////////

The auditorium was massive. Even though there were at least a hundred people there, it looked like the event was poorly attended.

Sanjib saw no familiar faces. John met someone from Calcutta, an old friend who had come for the panel. The moderator said he would be back after a visit to the campus's smoking zone. Sanjib looked around. Everyone's clothes fit so nicely, he noticed, only his were ill-fitting. He was also surprised how male students turned up in shorts and three-quarters and sleeveless vests. How carelessly the women wore their cotton saris—as if they were in bed until a moment ago—and yet how good they looked in them. He found a corner for himself and returned to the printed pages he would read soon. On the margins, he had written down the pronunciation of some English words in Assamese letters. He had practised reading the story with the translator. She had a posh accent—the kind of accent Riti had, the kind he would never be able to acquire. She had gone to an English-medium school that allowed them to wear skirts, unlike his Assamese-medium school where the girls had to wear green-bordered mekhela-sador and the boys had to wear khaki pants. For a long time, that khaki pair was the only one he had. He kept it well and, during festivals and weddings, sprinkled water on it and used a steel bowl filled with hot water to iron it. One day, when he told Riti that those were the only tailored pants he possessed until he moved to Guwahati to study chemistry, she blinked and said that it sounded like a fable. He said nothing. Later, when they broke up, he imagined her standing in front of him and said, there is nothing fabulous about it. It is how things are for many people. And it is my reality, too.

The moderator smelled good. He was wearing some cologne that was mild and powdery. So, what is your story about, he asked Sanjib. They were waiting for the rest of the panellists to arrive. Sanjib still couldn't get over the fact that the moderator hadn't read his story.

It is a folktale retold. Set during colonial times.

The moderator was excited. So, you are looking at the exploitation of your state from the colonial period?

No, not at all. It is just a popular story. I am just retelling it with some more twists and turns.

The moderator's eyebrows creased, and he looked disappointed. Why is it so popular?

Because the character, who is repeatedly killed by her stepmother, refuses to give up on life. You know, people find it inspiring. We have, after all, refused to give up on living, despite all the violence. The eighties and nineties were so horrible. Sanjib spoke slowly, in Hindi, which was better than his English. But he was annoyed that the moderator continued to ask him questions in English.

John hadn't returned yet. A young student from the organising committee was checking the microphone. Another student stood next to her with bouquets.

Why hide behind a folktale, Sanjib? You should write about those things that you just mentioned—the violence, human rights abuse, those are the real issues. That is where the real story from your region is; it is the kind of story that makes news and gets people to sit up and notice.

Sanjib was puzzled, not because every time the moderator used the word 'real', his voice became louder and more impatient, but because Sanjib didn't understand what he meant by a 'real story'. He just said, I am not hiding behind a folktale. There is a reason why people retell this story over and over—many contemporary writers have retold it, actually. It is because we find inspiration in the girl who refuses to die. And we are relieved that the stepmother is finally brought to justice. In reality, that doesn't happen. Delhi and its representatives are never made responsible.

Interesting, the moderator said, nodding, and asked, then why should people outside your state read this story?

I don't know. I never said they should or shouldn't. I wrote it in Assamese—the reader in Delhi never figured during the composition process.

Sanjib got a long, cold stare, and he thought, I am never making it to that coveted anthology.

//////////////

Maybe because of the guilt, for weeks, Romola didn't go to where Tejimola lay buried. So, one afternoon after lunch, when an emaciated beggarwoman came asking for gourds, she was surprised.

'Foolish beggar, you must be daydreaming. I haven't had a gourd in weeks, and, in fact, to cook the rohu fish for dinner, I just sent my son to look for a good mature one in someone's house. Where the hell have you seen gourds?'

'I wouldn't lie, aaideu,' the woman exclaimed. 'You are the owner of this house; if you don't want to give me a gourd when you have so many, I have nothing to say.' The beggarwoman turned to leave.

'I really don't know what you are talking about. If you have seen any, go help yourself. I have no problem,' Romola said and continued working her foot loom, trying to make a beautiful blue flower bloom. Irritated, she muttered about greedy beggarwomen.

Soon after, howling and crying, the woman came running and fainted right in front of her. Romola was stunned. Grumbling, she rushed indoors and returned with a glass of cold water that she sprinkled on the woman's eyes and face.

'Are you okay? Are you okay? What happened? What did you see?'

When the woman regained consciousness, she sat up, beads of perspiration still emerging on her forehead. 'There is a ghost in that creeper plant! It says it is Tejimola, and her stepmother killed her because of a silk dress! Who is she?'

Romola paced on the veranda. She was petrified because some people in the village were asking, and she had said that Teji never returned from her best friend's wedding. Bracing herself, Romola decided to do something about the situation—it's just a plant, Tejimola is dead! Romola took a huge machete and went to the backyard. She strained her ears and heard a parting song, sung at weddings, coming as if from a distance. Without wasting anymore time, she chopped the plant to pieces. The seeds of the gourd plant flew around, its juice stained her white dress, and she panted and sweated. There were 459 large gourds in the plant, 92 immature ones, and 3,045 flowers, which she picked up one by one, first on her own and later helped by her two sons who returned from the fields after their tang-guti games. The eldest, who had gone looking for a gourd, hadn't returned yet. Together, they dug a deep hole in the farthest corner of the garden and buried the rest of the plant.

This time, in that farthest corner, there grew a plant of reddish elephant lime. A few weeks later, when the yet-to-be-men village cowherds came asking for the ripe limes on a lush plant growing in the corner of her backyard garden, Romola told them to help themselves. She didn't think about it further until they began screaming at the top of their voices and fleeing.

She was sitting in her courtyard, grating a coconut. One of the boys flung himself on the ground in front of her, foaming at the mouth. Another one sat and cried like a baby. Before fainting, this second boy told her about a singing lime tree:

> *Don't you dare stretch your hands,*
> *I am not a lime tree,*
> *ground and buried*
> *because of a silk dress,*
> *it's me,*
> *it's me,*
> *Tejimola.*

///////////////

John's tale, set in New York and Kohima, was a love story between an Indian man and an American woman who visits Nagaland. The Mizo writer's story was set on the day when the state of Mizoram was bombarded by the Indian Air Force. The main character, a young girl displaced during the bombardment, is looking for her parents, and during her search, the writer provides a cinematic look at the ravaged portions of the city. The Khasi author's story was set in Bangalore and Shillong, about a man who has an affair with an injured Naga woman insurgent while his Bengali wife takes care of his family in Bangalore.

Sanjib was deeply impressed by most of the stories, but he liked the Mizo writer's story best. He couldn't stop thinking about the young girl, because it reminded him of his elder sister and mother, who had to flee their home when the soldiers surrounded their village and started burning houses to fish out insurgents. He hadn't even been born then. Sanjib also liked the Khasi author's story about the man's infidelity and wanted to read the story again to learn how to arrive at a language so intimate and descriptions so impartial that he didn't judge the man but felt sorry for all the characters torn apart by their desires. He didn't connect to John's story at all. He couldn't understand the point of bringing the American woman to Nagaland when they could have had that fight in New York as well. Nagaland was like a curtain; the characters didn't even eat Naga food in the story. They kept eating chow mein. But when John asked him later if he had liked it, he said it was excellent. When Sanjib read, the moderator walked out for four minutes during his ten-minute long reading. He felt insulted, and it affected the way he read. Sanjib wondered if the moderator was dealing with an emergency at home. He tried to forgive him and continued reading. At the end of the reading and discussion, a question-and-answer session started.

A young woman from the audience asked the first question. She introduced herself at length, but Sanjib didn't get her name or her profession. Perhaps it was her accent. She spoke with a lisp that made her sound sexy, but because he wasn't used to people talking that way, he found it difficult to follow most of what she said. She started by appreciating the panellists for their thoughtful conversations and also the university for organising the conference, and he wondered why she couldn't come to the point. Sanjib did manage to catch that she was writing her doctoral thesis on literature from Northeast India, but he didn't get the name of the university she was associated with. She sounded intelligent, he thought. She said her question was for Sanjib: why had he decided to write about this magical world, instead of the insurgencies, the violence, and the more immediate, the more topical stories? He was surprised because no audience member had ever asked him a question like that before. When she ended, the moderator said, good question, and a lot of people clapped, as if the woman was calling out Sanjib for doing something terrible. Sanjib paused and wondered how the moderator could comment on the quality of the question when he hadn't been present for much of the reading. Sanjib asked the young woman to repeat her question. There was an awkward silence before she responded to his request.

This is funny, Sanjib started to answer, because no one in Assam would ask me that question—why don't you write about the violence? The woman was in the front row, standing, with the microphone close to her lips and a smile on her face. When he said, this is funny, her smile vanished in an instant. As if he had said something hurtful and completely unexpected. He had spoken in his halting English, peppered with Hindi sentences, but because his Hindi was also thickly accented, he didn't sound serious. It seemed as if he was joking or making fun of the girl. But he wasn't. He continued, in fact, people thought it was a good break from the violence when it was conceived and published in Assamese. We read about violence and gun battles and rapes and dismembered bodies every day in the papers. So, people in Assam wouldn't mind reading this story. There is no burden of expectations on me when I write in Assamese. Back home, Assamese readers do not expect me to write about this or that topic. I am free to write anything. So, I really don't know how to answer your question.

The questioner thanked him, coldly, without the enthusiasm and warmth the question had. Sanjib wondered if she thought she had asked an excellent question and was disappointed he hadn't rewarded that brilliance with an answer that acknowledged its quality. He wanted to get out of there soon. And return home. The stories written by his co-panellists had humbled him, and that was all that mattered to him.

Gulab jamuns and samosas were served outside the auditorium. Sanjib was hungry. The other panellists were chatting with the moderator, signing books, or talking to the students. He didn't want to talk to anyone. Sanjib checked his cellphone for the time—the cab would come in a couple of hours and take him to the airport.

Excuse me, can I say something? It was the woman who had asked him that question. She seemed upset still, and her voice was quivering. She paused a little, creases forming on her forehead, as if she was about to say something unpleasant that she didn't want to articulate but had to because it would be the right thing to do. Sanjib smiled at her, but he was still thinking about the moderator who hadn't heard his story in its entirety, about the people who had clapped when the woman, who claimed to be a scholar on literature from India's Northeast, asked him that question. What was so right about her question that people had begun clapping even before he spoke? And why hadn't they clapped when he finished answering?

Yes, please?

I don't know how to say this, but I think it is important for me to express it.

Oh, sure. Sanjib tried to be encouraging.

I just wanted to say that I didn't appreciate your answer. I just felt so attacked—I just felt—I mean, I love literature from the Northeast, but I don't know why you got so defensive.

Sanjib was shocked. I wasn't attacking you. I was just telling you how things are back home. I was merely answering your question.

The woman became a bit more impatient. She asked him a question that further surprised him: do you think I asked you a question that I shouldn't have asked?

Sanjib shook his head. Not at all, you have every right to ask any question you want, but I just found it very amusing, and I wasn't insulting you. You know what is even funnier? Even when we write about violence, we are asked to be quiet and discreet. Write about violence, but don't name anyone. The non-threatening Northeastern who writes about real and topical issues is what everyone wants, and they're the one who is always garlanded with prizes and fellowships. And researchers like you base your doctoral research papers on their work. Do you have anything to say about that? I think the problem is that people only look at things in binaries. No one here knows that I have written several stories about the violence committed by the armies in the eighties and nineties.

There was an awkward silence. The woman did not appear mollified.

I am sorry, I have to leave. Perhaps this was a mistake, she said quickly, and rushed away.

Sanjib stood there, watching her back and her ponytail vanish into the crowd. He wasn't sure what he had done wrong, why she was offended, why she felt attacked just because he disagreed with her.

He felt a pat on his back. It was the moderator. You did well, he said, like an uncle who wanted to be the cool uncle when the parents were angry with a child. Your story got some good questions; you did well, the moderator repeated.

Sanjib turned to him and replied, but you didn't listen to my story. You weren't even there for the first four minutes.

By the time Dhaniram Saud reached his village, it was autumn. In Lower
Assam, he had met a guy who he thought would be the best for Tejimola.
Hardworking and muscular, he touched the feet of elders, listened to his
mother, helped his grandmother grind her betel with limestone until it was
bright red and sharp on the tongue. He wasn't a smoker. He slept early, rose
early. His skin was the colour of gold for he always bathed before sunrise. As
the boat approached the village, the boatman's song almost sent Dhaniram
Saud into a thin lull:

> *Kanai, take us to the other shore,*
> *The sun has created long shadows now.*
> *If you take too long to reach home,*
> *Your milk will curdle,*
> *Won't your mother scold you then?*
> *Won't your mother scold you then?*
> *Kanai, take us to the other shore,*
> *Otherwise your milk will curdle!*
> *As soon as you can!*

The excited chatter of one of his crewmembers woke him up.
'Look at that!'
'No, no, I have seen many, but this is divine.'
'Arrey, don't go, it might be charmed . . .'
'Yes, yes, we are not very far from Mayong—the land of sorcerers!'
'That's true; they turn human beings into buffaloes and make them
work in the fields.'
Dhaniram Saud sat up, wore his turban, checked if the tail fell grace-
fully on his spine, and walked out from his resting place. A most wonderful
sight awaited him: he had never seen a bigger, brighter, redder lotus in all
his life, as large as an umbrella crafted from bamboo. In the distance, he saw

the large steamers of the British companies moving slowly towards Calcutta, carrying goods and students who went to study in colleges there. 'I am going to pluck this for Tejimola, only a daughter like her, only a beautiful girl like her deserves it.'

The lotus sang, retelling a mournful story, starting with a rat and a tiny smouldering piece of wood, and ending with, "It is me, me, Tejimola! It is me, me, Tejimola!"

Dhaniram Saud didn't believe these words. He thought some evil spirit was playing tricks on him. But suddenly, when his workers were about to uproot the misleading, evil lotus, he said, 'Stop!' As if he had an inkling of the truth.

He looked closely at the blood-red flower and opened both his palms.

He placed a fresh piece of betel on one and spat out chewed betel on the other. 'If you are the real Tejimola, you will turn into a skylark and come and peck on the chewed betel on my right palm. If you are some ghost trying to delude me, you will come and chew the fresh piece of betel on my left palm. If I have lived a virtuous life, if I have respected my parents, if I truly believe in God, you will be compelled by the divine forces of nature to follow my command!'

The air was still.

A bee went near the lotus but did not sit on it.

A dragonfly flew to the centre of it but seemed to change its mind.

The steamer carrying goods and students to Calcutta was far away now. It looked like it was merging into the hills.

One man in the crew said, 'The lotus breathes, I felt it.'

'I command you. If I have lived a virtuous life, if I have respected my parents, if I truly believe in God . . .' Saud screamed again.

When he reached home that afternoon, he carried a caged brown skylark.

The stepmother didn't ask him about it. When Dhaniram Saud asked where Tejimola was, she began howling and said that his daughter had eloped with a man when she went to her best friend's wedding. So ashamed was Romola that she hadn't told the villagers. Her three sons, in varying stages of adolescence with varying lengths of incipient beards on their chins and upper lips, lied that they went to enquire in her best friend's village, and several people confessed secretly, saying they didn't want to taint the name of the famous Dhaniram Saud.

He took a long piece of red-bordered sador, walked up to the cage, and said, 'My daughter, now I command you to take your real form and wear this.'

BIZI COLONY

1.

Long before my younger brother, Bablu, began telling our neighbours that Ma sucked Papa's best friend Hriday Uncle's dick while Papa was away on official tours to New Delhi, he would touch the breasts of our forty-year-old maid and ask her how it felt. When the timid Geeta-baideo wept, saying that she was the one who had brought him up and washed his ass after he crapped as a baby, he beat her up with a cane. Bablu was around twelve. That evening, when Papa returned from work, he asked a sullen Geeta what had happened. She didn't say anything because she wanted to protect Bablu. Ma hesitantly told him bits and pieces of what had taken place. Papa beat up Bablu with whatever he could lay his hands on.

Back when Bablu was around nine, he broke the skull of a daily wager who came to weed our garden because the man had said that Bablu was crazy and muttered nonsense.

Ma complained to Papa that evening, 'Do you even care about what's going on here?'

Papa had had a long day at work. Tired and annoyed, he asked Ma, 'Are you his stepmother?' He accused her of loving her younger son less. 'You complain about your younger son all the time, like a stepmother! As if the elder one is a saint?'

Bablu pointed his finger at Ma. 'You are a stepmother.' He was young then. So young that he hadn't started calling Ma a 'bitch' and a 'slut'.

Ma cried all night. She screamed at Papa: how could you say that, how could you even think like that, how was she to deal with all this nonsense all day during her university's summer break, when he was two hours away by bus, sitting in his air-conditioned office where he had a sassy personal assistant to bring him tea. She used the word 'rosoki' actually, not 'sassy', and that irked Papa even more. Angered, he caned Bablu the next morning. Since Bablu was only nine years old then, Papa could hold him upside down by his legs. As he beat Bablu in a rage, Papa demanded to know if he would trouble Ma anymore. A petrified Ma called to our neighbours for help. They rebuked Papa. One shouldn't 'overdo' things, they said. It was truly sad, they said, to see Ma arguing with a whole band of Bangladeshi workers, who had arrived with their gang to corner her about the daily wager's injury. When she gave them money, they left without another word. Geeta-baideo said that that's what 'these Bangladeshis' wanted. Each and every person nodded, lips twisted with distaste. As if they had smelled fart—like the smell that came from the chemistry lab of the school nearby.

Papa sat down on a sofa, his head bowed. Ma went up to him and ran her fingers through his thick hair. She asked why he could not control his anger.

From the other room, Bablu roared. He said, when he grew up, he would kill Papa.

Our neighbours went in. They told him sweetly that he shouldn't say such things, only bad boys uttered such things, are you a bad boy? He said he wasn't a bad boy, but now he wanted to be one because he wanted to stab

Papa. When the kind-hearted, free-advice-dispensing neighbours repeated their counsel, Bablu asked them to get lost. Papa made a swift move towards the room, cane in hand.

2.

Bablu started to steal quite early. The second time he stole money, my cousin Junmoni was visiting. Junmoni had tried to take his seventh standard finals three times, in vain. So, my uncle wanted him to spend some days with Ma and Papa in a 'studious atmosphere'. Ma warned him that there was no such atmosphere, that her younger son was very unruly, fought with everyone who visited. But Uncle insisted. In the middle of the night, I sensed someone entering my room. I had left my door open because our cat, Munu, hadn't returned when I had gone to bed. He liked to sit on my table, watching me with half-shut eyes, purring loudly. If I slept with the door latched, he woke everyone up by meowing incessantly in front of my door until I opened it. So, when I heard soft sounds, I didn't bother to switch on the light. But the next morning, my wallet was empty. My hundred-rupee notes, four of them, were missing. When I told Papa that all my money was gone, he questioned Bablu. Ma began crying. She said it would be so embarrassing if Junmoni told everyone in her hometown about this. Junmoni kept assuring her that he wasn't much of a talker. When Bablu continued to deny that he'd taken the money, Papa started to thrash him. Bablu howled, saying that he would never do such a thing. But Ma kept quiet, held him in her arms, and said, don't cry, don't cry, don't cry.

When the pandemonium subsided—except for Bablu who continued to hurl abuses at Papa—Junmoni said he was too scared to stay on any longer and would go to Shillong with his friends before leaving for home. He returned late that night. The next morning, he showed us the hundred-rupee digital watch he had bought, the cheap green shades he must have picked up for a hundred-fifty from the kiosk at the bus stand, and a red T-shirt probably bought from the footpath vendor. I showed no interest. Ma looked hard at Junmoni and said, 'Your father loves you so much, gives you money whenever you want, why won't you study well?' He said he would return home and study well, because he wanted to go to Mumbai to learn acting and become a star. 'I am already learning breakdance,' he said and showed us a few steps, moving his head to the right, to the left.

No one was interested in discussing the topic, except Bablu. He asked Junmoni a thousand questions (How to go to Bombay? How to pursue a career as an underworld don? Which train must one take?) until Junmoni was so tired that he snapped at Bablu, 'STOPASKINGMETHESAMETHINGS.' Bablu hit him with a broom. Papa walked out of his study, Bablu ran out of the house, leaving a howling Junmoni sprawled on the floor. Junmoni left the next morning. In the evening, my uncle called. Papa picked up the phone, heard him out, and said, 'She is your sister, why would I scold her? You should scold her.' He handed the phone to Ma. At the end of what was evidently a monologue, Ma looked up at us and said, 'Who gave money to Junmoni? I didn't. He is drunk on moonshine, and my brother is inconsolable! Gosh, what is happening to the youth of this country?'

That night, Ma slept in Bablu's bed and wept a lot. Papa looked distressed and paced the veranda. 'Am I a failed father? Why do I get so angry?' he whispered.

3.

I had to tell Niyor about Bablu because I couldn't sleep the night before. I went to the kitchen in search of a sharp knife several times, but the thought of plunging it into my heart or stomach was so scary that I gave up the plan. I also fished out one of my 7 O'Clock blades (Super Stainless) from the black shaving kit and trailed it over the blue veins of my wrists over and over, never quite making contact with skin. In the other room, Papa and Ma were crying. From Bablu's room, the stench of shit. I wondered how the others were managing. How the others were breathing. I stayed awake, trying to study for the economics test.

We were returning from school in a crowded bus. It was evening. I told Niyor that I couldn't sleep the previous night. He said that meant I would pass the test with flying colours. I said that I wasn't awake studying for the test; we were at the police station until midnight because Bablu had been someplace fourteen-year-olds weren't supposed to be. When I told him exactly where, he didn't understand how serious the situation was. Then I gave him a description of the cow-dungy gunny bags and the blue plastic sheets that people covered themselves with when they slept, the smell of burnt marijuana leaves, the men in stained buttonless shirts staring at my mother, and the way she had covered her head with her sador. Niyor stopped speaking. I didn't tell him about the man who stood in front of Ma with his dick hanging out of his unzipped trousers like a banana. I didn't tell him that the police officer looked at Papa and said, 'Avoid'—a word of caution, to avoid attention from the man with the unzipped trousers who was probably trying to provoke us into a fight.

The crowded bus was so noisy, mostly full of people returning from their offices, and yet it felt to me that the world had come to a standstill— because that was the first time I had told anyone about Bablu. In a crowded bus. Full of tired people. Sweaty. Stuffy. In a crowded bus, I had finally spoken about Bablu. To Niyor, my best friend.

After a long time, he asked me if Bablu was the reason I never invited him to my house, and I said yes. But I wanted him to ask me more. I didn't want to tell him that Bablu said Ma sucked Hriday Uncle's cock. But I wanted to tell him about the things I had avoided that day, following the police officer's instructions. The drug peddlers I had seen and avoided. We had all gone because Ma didn't want Papa to go alone, and I wanted to accompany Ma. Ma held my hand firmly, as if we were on a tightrope. I wanted to tell him that I saw sex workers for the first time and avoided their gaze; their garish makeup, gaudy revealing dresses, deep cleavages. There were also men who wore lipstick and eyeliner, and gem-studded bangles flashed on their wrists. I wanted to tell him how, earlier, we had waited until eleven at night for Bablu to return. How none of his classmates had known where he was because he hadn't been to school. But Bablu had left home in the morning carrying his blue lunch box and school bag, wearing the grey school trousers, with Ma prompting him from the veranda to walk faster because he might miss the school bus.

In Bizi Colony, at around 1 a.m., when our shoes were caked with drying black scum and stomachs so filled with the smells of the neighbourhood that we might throw up on each other, we found Bablu. He was lying in a ditch. Actually, it was the police officer with the horrible breath who found him. How could Ma hug Bablu even though his clothes smelled so horrible? When he was brought home—released by the police officer without pressing charges because he was young and Ma was a professor—Geeta-baideo, who had been waiting for us, immediately threw up on the living-room floor because she had just finished dinner. She always ate late anyway after watching soap operas. But today it had been delayed because she was stressed about the whole situation.

In the crowded bus, I told Niyor that, last night, when I couldn't sleep, I'd looked around for the room freshener. When I couldn't find it, I went out to the veranda, where I saw the huge container of Dendrite and the many white handkerchiefs we had discovered earlier that night. Bablu had poured out the adhesive on those cloths and inhaled compulsively. 'Perhaps he sniffed it all day,' the police officer told Ma after we found Bablu. His alcohol breath filled the air, and Ma moved her face away and murmured, 'I have lived in this city for so many years, never heard of this strange place called Bizi Colony.' Later, standing on the veranda, with the Dendrite container in front of me, I'd thought only thieves could identify the legs of thieves.

Niyor didn't ask me anything else. Not the next day, or in the next few weeks. I wanted to tell him because he wouldn't pity me, he'd provide me with solutions. As if we hadn't consulted psychiatrists, tantrics, sadhus, and women oracles with large red bindis and open hair. Niyor didn't ask me more until he came to spend the night at the filthy Guwahati Medical College Hospital general ward as my attendant after I'd gulped down fifty-nine sleeping tablets.

Bablu had been having extended fights with Papa every morning and every evening around the time I usually sat down to study. He roamed around during the day, returned home to fight with us, demanded more money to procure substances we didn't know the names of. He'd stopped going to school. Even when he went—cajoled, threatened, and persuaded by Ma—he jumped the wall before lunch break. One day, he broke all the windows of the house. The next day, the chinaware. We stayed under the beds for hours as he pelted stones on the glass windows.

That night in the hospital, Niyor didn't ask me about the sleeping tablets, he asked why the hospital authorities had caught me trying to jump from the fourth-floor window two days after they had held me down and pumped out all the molten tablets from my stomach. The tablets had looked like tiny runny egg yolks, only almost white, not yellow. When we were young, we had planned to marry the same girl. Later, we had planned to marry on the same day (two different girls, of course). We had conversations that no one else understood. So, I knew that what he was really asking was what this was all about, but that day, I just couldn't tell him. I was sleepy. All I remember was him sitting on the chair beside the bed, staring at me, and the smell of Dettol and the jute rope that bound my legs tightly to the bed.

By the time my parents sent me away from Assam to New Delhi for further studies, Bablu had turned into a crackling fire that refused to be doused, demanding to be fed with wood, oil, fat, tears. Each of us took turns to let it feed upon us. Niyor stayed back in our city. He would visit my parents sometimes, help them douse the fire, sprinkle some water with his laughter and jokes, but that was only for a few minutes. How much more could a friend do?

4.

Ma didn't come to pick me up from the airport when I visited Guwahati during my first winter break. Papa came with our new driver, who spoke a lot while he drove. I asked Papa in English when he'd hired the driver, how sincere he was, if his driving was smooth, if he stole oil. When the driver heard me speak in English, he fell silent.

Ma had a thick white bandage around her head, with orange blood seeping through at one spot on the right. When I asked her what had happened, she said she would tell me everything 'gradually', but I wanted to know right away because I knew who was responsible for it. After dinner, I almost cried in my room.

But I didn't because I was ashamed of crying, even though I was alone. I felt a strange burning sensation in my chest and a strange choking lump in my throat.

Ma didn't tell me how Bablu broke the tall, thick juice glass on her head because she'd refused to give him money to buy Dendrite or Eraz-ex. Geeta-baideo told me about it when she came to my room with the bottle of water that I'd need at night and the glass of hot milk that I drank before going to bed. 'If we don't pick up the phone when you call, please call Niyor to come and check on us.' She paused and looked around my room. 'At least you'll know for sure if we've been killed by that demon. We are living in the shadow of a constant reign of terror.' Ordinarily, I'd have laughed and asked where she learnt to speak like that, and she would have just smiled without confessing that she'd picked up phrases from the laments of my parents who talked like characters from historical plays whenever they were sad.

I woke up the next morning to the sounds of chairs being upturned, slamming wooden doors, and Papa's hoarse wailing. The sound of a fifty-year-old man crying loudly is horrible, especially if you were so scared of him when you were young, especially if he was once the apex court whose decisions couldn't be overruled. Bablu was fighting for money again, to buy Eraz-ex, to buy Dendrite, to buy pot.

I went out for a walk across the flyover. Young men from the engineering college were exercising, and housewives wrapped in colourful shawls were taking brisk walks with their neighbours, bitching about their in-laws. The morning sun was golden. The leaves that were still on their branches had curled up like centipedes that had been touched. I looked at the street-lights and wondered how I'd managed to study for my twelfth-grade board exams under them, sitting on a step nearby. I had just returned from hospital. Back then, I had badly wanted to blend in with the young crowd that returned from private tuition and coaching classes, who discussed their test papers standing around, cracking peanuts or opening bottles of Kingfisher beer. But I knew I stood apart because I wasn't relaxed like them.

5.

The summer I returned home after the final year exams, I noticed Ma's eyes had sunken in too deep. She told me insulin injections weren't working for her. 'All because of tension. Have a good look at me, I could die soon,' she declared in a tone that was both grim and funny. Her face was wrapped in sadness, but in a second, she smiled, as if she was laughing at some joke. When Ma acted like that, I didn't know whether to think it was mysterious or amusing or tragic.

But I wasn't worried about her because I knew she had this way of bouncing back. Shahnaz Husain (Perfect Blend of Nature's Secret for Youthful Skin) or Vandana Luthra Curls and Curves clinic (Slimming. Beauty. Fitness.) would take care of her sunken eyes, her darkened skin, and the thinning hair. Fact was, she kept herself happy. Under thick make-up and her million-dollar smile, she could hide everything.

I was more worried about Papa. He only slept fitfully. At night, while Bablu slept, smeared in his own urine and shit, after taking twelve pills of different sizes and shapes and colours, Papa walked around our home like an old house fairy. Since he was awake, we couldn't sleep, either. Like that time before my school-leaving boards, the summer after my graduation, I stayed up. But he looked fine. Even if he couldn't sleep because he was scared that Bablu would wake up and break windowpanes, kill Ma, rape Geeta-baideo. He drank warm milk, washed his feet, jogged. In the mornings, when Bablu woke up, they fought. Papa refused to give him money. Bablu called him a dog. Papa said if he was a dog, then Bablu was one, too. Bablu called him a rapist, a sodomite, which angered Papa. They wrestled. Ma screamed. By this time, the neighbours had stopped rushing over. We only called the security when it was needed. After about an hour, when Ma would threaten to jump off the terrace, Bablu would fall at her feet and ask her not to die because she was 'the only person in the world who loves me, truly'.

'Then why don't you listen to me? We are trying to help you. Who'd look after you if we died?'

He pleaded, 'Just today, give me the money only for today; I will never consume those harmful things again. Otherwise I am going to kill myself.'

Sometimes, I took out money from my Hidesign wallet, at other times Papa did, or Ma, from her vanity bag or the steel almirah. When Bablu left, Papa looked at his retreating back and said, 'Shanti kinisu!' We are buying peace. Papa often started weeping at this point. I liked it when he pulled out the book of chants for the Mother Goddess and recited.

'Kill him, Mother, kill him! I will sacrifice a black goat if you listen to my prayers. Otherwise, one day I will kill him and go to jail, but then what will happen to my other son, my wife!' Ma told me he'd been praying like that for months, and when he heard her telling me, he responded, 'But the Mother hasn't listened to me.'

Geeta-baideo added in her feeble voice, 'If parents wish ill for their children, it really doesn't work. Because they are parents.' Later, she told me she was worried both of them were losing it. 'One day, all of us will run naked on the streets, and you will get to read about it in the Delhi papers.'

I didn't tell her that her 'Delhi papers' rarely published news about Assam.

Instead, I tried to remember that Papa used to be the one who sang songs ('We are in the same boat, brother') as he dusted the books, sticking 'we do not lend books' notes in red ink on the steel and wooden bookshelves.

6.

The beds stood in a row, and the ward smelled of sweat, damp clothes, antiseptic liquid, and, underneath it all, something rotten. Government hospitals in India are dirtier than anywhere else in the world, I'm sure, and perhaps this one was the dirtiest of them all. I didn't know what ward it was. When I entered its damp white premises, I just followed Papa's slouched back. I walked without lingering on the large clogged drain on my right, filled with brackish garbage, or the huge festering spittoons where rats ran around, lifting their noses and sniffing the air. I was back home, in Guwahati, after finishing college. I had tried to run away from this city, but I couldn't.

Since it was a case of attempted suicide, no private hospitals would take him in, even though we explained to each one of them, reception after reception, how he'd jumped from the flyover, how he wasn't responding at all, how yellow goo was coming out of his behind, and how its stench filled our Honda City, which usually smelled of rose or jasmine. Papa had been in attendance for the last six days, and Ma wanted him to take a break. 'He will fall sick,' she told me. 'You have to go and spend the night today. Take a book and read. We will get some help by tomorrow from your uncles. Your aunt said she would come to stay.' Not long after Papa left at around nine, giving me a million instructions on his way out, I wanted to run away, because the five other people in that general ward were staring at me.

'Why are you here? To gloat?' Bablu should have a shave, I thought, looking at the stubble around his seventeen-year-old face. After two minutes, he said, 'Fuck off, I don't want you here: go and fuck Geeta-baideo now that you are done sodomising Niyor's ass. Ja-ja eitiai ja.' I kept quiet. He said again, 'Go and fuck Geeta-baideo now that you are done sodomising Niyor's ass.' I'd noticed he'd developed this manner of 'Go fuck Geeta-baideo, GO FUCK GEETA-BAIDEO' until it got on your nerves.

'Alright, I am leaving. You are alone for the rest of the night.'

'PLEASE COME BACK!!!'

I was amazed at the energy and the longing and helplessness. I stopped. 'Then stop hurling obscenities. Try to think about other things,' I said.

'I am sorry; you know that's my disease, I like to say such things. What can I do? Give me your hand please.' Tears streamed from reddish eyes.

'Why?'

'I want to hold your hand and apologise.'

'It's fine; I have accepted your apology.'

'No, please let me hold your hand and apologise, otherwise I won't be able to sleep, and I will slash my wrists.'

He spat on my hand when I let him hold it, and when I went to wash my hand, I was in tears. Not out of anger. Not out of exasperation, either. I was thinking about Ma, about Papa, about Geeta-baideo. Bablu started to scream for the nurses and doctors when I left the ward. He thought I was abandoning him. The nurses in white skirts and saris tried to calm him, told him to control his anger. When I returned, I saw a tall, plump woman sitting beside him, humming him a song. Saliva dripped from the corners of her lips. She was wearing an ash-grey cotton sari with yellow turmeric stains, but no earrings or even a necklace.

'Come to me, I will sing the song for you, too,' she said to me, smiling. A vague smile. 'Everyone must learn this song. It's beautiful.'

The other men in the ward, old and young, urged me to go closer. 'Go near her, she will sing you a song, and we will play the music.'

'Go to her!' the skinny old man with a white beard said, scratching his crotch.

'Go, brother, go,' a young guy in his twenties, who kept looking at the mirror, said.

I had noticed that this man had a mug of water beside his bed; all the other patients had bottles to drink water from, but he had a mug, too. Occasionally, he would dip his comb in the water and run it through his hair, trying to give it shape. But he never seemed satisfied with the way it looked in the mirror.

At the entrance, I stood transfixed. Soon, they all took out their shiny steel dishes and started to play different rhythms on it, asking me to go to her, listen to the song, and learn it. Amidst that cacophony, the woman climbed up on a stool and started to sing loudly, no longer waiting. When I went closer, Bablu muttered to me, as if he were sharing a secret, that I should just ignore her, not say anything, because she was a lunatic. He said, giggling, she'd fight with me if I said something to her.

It wasn't a song. She recited a string of sentences in a singsong manner about how a woman should give a glass of water to her husband when he returns from work. At the end of the song, she looked into my eyes and said, 'Tell your mother, giving a cold glass of water to your father after he returns from work is the same thing as burning an incense stick in front of Lord Shiva.'

The next morning, when one of my uncles went to attend to Bablu, the rest of us stayed at home together. I told Ma about the incident. She started to laugh loudly, called Papa, and asked me to sing the 'song' to him. When I sang, the three of us laughed uncontrollably. I laughed the most—not because the song was silly and funny, but because I had sung it worse than that woman in the psychiatric ward. *Giving a glass of water to your husband / is the same thing as lighting incense / for Lord Shiva / same thing, same thing.* Geeta-baideo joined us, saying she, too, wanted to listen and learn. Ma said this should become the anthem of our house. When Geeta-baideo laughed, Ma laughed even louder, saying that Geeta's laughter was squeaky like a rat's. Geeta-baideo didn't mind, she continued to laugh squeakily, and I couldn't tell whether she was laughing at herself or the anthem of our house or the way Ma was laughing, holding her stomach, with tears streaming from her eyes. My eyes streamed tears, my stomach ached, I couldn't breathe. I was worried I would pee in the living room right then. For a moment, we couldn't feel the hurt of the doctors' verdict: Bablu would never walk again.

7.

I decided to walk back home from the high school I taught at, where they didn't pay me too well because I didn't have a master's yet. Walking back would slow down time. It was around 3 p.m. I realised how much I loved the Guwahati winters: not too warm, not too cold, just the weather to spread the folding bed out in the courtyard with a large basket of oranges on it.

Long ago, Ma, Papa, Bablu, and I used to do that. We would finish about a dozen in just a few hours. Those were the days when we didn't buy greeting cards but made them at home during the winter break with love and care. On the first of January, Ma used to take us to each of our neighbours' houses, where they would give us chocolates or printed cards in return and tell us that we had drawn lovely cars and airplanes.

'How was your day?' Bablu asked me with concern when I reached home.

'Good.'

'Why are you so late today?'

'I walked.'

I was yet to get used to his docility. Miracle. That's what the doctor had said. 'A miracle could change things for the better,' because he was 'still so young'. Often, I would tell Papa and Ma that we shouldn't complain, shouldn't talk about suing the doctor because we'd signed those papers, because he'd warned us that there was almost no chance of Bablu's spinal cord becoming normal, because we were eating our meals in peace after fifteen years, because we could sleep peacefully these days.

Papa was quiet. They often worried about what would happen to Bablu when he grew up, who'd wash him, change his bedpan. 'Only parents will do such dirty stuff,' Ma would comment, going on to list names of wives who had run away with other men after their husbands were paralysed because of blood pressure strokes or accidents. I didn't ask where she'd carried out that survey. We knew she chatted with patients and their attendants when she was Bablu's attendant at the hospital. All of us teased her and said that she should join politics because she would win all the votes

MINNESOTA NICE

On his first day in America, Himjyoti didn't mind when his new roommate took him to the bathroom, shut the door, and showed him how to lock it. 'Push and turn,' he said and then pulled the knob to show it was locked. 'Now push, hold for a sec, turn, and then pull,' he said, opening the door. 'Why don't you do it now?'

Himjyoti copied Mike, nervous. He was terrible with doorknobs. A few years ago, when he and his father had gone to consult a doctor back home, Himjyoti had accidentally locked himself in the chamber's bathroom. By the time he heard his father's voice at the door, Himjyoti was highly agitated, having already imagined everyone leaving, his father looking for him on the streets and then filing a complaint at the police station. Finally, the doctor had had to come out, leaving a patient sprawled on the examination table. He spoke loudly across the bathroom door, instructing Himjyoti on the door's locking mechanism, over and over. When Himjyoti eventually walked out, he hugged his father and cried. He was embarrassed about that later. His father had tried to smile, to ease the situation, clearly embarrassed. Yet, he wanted to soothe the nerves of this forever-nervous, oversensitive son.

Himjyoti had always been paranoid. Since he was scared of sleeping under mosquito nets, his parents bought chemical repellents—much to his grandmother's dismay, for she believed they reduced a person's lifespan. In his hometown, they lived in a safe, protected apartment complex. It was old, with moss sprouting from its walls. Once, his mother had latched the main door to go out for a walk, not wanting to wake him from his post-school siesta. He'd panicked on waking up and ended up calling the cops. The police alerted the security agency that guarded their neighbourhood. By the time his mother returned with vegetable bags in both hands and droplets of sweat sparkling on her forehead, he was faint with fear and fore-boding. The cops rang the doorbell soon after she arrived.

People have strange phobias. People laughed at Himjyoti's harmless phobias, and sometimes he joined in, too. So, he listened to Mike dili-gently. He didn't want to get locked in the bathroom. He knew that in the US, people didn't drop in unannounced, unlike his neighbourhood in Guwahati, where everyone knew everyone else and dropped in at each oth-er's houses in the evening, staying back for tea and long conversations. His Indian friends who studied in the US had told him about the choking lone-liness of this country. About the absence of the kind of friend who would go with you to Cub Foods even when he had work to finish. He couldn't say why people back home accompanied each other to grocery shops, to news-paper stands, to have a cup of tea—why they adjusted so much for each other. The girls even went to the loo in groups. One or two always waited outside.

But he didn't think it was 'cultural', as his American roommate said one day. In fact, he didn't understand what that meant. By then, he had heard so many people using that word to describe something puzzling, confusing, or incomprehensible in a foreigner that it had started to annoy him. A few days ago, when the Nepali student in his class spoke out of turn and a bit too loudly, Himjyoti's classmate Diana told him that it wasn't rude, it was 'cultural'. But Lakpa had been in the US for eight years, and he knew the codes of courtesy. That day in class, he had just been very passionate about the topic under discussion. Himjyoti wondered if Diana was afraid to call him rude. Calling the behaviour 'cultural' allowed her to create distance, disengagement, and dismissal. It allowed her not to analyse it, bring it closer.

'No, it's not cultural, Mike,' Himjyoti had corrected him. 'That's how things are in India. We like to be with people, and it's no different if you are a recluse by nature.'

On the first day, Mike had picked him up from the Minneapolis–Saint Paul International Airport. Himjyoti's friend Zutimala, who studied in Boston, told him that settling down in America was like digging a tunnel through the bed of the Atlantic Ocean from the Bay of Bengal with only a pickaxe. She had heard of Indians doing such favours for newly arrived Indians, not Americans. Himjyoti replied that he had heard people in Minnesota were nicer than people on the West and East Coasts.

'Good for you,' she said in an unconvinced tone. 'But make sure you make some Indian friends. They are the ones who will take care of you, come to you when you have a fever. Your American friends will leave 'xoxos' in your inbox. They won't sit beside you when you have a cold. It's a nation afraid of germs.' She said 'your American friends' in the same tone that little children sang 'yellow-yellow-dirty-fellow' to tease each other.

Oh god, Himjyoti thought, why is she always so cynical?

While Mike was driving Himjyoti from the airport that first day, he said that he had a lot of 'South Asian friends' because his girlfriend was 'South Asian'. When Himjyoti asked Mike which country she was from, what language she spoke, Mike couldn't tell him. Cheerfully, he said she cooked 'South Asian food on the weekends' and that he loved 'daaal'. The word 'dal' sounded odd in Mike's tongue, somewhat cute. It made the everyday dal so amazing and special that Himjyoti didn't want to correct the pronunciation.

Himjyoti was pleased to find that Mike's girlfriend was from India. Her father worked in the army, so she had grown up in a major or minor city in almost every part of India: Delhi, Srinagar, Coimbatore, Cherrapunjee, Darjeeling, Ambala, Jalandhar, Thiruvananthapuram, Chandigarh, Kolkata, Pasighat. She spoke Tamil fluently because she went to high school in Chennai. She could make momos because she studied in Darjeeling before enrolling in college and had 'lots of Nepali friends'. She firmly believed that Suniel Shetty was the sexiest man in the world. Her name was Neelakshi Rai. On the first day, when they met, Himjyoti thanked her for making his bed, for writing the wonderful welcome note, in blue and red ink, that was pasted on his door.

//////////////

A week later, Neelakshi didn't laugh at him when he locked himself in the bathroom and screamed, 'Neelakshi, Neelakshi!'

She was making dinner then but rushed to help. 'Push, keep it in for a while, and now pull,' she kept saying, until he tumbled out of the bathroom in his black briefs, looking terrified. He went back in immediately. But he didn't turn that complicated knob. He just shut the door firmly against the frame.

When he finally came out, dressed, drying his hair with a towel, Himjyoti wasn't annoyed when Mike, who was now seated at the dining table, laughed at him. He knew he'd been foolish. But he didn't like it when Mike asked him, laughing, whether India had such sophisticated bathrooms. 'I have heard you guys bathe in the river?"

'No, we don't! And this isn't a sophisticated bathroom! I don't really know what you mean by sophisticated bathroom because my own bathroom has everything this one has, except the bathtub because none of us like bathing in tubs. I am just not very comfortable with gadgets. I still don't have a smartphone, you know. And I want to buy a new camera such as a DSLR, but I haven't gathered the courage to.'

Himjyoti couldn't understand why he was being so defensive. So apologetic. It annoyed him that he was. He was even more annoyed when Mike asked him, with a polite smile on his face, if people really used smartphones in India and if computers were popular at all. He looked curious, genuinely interested. Too genuine, too polite, Himjyoti wondered.

Neelakshi ignored Himjyoti's surprised look that probably meant, 'Haven't you told him anything about India?' She was looking away, as if she hadn't heard the conversation at all.

At dinner, they talked about home. Neelakshi said how she missed freshly cooked food, how bored she was of eating frozen items. Himjyoti said that he would soon go to Target and buy all the utensils he needed to cook. Neelakshi said he should buy from Walmart because it was cheaper there.

'I love South Asian food,' Mike said cheerfully, loudly.

Himjyoti pointed out that 'South Asian food' was a very vague term. Mike didn't look pleased but asked him what was wrong with that: 'Aren't you South Asian?'

At this, Himjyoti laughed. How would it feel if he called Mike a 'North American' or a 'northern hemispherian'? Mike said in a slightly peevish tone that that 'didn't make any sense' and 'you shouldn't mind it because Africans don't mind being called Africans'.

Himjyoti cleaned his plate slowly. He was at the sink when he replied that he didn't mind. He was only asking Mike to be more precise. Mike pretended he didn't hear.

Neelakshi said, 'Jeez, you know Anna didn't say hi to me today?' A strange lilt in her speech. Like a drunken man talking to unresponsive passers-by.

'Jeez, how rude! Did she at least smile?' Mike asked.

///////////////

But Himjyoti was able to start cooking only a month later, when he was bored of eating pizzas and frozen food, and after his mother lectured him about the benefits of healthy home-cooked meals. When his grandmother grabbed the phone to repeat the same series of orders, sprinkled with retro Assamese proverbs, he told her that he was running out of minutes.

She didn't understand. 'What do you mean?'

When he explained, she barked out at him, 'WHAT? You don't have time to talk to your grandmother?'

'Aaita, please, we have been speaking for almost an hour.'

She disconnected the phone only when he promised to cook food at home and return to India as the same 'healthy boy we brought up'. Later, his mother called again. She asked him about his friends and roommates; she worried they would 'exploit' him.

'What do you mean, Ma? Will they make me work in the factory and take all my earnings?'

When he cooked that first time, the three of them ate together. Mike said how much he loved South Asian food (too loudly) and Neelakshi had gasped, 'So good, so good.' Himjyoti wondered why Neelakshi didn't tell him frankly that the chicken wasn't very good. The preservative in the Great Value minced garlic had given it a taste and smell that he hated. He ate less than usual. Mike expressed his love for South Asian food one last time (too cheerfully) before dumping his plate in the sink. Neelakshi showed Himjyoti how he could save the food in boxes for heating up and eating later. She suggested that he cook no more than twice a week to save time.

////////////

Mike and Neelakshi had gone to his home in Owatonna because it was a long weekend. When they were packing, Himjyoti noticed the spices that Neelakshi was carrying to cook Indian dishes. He teased her that she was visiting to 'do bahurani duty' and impress her would-be in-laws. When both of them laughed, she explained to Mike that 'bahurani' meant daughter-in-law.

With the whole house to himself, Himjyoti played music on his stereo. He sat in the living room, something he couldn't usually do because he felt uncomfortable when Mike and Neelakshi sat there, groping each other, smooching. It made his cheeks warm and ears hot. What would his parents think if they knew about it—though there wasn't a chance such a thing could happen. He had felt that Mike and Neelakshi didn't like it when he sat in the living room or the dining table, a little away from the couch where they'd sit, looking into each other's eyes. Perhaps Neelakshi disliked it more than Mike.

Neelakshi didn't have a graduate assistantship like Mike did since she was an undergrad student. She worked at a shelter home until late at night and probably slept only three, four hours a day. He wondered how she functioned, how she managed to wake up half an hour before Mike returned from his second job at nine in the evening so that she could take a bath, put on make-up, change into a new dress, and wait for him on that couch. Sometimes, she called him up to ask what he would like to eat. She'd keep the cheese melted for him and place the pizza in the oven, so all he had to do was switch off the oven and pull on the gloves that she'd taken out from the drawer and placed on the counter.

When Mike was very tired, he would drawl, 'Aww, can you please bring it here?'

He made that request often, and she always complied. Neelakshi ate very little. She also used very few dishes because it was she who washed the dishes every day—dishes that Mike piled up on the sink one by one until all the dishes in the house were in use. He made a face when washing the dishes, holding them like fragile crystal dolls. Neelakshi teased him that it wasn't a small bird he was holding, that he had to rub the steel scrubber hard.

Mike would whine, 'Show me again, daaarrrlinggg.'

She'd show him how, but Mike never said, 'Let me try.' He waited for her to finish all the dishes. She did them, demonstrating how to wash, scrub hard, not do it like he was caressing the cheeks of a little girl.

Sometimes Himjyoti felt sorry for Neelakshi. In the second week after he had moved in, they had a conversation where she'd said her life would be destroyed if Mike didn't marry her because once her visa expired, she'd have to return to the dust and grime of India and work in cities she didn't want to live in. Himjyoti just told her not to worry, Mike would surely marry her, and besides, everything had already been set up for next year: the cards, the dates, the hall, the wedding gown, and the four tubes of Fair and Lovely, the skin lightening cream that she had requested Himjyoti bring along once it was finalised that he would be their roommate. He had contacted them through Craigslist.

When they returned from Owatonna, Mike didn't greet him the way he usually did, the way Himjyoti was now accustomed to. While heating lunch, Mike told Himjyoti that he should open the sliding door that led to the patio when he cooked. He moved his hands a lot when he said that. His voice was a bit strained. At some point, Himjyoti thought Mike would break into a dance as he spoke. He felt Mike was trying too hard to make the conversation casual, like chatting about the security deposit they had made to their landlord. Or about the bathroom knob.

Later, when he was back in his own room, he overheard an argument. Bits of sentences were audible—too audible.

Mike was saying loudly to Neelakshi that he would have to cancel the invitation he sent out for the dinner guests now. Neelakshi said it had been his idea to send around that bleep for a roommate on Craigslist. Unusually, her tone was sharp, even peevish.

Mike left the house in a huff, frowning hard, but returned quickly. Maybe he'd gone to Walmart because he now had a Lysol Neutra Air Sanitising Spray in his hand, new and unopened.

He didn't acknowledge Himjyoti who had taken his lunch to the dining table. He went around the living room, kitchen, and dining room (where Himjyoti was eating) with a frown on his face and sprayed. 'Sorry, this is not toxic. I made sure I didn't spray it near you. Actually, we have guests coming in a few hours, so we need to get rid of the Indian smell.'

Himjyoti said it was all right, but he didn't feel like finishing his meal— the chicken he'd spent two hours cooking so that he could go back home the same healthy boy that his mother and grandmother expected, the dal that Mike loved so much. It felt as if someone had sneezed on this food.

After clearing his white china plate, he went in to his room and stayed there all day, reading. In the evening, when he came out to make some tea so that he didn't fall asleep and could read more, he saw *Glamour* magazine open on the dining table. '29 things to do with a naked man' and 'Get your WonderBra today!'

From his bedroom, Himjyoti heard Mike apologising. 'We have a new roommate, a South Asian, sorry about the smell.'

After a while, he heard a loud female voice, 'Oh, it's cultural.'

Mike said, 'He will learn. We will also learn to adjust.'

Himjyoti wondered what exactly WonderBras were. He thought about the way Mike had pronounced dal on the first day when he had driven him in from the airport, telling him about the winter here. He wondered about the twenty-nine things a woman could do with a naked man and smiled to himself.

BEFORE THE BULLET

Minutes before the bullet was fired, Digonto was standing impatiently in front of the officer at the army camp in Teteliguri village, Kamrup district, Assam. He had just returned from a six-year stay in Indiana, United States, having completed his PhD on the effects of neighbouring perturbation on drop coalescence in colloid/polymer mixtures.

The military officer, commanding Digonto to stand straight, asked about the weather in America. About the snow. About 'American women who wear short skirts and fuck men as often as they change bras'. And Digonto answered to satisfy his curiosity: yes, it is cold, it snows, but there are no issues with that because everything is internally heated, and during the winter months, though it is unbearably cold, the best thing is cups of hot coffee. Yes, American women sleep around (he didn't want to debate), change boyfriends like their underpants. The officer asked if he had brought Assam tea with him. Digonto replied, yes, but by the end of the first year, it had run out, and he'd had to depend on various blends of American coffee bought from Walmart. The officer said, 'The whites should be posted to

Siachen, Kashmir, and they will forget their snow for life.' Digonto said, 'Yes, they should be sent to Siachen, in Kashmir—the highest battlefield in the world.'

The army camp was at the edge of the village. Digonto hadn't known of its existence until that day. It wasn't there when he had left in 1997. Their village had no insurgents, unlike the remote places of Assam. He had been stopped because he wasn't supposed to pass the camp on his bicycle; he was supposed to stop and disembark as a mark of respect to the Sikh regiment officers and soldiers stationed there and who hung around carrying their AK-47s like khadi-clad leftist students might carry their satchels. Digonto, who did his high school in Guwahati and then left to study in the US, was returning home after six years and didn't know that the once-free village now had certain rules and regulations. Rules that were not made by the village council, but made and monitored by men in olive-green uniforms who had set up camp there around five years ago.

When the officer had stopped him, Digonto was puzzled. He'd stopped pedalling and asked, 'Are you asking me to step down?' That was about half an hour before the bullet was fired.

/////////////////

About an hour before the bullet flew into the air, Digonto deboarded with his luggage at the Tetelia bus stop. He took the regular route to Teteliguri, where he had grown up, a village he had left less than a decade ago, a village that was named after a 350-year-old tamarind tree. He inhaled the smell he so loved, of dust mixed with dried cow dung. When he saw the newborn calves, he knew he would get to drink 'real milk' after a long time. Milk that you couldn't store for long because it didn't have preservatives. Milk that you needed to boil thrice a day during summers and twice a day during winters so that it didn't curdle, in a village that had no refrigerators.

How many calves had their cow had over these years? But it had been six years: did cows live that long? After six years of drinking Hy-Vee and Walmart whole milk, he was eager for home milk, unfrozen vegetables, and real rotis (not tortillas, which were a poor substitute). But, of course, like every Assamese, he preferred rice.

Digonto was in a hurry to reach home, but he didn't quicken his pace, even though he had borrowed a bicycle from a neighbour he had met at the bus stop. He wheeled the cycle and walked. He wanted to smell the forests that the dusty gravel road cut through and gaze at the light-brown empty paddy fields interrupted only by patches of first-rain grasses raising their adamant heads. Soon, it would rain a lot, and the fields would be under water, ready to receive the rice seedlings. For some reason, that scene reminded him of his American university. There was farmland around the university, too, but no laburnum trees. When he reached the gravel path under the silk cotton tree, a little ahead of the primary school, he mounted the bicycle. He would cycle for a while, walk a little; he would enjoy the fresh air properly.

He shouldn't have sat on the bicycle.

//////////////

Arrangements had been made: he'd sent an email to his friend in Guwahati; his friend's father had called up his uncle's mobile phone; his uncle had cycled two miles (and crossed two rickety bridges: one wooden, one bamboo) to tell his mother, grandfather, brother, and sister-in-law the exact date he'd arrive. 'On the twenty-fifth, he will land in Delhi, stay back with a friend at the university there, before boarding the connecting fight to Guwahati—'

Konmai, his mother, had interrupted her brother in a shrill, displeased voice. 'What? His friends are more important than his mother who hasn't seen him in six years? I knew this would happen. I knew he would go mad staring at those glass tubes inside that lab or whatever he calls it.' Konmai sat on the blackened wooden chair, on which only men were supposed to sit, and shed tears.

Her mother-in-law raised an eyebrow when she saw Konmai sitting there in front of so many men, but then she thought, let it be, I can understand. She caressed Konmai's head with her wrinkled hands, smiling with her wrinkled face. 'Get up, my dear; it's not a big deal. He mustn't have gotten a ticket in that Flying Ship on the preferred date.'

'I knew this would happen!' Konmai continued to weep. 'What's the point of such university degrees that keep you away from loved ones for so long?'

'But he has sent money. Look, this is not the old thatched house,' her brother consoled her. 'Don't forget the US dollars over the years, savings from his scholarship.'

Wiping her tears at her brother's consolations, Konmai thought of the small and big sacrifices he must have made to send those dollars that had turned into many rupees when they reached the State Bank in Maloybari village. She never understood the mystery of how a few dollars turned into so many rupees. But when was there time to worry about such things? Certainly not after his father had passed away. The debts the man had taken to educate his son, the holes in the roof, raising money for her twenty-year-old daughter's wedding—these were the worries that occupied her, not the mystery of dollars and rupees or small sacrifices.

But his American trip was a sort of lucky charm. The first prospective groom who had come to see Digonto's sister Poree, the young moustached boy who taught physics in the government school a few villages away, had asked them where her brother was, right after Konmai had proudly displayed Poree's embroidery and footloom work.

'Aamerikaa.'

The boy's eyes twinkled. 'What does he do?' he asked eagerly.

'He teaches,' Digonto's mother said.

Poree, embarrassed, corrected her mother, 'Actually, he is doing a PhD, and he has a teaching assistantship.' But they didn't understand what that meant. Since Poree had passed high school, she could at least repeat the things he wrote to them.

The middle-aged prospective mother-in-law said pejoratively, 'Oh, assistant?' She had a black mole on her upper lip. Four strands of hair sprouted from it; one of them was greyish. 'I guess he cleans desks and benches at the university?'

The boy's aunt, who supported the prospective mother-in-law in everything she uttered, added, 'Must be like our Komol in Delhi. He even bathes his professor's dog, gets them groceries. You have to do a lot of humiliating jobs when you are an assistant.'

Later that afternoon, after they had left, Konmai sat in a corner and howled, 'Who will marry you? You just can't keep your loud mouth shut!'

Poree stared at her mother, furious. 'I don't care. Why do you go about bragging that your Great Son is a professor in an American university? He has gone there to be taught, not teach. That assistantship is a part of his scholarship—he said all this very clearly in his letter.'

Konmai didn't like the way Poree spoke. 'I don't know from which angle I am lying. It is not a joke: teaching sums to American kids. How many people from our village have done that? How many from all the villages in this region?' She spoke with such confidence that anyone would think she had travelled around the world, knew just how difficult it was to teach in America. But the truth was that after she had eloped with Digonto's father at the age of sixteen, she hadn't travelled out of that region. She hadn't even been to Guwahati, and that was only about an hour away.

Konmai had predicted that no mother-in-law would like to have a daughter-in-law who interrupted elders' conversations. But so wrong she was. Two years before the bullet went off one afternoon under the laburnum tree, that man with twinkling eyes had coloured the white middle parting of Poree's hair with red vermillion powder. He was proud to have a wife whose brother worked abroad. Proud to have a brother-in-law who sent him an America-bought shirt with a hundred-dollar bill pinned inside its pocket.

///////////////

When the soldiers first stopped him, Digonto had told the officer, in Hindi, that he was returning to his village after many years to be with his family. The bicycle didn't belong to him. He had borrowed it from their neighbour at the little kiosk near the bus stop. He didn't tell them that he knew his mother was waiting with cooked food. That his sister would have woven for him traditional gamusas with large flowers on them. That his brother-in-law would have arranged a duck from somewhere, or a turtle, to be eaten with rice. But his movements, his quick, polite, and firm replies, told the officers that he wanted to be on his way as soon as possible.

When the officer called him a bastard, Digonto looked at him, surprised, and, without dismounting, asked him in English why he was behaving like that.

The officer looked astonished, as did the soldier standing beside him. 'Where are you coming from after so many years?' They wanted to see his passport, the official identity card of his university. The soldier told him, 'It's a rule that people dismount from cycles and bullock carts on this path, this path that runs in front of the army camp.'

Digonto dismounted.

'It was also a rule a few years ago to take off any footwear and place it on the head to cross this stretch. But the days are peaceful now, so you don't need to do that anymore. The elderly men are not made to frog-jump for kilometres for criminally sheltering insurgents or serving them meals when they came knocking at the door with guns hanging from their shoulders,' the heavy-built officer said. He then asked Digonto about Assam tea and snow and how cold it got when it snowed in America.

The disbelief and disgust on Digonto's curled lips didn't go down well. They looked at his passport, went through its pages several times. They took a long time, like a cat might smell strange food from several angles before taking a tiny bite.

Digonto wanted the ordeal over with. They had no right to search him like that, he thought. He distracted himself with thoughts of the dishes his mother would have prepared. He looked at the laburnum tree a little farther on and felt better. It was fifteen minutes before the bullet, and the crows and sparrows were peaceful, perching, fluttering their wings on the branches. Digonto yearned to stand under the laburnum while the officer interrogated him. The birds had gathered to discuss, as they did daily, which group would occupy how much space among the blooms on those robust branches. So many flowers, so yellow, a tree made of round gold coins. During dark nights, when someone holding a bright lamp walked under it, the tree looked like a tall woman dressed in a glowing dress. He wanted to go closer. They were still looking at his passport.

He asked in English, 'Are you done?'

Giving him a long stare, the officer replied, also in English, 'Yes, you can go now.'

The officer hadn't expected someone in the area to know English, speak in fluent Hindi, to be America-returned. He didn't like the confidence, the stamp on his visa that allowed him to work in the States, the swagger Digonto had when he spoke, when he remounted his cycle. The officers were used to submission, earned from the fear that they had spread in the past five years. Last night, there had been a roundtable conference in the army camp discussing the funds that had come for counterinsurgency operations: the money needed to be used up or it would be summoned back to the capital. The best way to use it was by demonstrating corpses.

In this business, only the dead spoke to the government agencies. If there was no unrest (deaths, chases, corpses), the camp would be called off: the camp that laid golden eggs for the soldiers and officers here. What if the story of a young local man who didn't dismount from his bicycle, who spoke in English at the army camp in a village where people didn't even know how to speak in Hindi, went around? It could create a hushed confidence in the minds of the villagers.

The officer looked at Digonto's retreating figure. He was just reaching the laburnum tree. The officer's voice was calm. 'Aim at his head.'

'Sir?'

'Do as I say, and if you miss, I will shoot your head.'

The soldier shivered. He didn't want to do it. All he wanted was to go home. It wasn't he who had been complaining about the lack of excitement in the last few months: no chases, no corpses, no gunshots, no skirmishes.

///////////////

The birds scattered. Blood splattered onto the tree trunk. A few petals fell, turning in the wind like a spinning cricket ball. But they would have fallen anyway, because the wind had weakened the hold of their light-green stems in the past few days. The cows were the most frightened, grazing in the fields below, shaking their heads. When they heard the bullet (they didn't see the blood and the creamy brain), they raised their ears and stood stiff, as if struck by lightning. There were a few wobbly-footed calves. Confused, they curled their long tails like touched centipedes, sat down, dropped dung or repeatedly ran in circles round their mothers. From a distance, it was impossible to guess whether they were happy or frightened.

Digonto's mother heard the bullet very clearly even though she was in the kitchen, which was filled with the noise of sautéing, boiling, sizzling food. She was, as he had imagined, cooking fish curry for him and the chicken curry that he loved so much.

Poree said, 'Ah, don't worry, why are you shivering like that? The army must be practising.'

Konmai pushed a log of wood into the hearth, took the lid from the iron pan where the chicken curry was simmering, and stirred it twice with her shiny, fat steel ladle. 'Hope they are! Nowadays, I have lost trust totally. In just the last ten years, I have seen so many bodies. That ten-year-old boy, what had he done? They shot him because he ran away. What do you expect when you go to talk to a ten-year-old with guns hanging from your shoulders?'

'That Punjabi soldier who is having an affair with Nirmali? He really cares for her parents. He has helped them rebuild their house and even promised to marry her. Next month, his parents are coming over all the way from Delhi to see her. I wonder how they will talk! His parents don't know Assamese and Nirmali's don't know how to speak Hindi or Punjabi. But the boy is nice. The way he respectfully addresses every woman in the village as Maaji-Maaji is really heartening.'

Konmai scratched her back with a long twig and pushed it into the fire. 'Yes, this camp's soldiers haven't put their hands on the bodies of women in our village, but in other villages, they have. I guess it's because our MLA is from a nearby village. But don't forget the number of boys they maimed and beat to death four years ago. Don't trust so easily. They speak another language.'

By then, the laburnum flowers had covered Digonto's smashed brain.

THE LOVE LIVES
OF PEOPLE WHO
LOOK LIKE KAL PENN

A friendly woman sits next to Arunabh on the flight. She carries a bottle of green liquid. Must be vitamin water; people here drink a lot of vitamin water, he thinks. She introduces herself as Sandy. Sandy is chatty. She tells him she teaches history in a community college and asks if he is from New York. He says he is from India, though he recently moved to Shakopee, Minnesota. He doesn't say that he is from Tinsukia since he is sure she has never heard of his hometown. There is no reason for her to know of it, just as there is no reason for him to visit East Lansing, Michigan, had it not been for this conference. He has been in this country only for a few months. When the flight takes off, Sandy unties her red hair and asks him if he grew up in New York (for the third time), and he says, no, he didn't (for the third time). He wants to look out of the window, but she has the window seat, and he is worried that if he looks that way, she will ask him more questions, try to pronounce the name of his hometown, fail and laugh, and ask him to teach her how to pronounce it, fail again, apologise, laugh again, and that's how they will be likely to spend the next half an hour. So, he doesn't look out. He tries to nap instead, but she wakes him up when she has to use the restroom and apologises profusely. It is okay, he says, though he is irritated. It is not her fault, he thinks. When she returns, she requests the air hostess for a bottle of chilled water and some peanuts, then calls her again and specifies that she wants roasted but unsalted peanuts. The air hostess says she will check and get back to her.

It will be snowing soon in Michigan when they arrive, Sandy says. She is worried about the snowfall, but he says it is okay, he has never seen snow and would love to see and feel it for the first time. She is surprised and asks him how far the Himalayas are from his hometown, and he says, very far, as far as Alaska. He doesn't mean it and doesn't care if she believes it. They talk about climate change and online dating, about travelling to Greece when they have money, about the lack of tenure-track jobs. But he doesn't tell her that he is still new in America, that small-town Minnesota, all this conversation about the impending winter, people saying 'jeez' and 'sorry' and 'thank you' all the time are his first glimpses of the country. He doesn't tell her that he is going for a conference, that when he signed up for it earlier that year, he didn't know the venue would be in the middle of nowhere, or that his flight would be so small, with only two rows of seats, small enough that a strong gust of wind might cause it to crash.

There are no shuttles from the airport to the university. The cab costs 185 dollars. He is upset but has no choice. It is November, and the air is nippy, even chilly. At the airport lounge, Sandy and Arunabh wait together for their rides after she calls her boyfriend. When her ride arrives, they shake hands and say their goodbyes. She smiles and says she will find him on Facebook, to which he nods and smiles back—the kind of smile that doesn't show teeth but conveys measured warmth. Then he adds that it would be good to connect and worries if she will get his last name right:

Borkakoti. She says she loves India and has plans to visit once she is married. She is going to marry the man who is coming to pick her up.

'And I am not marrying the person who is coming to pick me up,' he jokes. Before leaving, she pauses and asks if she can tell him something.

'Yes, sure.'

'Alright, you know, I have been thinking this since I met you, and I wasn't sure if I should say it.'

'Oh, come on, just say it,' he laughs.

'Alright, alright. You know, you remind me so much of Kal Penn. He is, like, my favourite actor! I mean, he has grown older and put on a little weight, but he is absolutely adorable. And I think you look like him, quite a lot, do you know?'

Arunabh's heart sinks a little. 'Hah!' He forces out a smile and says, 'Never thought about that.'

Sandy's lips form an inverted U. It is the kind of expression that people make when they know they have said something offensive but also know that it isn't very offensive and this show absolves them of it. But Arunabh is silent for several seconds, not knowing what her expression is all about. She rolls her eyes, moves the inverted U slightly to her left, and adds quickly, as if to fill the awkward silence, 'As in, a younger, handsome Kal Penn Moody?'

He wants to say, actually, it is Modi, not Moody, but all he can say is, 'Oh, haha.' He knows his smile isn't reaching his eyes, so he exerts a mild force on his lips to keep up the smile for a little longer. But he can feel his smile and the goodbye expression slipping. He decides to reject her friend request on Facebook even if she gets his last name right.

'See you. Will connect later.'

'See you,' he says.

He isn't flattered that she thinks he looks like Kal Penn. His cab driver, Jim, can't pronounce his last name, either. 'Mr Bukkake? Hi, I am from

Clinton County Cabs.' Arunabh tries not to laugh and wonders if Jim knows the meaning of bukkake. He doesn't mind because there isn't a chance that they will send each other friend requests. Jim wears a blue denim jacket, has black hair, and one of his front teeth is missing. He has tobacco stains on his gums but smiles broadly. His name is easy to pronounce. He is six feet tall.

It is five in the evening. The pre-winter November air in Michigan is sharp on his face and neck. Jim mumbles that it is going to snow and starts the car. Inside the car, Arunabh takes off his cap, sits comfortably, pulls down the zip of his woollen coat, looks at the sky, and hopes it will snow. He wants to see snow, touch snow, and walk on snow. He doesn't say that to Jim, of course. Because then Jim would know that he is new in America. Jim turns on the heating, and Arunabh feels warm and sleepy, but he doesn't want to sleep, even though the journey is going to be long and lonely. In twenty minutes, they have left the city behind, and for miles and miles, he sees no human beings or houses.

Not even birds. He looks out, enjoying the fall colours. The comfortable car makes him feel lazy, and he doesn't feel like revising his conference paper or making calls or checking Facebook.

Years later, when he speaks about this journey, he won't remember whether the cab drove through downtown East Lansing, cutting through the campus of the large state university, or even if East Lansing had a downtown at all. He won't remember whether he saw Jimmy John's, Papa Johns, Olive Garden, Applebee's, Burger King, or other restaurants. But he will remember how the trees were running away from him. He will remember that he didn't want to look like Kal Penn, and that he studied his reflection in the rear-view mirror and more than once considered asking Jim whether he saw any resemblance to Kal Penn. And he will always remember the fall colours, his first fall in America: the gold, the yellow, the orange, the red; the blue sky that was slowly turning grey; and his yearning for snow.

At the reception desk, Arunabh meets a young man who is also attending the conference. He is training to be a journalist with a programme in New York City. He grew up in New Jersey but was born in Delhi, where Arunabh had moved to study for a few years. They don't hit it off because the young man says he is working on a project that tries to understand, not justify, the philosophical reasons—he uses the word 'underpinnings'— behind the attack on artists by the Indian right-wing. Arunabh cannot imagine how that qualifies as a subject of research. He takes out his credit card, swipes, signs the receipt, thanks the receptionist, and asks him how his work does not condone something heinous. The young man develops a cranky tone, an unpleasant swagger. This man who 1) is training to be a journalist, 2) is working on a project that tries to psychoanalyse and philosophically understand why the conservatives attack artists and shoot writers, and 3) is claiming the project isn't trying to justify violence is called Adit.

'I thought this conference is about human rights and literature,' Arunabh quips. He decides not to attend Adit's session.

Adit asks him if he would like to grab a cup of coffee. Arunabh has no idea why he agrees, but they walk to the other end of the room, where some people who look like Serious Conference Attendees are sitting. On a desk, there are four large coffee dispensers: hazelnut, dark roast, medium roast, decaffeinated. There are cookies and pretzels and green apples and bananas on a large tray engraved with the name of the hotel. Adit asks about Arunabh's paper, and he says, oh, you won't be interested. He hears the sarcasm in his own tone and decides he must dial it down. It is cold outside, but there is no sign of snow.

Arunabh tries to change the topic. 'I don't understand the point of decaffeinated coffee. Isn't it just brown water?' They agree on something finally. Adit chuckles. Arunabh doesn't understand why this man has taken a liking to him.

'America is a funny country,' Adit says in a deliberate Indian accent. 'Now, come on, tell me about your paper.'

'Why don't you come to listen to me tomorrow?' He is a bit irritated now.

'My god, you are adamant.'

'One has to hold one's ground, don't you think?'

'I will come for your paper. I like to listen to people who make a career out of dissing their country!' He winks, raising a thumb at Arunabh.

Perhaps he is trying to make the threat sound like a joke, or the joke sound like a threat, but Arunabh finds it neither funny nor threatening. He doesn't smile back, doesn't wink back, just leaves the lobby. He looks outside and hopes it will snow at night. He will then open the window, take a picture with his new smartphone, and share it with his friends in India. So beautiful, he can already hear them exclaiming. His friends in Assam have never seen snow. His mother is worried Arunabh won't be able to cope with the snow and will catch a cold.

///////////////

On the third floor, he looks for his room. Most American hotels feel like mazes to him, so easy it is to lose one's way. He remembers the conference hotel in Madison, where he could not find his room on the first try, and this hotel feels the same. When he finally locates his room, he cannot unlock it. He tries, with his laptop and duffel bag hanging from his right shoulder. Then he gently places them on the carpeted floor and tries again. He tries for a very long time, and he is tired and unhappy and realises he hates people like Adit and doesn't want to look like Kal Penn.

'There is a trick to opening that door.' A husky, resonant voice.

He turns around. Never in his life has he seen such a beautiful woman. An indigo scarf covers her head. Everything else she is wearing is pitch black, except the bright, silk muffler around her neck, giving her a radiance that matches her expressive eyes. He almost drops the key. She says, 'May I?' but doesn't wait for him to say yes. She takes the key from his hand and unlocks the door in a second.

'Oh my god, that looked easy.'

'But it is not.' Her voice is deep and sonorous. She speaks from her heart, he thinks and immediately considers the thought stupid. He smiles.

'I am sorry—? Did I say anything funny? I am sorry if I did. I didn't mean to—'

He smiles more broadly. 'No, you didn't say anything funny. I was just thinking of something else.'

'Oh, I am sorry. I thought—'

He does the rude thing. He interrupts. 'Any chance you are from Minnesota?'

For a second, she looks stunned. Then she bursts out laughing. It is a loud, throaty, crackling laughter, a confident and happy laughter. He laughs, too.

'I am not gonna ask how you know.'

'You don't have to,' he says. 'Hi, I am Arunabh. I live in Shakopee. I'm here for the conference.'

'What a small world!' she says.

He notices how skilfully she unlocks her own door, which is opposite from his. She knows the trick well. He wants to tell her not to go. To stand there and chat. She pushes her door open, slots the key in the main switch, and waits. 'I am really sorry, I haven't even told you my name. I am Adayomi.' She comes forward to shake hands with him, and the door shuts behind her with a thud. She gasps as soon as their hands touch. 'Fuck. My key is stuck in the room!'

'Oh no. Don't you have a spare key?'

'Yes, I do.' She feels the pockets in her jacket. 'I am so sorry I swore.' Her fingers rush through the pockets but return empty. 'But I think I left it on the table inside when I went to get some coffee downstairs. Oh no, I am so sorry.'

He pushes his door open. For a second, he isn't sure whether he should invite her into his room so she can wait while the hotel staff arrive with their master key. If he invites her in, he may come across as creepy. If he shuts the door in her face, it would be rude—rude to the person who helped him unlock his door, to the person who says so many sorries, to the person who is also from Minnesota. And she is beautiful. He wants to hang out with her. In a second, he has decided. He props the door open with his luggage and says he will go in to call the main desk. She waits at the door. Perhaps she can see him from there, picking up the phone on the bedside table and speaking. Maybe she can also see the white curtains and beyond that, through huge glass windows, the yellow streetlights, the racing cars, the orange-coloured tree that is shedding the last of its leaves to welcome the winter.

'I am so, so sorry; you must be so tired,' she says.

'It is alright, and you don't have to apologise. It happens to everyone, I am sure.'

She rolls her eyes. His door is still open, and if she wanted to, she could come in and look outside the window, where she would see the orange leaves falling and the group of people walking on the road. She says, 'I am sorry I am delaying you. The dinner is at 8.30, and it is almost 7.30. You won't have any time to rest.' She folds her arms and looks at him.

'That's alright! I am from India, by the way. We don't say "sorry" and "thank you" that much, so all of this is a bit odd for me.'

She smiles and looks down at the brown carpet. It has chrome-yellow patterns.

He adds, 'You know, I have to say this, my god, Minnesotans apologise all the time. My friend Kate apologises for apologising too much.'

She shakes her head and laughs again. A bit of her red muffler comes undone, revealing her neck. It is longer than he expected. 'I get that a lot. I came to attend school in Minnesota eight years ago and have been living there since. But my family is still in New York. And guess what, I now think them rude!'

Now Arunabh rolls his eyes. 'I am not sure if it is really about being polite. My awful roommate leaves these stickers on my door, which I find after a long day.' He puts on a poor American accent to mimic his roommate: 'I would really appreciate it if you could please spray the antibacterial liquid on the kitchen counter after you make tea and then mop it with the kitchen rolls.'

'Seriously?' Adayomi says, as if offended on his behalf.

When a housekeeper comes with a set of keys, Arunabh hates him for arriving too soon. He hopes there is something wrong with the key and that it takes longer to open the door, but he opens it just fine.

'Have a comfortable stay,' he drawls and leaves.

Arunabh wants to kick his ass. 'I didn't even ask what your paper's about.'

'Oh, don't worry, it is not scintillating.'

How effortlessly she unlocks the door and pushes it open. She has long fingers, and her nails are painted blue. 'Shall we meet at 8.25 downstairs?' Adayomi asks. 'It will be good to meet the rest of the presenters.'

'I think so,' he says.

She doesn't leave. 'It is very cold outside. So, bundle up.' She sounds like a caring friend—like his new friends in Minnesota who regularly offer rides for winter shopping. 'It may even snow.'

'Ah, well, it is two degrees already.'

She gasps. 'What!'

'Oh, wait, I mean in Celsius. I am still getting used to Fahrenheit. It doesn't make sense to me. Why do you guys have to do everything differently?'

'Don't blame me. My father is Nigerian. I was born in Canberra, and we moved here when I was fourteen. I am all for Celsius, only I don't understand how that works!' She stands there for a few seconds more. As if waiting for him to say something. She looks beautiful when she smiles.

'I see,' he says. 'Don't tell me your paper is on Chinua Achebe.'

She laughs again. Throaty and loud. The laughter of a joyful person. More than ever, he wants to see snow, touch snow, and walk on snow.

////////////////

There are sixteen conference delegates at the hotel. They meet in the lobby but soon break up into groups of four or five. Some of them had arrived earlier in the day and have already formed their own circles. Arunabh's group, which includes Adayomi and Adit, walks to the pizza restaurant nearby. He doesn't like pizza but goes along anyway. It looks like a cheap place, and he doesn't want to spend a lot of money. He is still converting US dollars to rupees in his mind, he is embarrassed to admit. There is a woman called Elena with them who moved to Boston several years ago from Wyoming. She makes sure everyone knows that. And that she is working with a famous academic, and that she ran into Derek Walcott several times while waiting for the elevator. Adayomi and Arunabh are sitting next to each other. She turns to look at him, and he sees that her lips have formed a soft inverted U. He looks away, worried he will burst out laughing, and the woman from Boston who met Derek Walcott won't like that.

Elena dominates the dinner conversation and, like many people here, uses a few words repeatedly. They are: 'excited' (variations of it), 'amazing', 'cool', 'awesome', and 'that sucks'. She is the one who reads out the menu, asks everyone about their preferences, and then places the order. She says that if the waiter walks around the table asking people what they would like to eat, it would drive her nuts. She repeatedly touches her blond hair and rattles off the list of things she is allergic to and what she likes or dislikes eating and also provides a list of pizzas she strongly recommends. When Tara, from Mumbai, wants to order one with olives and tomatoes, Elena asks if Tara is sure that she wouldn't want to add pepperoni. Tara says no. She asks again, 'Are you sure?' Later, when they wait for the food, she talks about her ex-boyfriend, the athletic sex they had, and the perils of online dating in America. Arunabh doesn't want to know any of this.

Adayomi is quiet. Arunabh is quiet. Adit is not so quiet. Tara is wearing a sari. She is smiling so much that he wonders if she is jet-lagged because, between Elena's anecdotes, she manages to say that she landed in Chicago only that afternoon. After Elena finishes talking about her sex life and dating life, she wants to know about everyone's papers and responds with one of her stock words. Arunabh feels he is in the middle of a panel discussion and she is the moderator—a bad one. She uses the word 'awesome' in response to Arunabh's abstract. Tara is the last one, and she speaks for at least four minutes and fifty seconds. He wonders if everyone has now decided not to go to her panel the day after. She continues to speak until Adit interrupts her with a question that is clearly meant to disrupt her, not out of any curiosity. Elena takes the window to respond to Tara's narration of her abstract. She uses a different word: 'interesting'. Tara looks disappointed. Perhaps she wanted to hear one of the other superlatives that Elena has been using.

'So, did you grow up in Nigeria? Kedu?' Elena asks Adayomi. 'I have read a lot of Nigerian novels.'

'No, I grew up in Paris and New York, and I don't know the meaning of "kedu".'

Elena's disappointment is visible. She stops mid-sentence, her lips parted just wide enough for a fly to enter. 'So, how did you get interested in Nigerian literature?'

Adayomi fumbles. 'Oh, I mean, everyone has heard of the civil war, and we have all read Achebe.'

Arunabh says, 'So, your paper *is* actually about Achebe.'

'Yeah,' she says in a bored tone. 'All Nigerian English PhDs are about Achebe, you know.' Tara bursts out laughing. She is so loud and her voice so thin that it startles the baby at the next table. The baby starts to cry loudly, looking at Tara, and the mother is annoyed. She tries to whisper, 'I am sorry. I am just jet-lagged.' She fails at whispering. It seems she is a generally loud person.

Elena is unrelenting. She asks Adayomi, 'But, I mean, your upbringing must have helped you gain some interest in Nigerian writing, right?'

'My father is an engineer. He doesn't even read the papers, forget Achebe. And my mother is a nurse. She had no time to read books, and she is Bangladeshi.'

Arunabh looks at her, pleasantly surprised, and she responds with a soft nod that no one else can see. Perhaps, it is a nod to the bond that they have suddenly found in their common South Asian-ness.

'Oh,' Elena sounds defeated. But she bounces back to ask cheerfully, 'You must have visited Nigeria, though?'

'Once.' Adayomi sips her Coke.

The pizzas are on the table. The waiter asks if he can get them anything else. Arunabh knows that he will come back and ask if they are enjoying everything, and everyone will say 'food is great' and 'awesome'. How are people always so cheerful and enthusiastic here? He doesn't want to be cheerful and enthusiastic all the time. He wants to see snow. And he is still irked by Elena's questions.

'Elena, but you must have grown up in Somalia, right?' Arunabh asks her.

She looks shocked. 'Of course not.' She places her piece of pizza on the white plastic plate. 'Oh no, not at all. Why do you think so?'

'No, since you are presenting your research on Nuruddin Farah. How did you get interested in him?'

Elena's annoyed expression is enough, so he wants to leave it there; he has made his point. He allows her to concentrate on her pizza and contemplate what has just happened. But Adayomi ruins it. She places her water bottle with a thud on the table, covers her mouth and coughs a little, then says loudly, 'You're killing it,' and bursts out laughing. Water dribbles from the corner of her lips. She uses a tissue to cover her face and swallows the remaining water in her mouth, gasping. 'That's a good point, Arunabh,' says Tara, grinning. The baby at the next table starts to cry loudly, and the mother gives their table a dirty look. Elena eats her dinner in silence and avoids him for the next three days.

///////////////

Twenty minutes later, they are walking towards the university campus, laughing. Adayomi intersperses her gasps with 'oh my god' and 'you are too much'. She asks, 'Why did you do that?' But he is laughing, too, and in no state to respond. The large red-brick buildings of the university welcome them. It is 9 p.m., and they should be going to bed if they are to wake up in time for the conference, but they walk on. She says she owes him a treat. He says he will accept on one condition—they have to sit on one of those large plastic benches outside and eat. She says it is cold and adds, mimicking him, 'Two degrees Celsius.' But later, when she buys him baklava, they sit outside. They eat slowly.

'What did you think about that guy? The other Indian guy,' she asks him.

'Oh, he is an ABCD.'

'I know that term—it is not a nice term. My mother uses it a lot!' She laughs again. 'I didn't bring water, don't make me laugh. When I laugh a lot, I choke.'

'Okay, then I won't tell you what ABCND means.'

She gives him a look full of question marks.

'American Born Confused Nationalist Desi.'

'What?' she gasps. 'Where do you even learn these things?'

'I think he is going to come to troll me during my presentation. But never mind him—tell me about your mother. How did your parents meet? And which part of Bangladesh is she from?' His voice is full of excitement.

'She's from Chittagong. It is a long story, but my father tells everyone that he met my mother in bed.'

'What does that mean!' Arunabh laughs so much that he has to put his plate of baklava down on the bench. 'Sounds like a poor joke!'

'Yes.' Her eyes become large. 'My sisters and I banned that joke in the house, but later we found out that my mother really loves this awful joke, so the ban was lifted. Now we are filled with dread when someone asks him where they met. He had an operation in a Dubai hospital where she was working as a nurse.'

Arunabh nibbles on the sweet, shaking his head. He takes a sip of his coffee and watches her drinking hers, decaffeinated. He doesn't tease her. The temperature is dropping fast. He tightens the muffler around his neck. She sits in a heat-preserving position: arms folded, hands inside warm coat pockets.

'I don't know what I am doing here with you. We should go! My blood is going to freeze,' she says.

'You are buying me baklava in appreciation of my brilliant trolling of Madam Elena.'

It starts to snow. Arunabh stands up. He feels the snow on his hands. The snow looks like cotton swabs, and he watches the flakes melt as soon as they kiss the ground. He hears a mild sound: *kit-kit-kit*. It is the sound of snow falling on warm ground and melting on contact. But snow is relentless and adamant. It falls again. *Kit-kit-kit. Kit-kit-kit.* He is amazed at the sight and sound of it. Adayomi stands next to him.

'Let's go,' she says, and he says, 'Wait, let's wait.'

She is loud now. 'You will see so much snow in your life in Minnesota that you will want to return to India. You will hate snow. You will have to memorise the size and design of your friends' coats in order to recognise people during winter. Fuck, it is cold.'

'Adayomi.'

'Yes? I am leaving if you aren't coming with me!'

He wants to say, I know you won't go, but asks, 'What is the meaning of your name?'

'You want to know that now?'

'Because I am sure there is a meaning.'

'Will you fucking go if I tell you the meaning of my name?'

'Yes, I will.'

'I think it means something like "she brings me joy". I don't know. I don't speak Igbo. Although, I do know the meaning of "kedu", but I just didn't want to talk to that stupid woman.'

They start to walk back. She is still in the heat-preserving posture. 'And what does your name mean?'

He doesn't want to tell her that his name means sunrays—sunrays that bring mornings, that melt snow. He doesn't want the snow to melt. Arunabh, whose name means sunrays, looks straight into her eyes and says, 'Promise me you will meet me in Minneapolis. I will tell you the meaning of my name.'

She smiles. Her eyes dance. She holds his hand as they walk into the lobby. When he takes her in his arms, he believes his kidneys are moving around his body and his heart has stopped forever. At that moment, he realises, he could die, and there would be no regrets.

FOR THE GREATER COMMON GOOD

Neerumoni was the first one in the family to suspect the bark manuscripts. Anil had stared at her in silence. Where on earth had she heard of books being haunted? She said firmly that it wasn't the soul of her dead husband—his father, Horokanto—whom she had first suspected, but the souls trapped in the manuscripts. She stood up and went out to the one-acre pond behind her house, bamboo creel in hand. She would spend some time there. Washing the rice, vegetables, clothes, and vessels from the afternoon's meal wouldn't take long. Chores done, she changed into a petticoat, tied just above her breasts, and swam for at least an hour.

Winters weren't harsh in Teteliguri, not like the villages at the foot of the Jaintia Hills on the Meghalaya border. The wind from the hills entered every nook and cranny there. Meghalaya was the abode of clouds. The white clouds descended as quiet as cats' paws, and soon people would be in the middle of a fog, even before the cat's tongue could scrape their bones.

No, here, in Teteliguri village, things were better. There were huge paddy fields. There were many houses and many people in those houses. Here, the climate remained warm and comfortable. Of course, when the trees in the stunted hills that guarded the village started to sway, there was a storm. But the chill reigned only on nights when the winds froze the stones and then carried the bite of it into the houses of the village, an uninvited guest. That was why, when Neerumoni first said she was hearing things, Anil had suggested it was the wind. It was usual for the wind to knock at the door, hover over the straw roof of their thatched hut. They had never finished reinforcing the walls with mud.

Back then, she had been confident that it was the soul of her spiteful husband, Horokanto, who had had many unfulfilled desires before he died in that accident last year. He wanted to return to the mortal world, she thought. In the process, he would rob them of all peace. Eventually, Anil took her seriously, as did most other women in the village. They prayed. They left a meal with Horokanto's favourite dishes on the western side of the house. But the manuscripts still opened and shut in the middle of the night (mainly on Saturdays and Tuesdays) all by themselves. Nor did strange souls stop troubling Neerumoni: they left earthworm mounds on the food she cooked and strange handprints on the bedsheets she washed with khar. And one day, when she had cooked duck meat with banana flower, they dropped a ball of curly hair in the pot.

Gradually, those murmurs, faint songs, the rustle of bark as the manuscripts turned their own pages, invaded the dreams of Neerumoni, and Anil, too. On lonely afternoons, when everything was quiet, those sounds were louder, quicker, more restless. One night, Neerumoni woke up, disturbed by the choric melody of the singing crickets. She saw four lanky men standing over the small wooden box where the manuscripts were kept. They were trying to open the lock with a knife that had a blue plastic handle. When she shouted at them, they turned towards her, grew black wings, and flew off through the ceiling, leaving it undisturbed. Her screams woke up the rest of the family, and she told them one of the figures had worn a long green dress, and the others three white turbans and dhotis. They looked as if they were from a royal family. They didn't wear ornaments, though.

No one believed her. Her suspicions were fortified when she saw one of the manuscripts take the shape of an old man in her dreams. He was crying, asking her to set him free, telling her that he was trapped there by mistake, unlike the other souls who had committed sins. He promised never to disturb her if she freed him from the fetters of the spells in the bark manuscripts. When she said that she hadn't trapped him, she wasn't holding him there, he got angry and screamed, called her a liar. Anil laughed it away. But Anju, who would have said many sarcastic things about her mother's superstitions, who would have fought with her even a month ago, was quiet.

Anil looked at Anju and felt again that, after she had been raped, he required inhuman strength just to look at her face, let alone her eyes. She was sitting in a corner when her brother and mother were speaking about the old man trapped in the manuscripts, fingering the crisscross of welts on her wrists, the result of being tied to a bed with steel threads ordinarily used to tie bamboo. Everyone had been away. It was the death anniversary of the village headman's mother. Neerumoni had asked her to come along, tried to tempt her by saying that she'd get to eat porridge at the function, but Anju said that Biren was coming to leave his baby son with her. His wife was away, and the little one wouldn't sleep until Anju sang him a lullaby. Even that day, Neerumoni reminded Anju that she shouldn't forget that Biren was, after all, a man. Though he was her first cousin, the sudden intimacy between them over the last two years was the talk among certain sections of the village.

But Anju was a popular girl. Everyone loved her. Almost every household in the village was indebted to her in some way or the other. 'Anju, would you please weave this mekhela for me? I won't pay you the full price, but I will give you something as a token of love.' Anju turned into Mother Teresa when phrases such as 'token of love' were mentioned. 'Anju, could you come to our house tomorrow morning? I have asked everyone in the village, but you know how the girls in our village have become after the cinema hall opened in Sonapur; they are afraid their hands will melt away like a leper's if they so much as touch the mix of cow dung and loamy soil. Who else will I ask?' Anju nodded vigorously, agreeing with the old woman. 'Anju, don't you dare forget to come a week before the wedding. You know there is no one else I can trust with keys to the money, the ornaments, with supervising . . . oh, you are such an angel, what would I do without you!'

So, while some tongues were wagging, others remained quiet. Why should anyone suspect the relationship between first cousins? Those tongue-waggers said 'first cousins' in a dismissive, mocking tone, and suggested that Biren was 'woman-hungry'.

Thus, the day after Neerumoni found an unconscious Anju lying on the bed with bleeding wrists, the whole village blamed Biren and accompanied a near-crazy Anil to the police station to lodge a complaint. Biren was in jail now for raping Anju. And inside that haunted house, where books with souls created strange noises, a new Anju lived with a constantly growing belly. This new Anju didn't speak and often cried silently.

Slopp-slopp-slopp! The sound brought him back to the present. His mother had rushed in and was now standing in front of him, her adult son, in wet clothes that had become translucent. She hadn't brought her bamboo creel back and looked terrified. When he asked what was wrong, she told him that a rough, hairy hand had pulled her down by the leg while she was bathing in the pond. 'I didn't see it, Anil, but it was a man's hand. Hairy. It's the manuscripts, I am telling you.'

////////////////

Anil's father, Horokanto, learnt sorcery from Neerumoni's father, Doityo-burha, long before the Indian army camp in this village became an integral part of the lives of people here.

As the result of a small disagreement with his own father, Horokanto left home for good. He took shelter in the house of his closest friend, Neerumoni's brother, Nilambor. The next day, when they were having breakfast in the kitchen, Neerumoni's father had asked him what he was interested in. Horokanto replied that he would like to learn the art of sorcery from Doityo-burha. It wasn't an easy art, said the man who was known across seven villages as a great magician, the man who controlled the souls of many rowdy ghosts and forced snakes to come crawling back to suck poison out from the wound of a dying man. Doityo-burha sipped his hot milk and looked at the younger man. But Horokanto was determined to learn. He promised to follow all the rules and regulations. The old man with the long white beard warned him again: if he neglected the rituals for even one day, the bark manuscripts that held the trapped spirits of wild but dead men would strike him dead.

In fact, when he was finally a master of the art, Horokanto managed to imprison a bidaa, a ghost who would be under his command like a genie in a bottle. But the only way to keep the bidaa under control was to give him more and more work. In the next room, Neerumoni, who was a seventeen-year-old girl then, laughed and told her elder sister that it wasn't difficult at all—one could just send the bidaa to a desert and ask him to dig as many wells as possible.

Neerumoni saw Horokanto for the first time three days later. He was swimming in the pond wearing a white gamusa around his waist. It clung to his buttocks. She remembered a long-forgotten feeling. The strange and disturbing pleasure she had felt when her pot-bellied thirty-year-old cousin, who had come to invite them to the rice ceremony for his second son, had pushed up her petticoat, taken out his penis, rubbed it against her inner thighs, asked her to hold it and move her hand slowly up and down. When he started to moan strangely, she got suddenly scared and fled, but not before he had kissed her lips, pushed his tongue inside her mouth, and sucked her upper lip. That was her first time with a man. After a long time, seeing Horokanto, she wanted to lie down beside him.

They had sex for the first time on a rainy winter afternoon, just after the grains were harvested. It wasn't the sort of sudden winter rain that farmers worried would blacken the leaves of the potato. The day had been windy since morning. Clouds gathered little by little in the sky, leisurely, like people trickling into a wedding reception. Her grandmother had advised everyone not to spread out the new grains for drying in the courtyard that day because it might rain. Though it was winter, the sun was strong—you had to drink at least two glasses of water after a half-hour walk. When it finally rained, everyone was ready for it and had taken to their beds or settled down near the hearth with a drink of tea. The cold, the fresh smell of water on earth, the wind: it was ideal. When she reached her house, the quietness of it and the empty veranda seemed to instruct her to go straight to the room that Horokanto shared with Nilambor. Inside, he was lying on his stomach. She latched the door. He looked at her, startled, and tried to smile, but she knew he found her sudden entry odd. She started taking off her clothes. When she was finished, she moved to Horokanto who was staring at her with rapid breaths. Later, lying naked beside her, he pulled her closer and said he had never seen a more beautiful woman in his life. They smelled like coconut water.

After four months of random, wild lovemaking, behind the house at midnight, beside the pond early in the morning, in the mud of the Tamulidobha River, behind cowsheds, on hay stored to serve as fodder, they eloped. They knew her father would rather kill her than let her marry him. He stole most of the manuscripts. Her father died ten years later; by then, Nilambor had died unmarried, and Neerumoni had given birth to three daughters and a son. Anju was her first-born. Anil her second. On his deathbed, her father had seen Horokanto finally, had given him the rest of the manuscripts, cautioned him to use them carefully and for the good of humanity. Doityo-burha also mentioned that since he had eloped with Neerumoni against her father's wishes, he would not be able to use the spells when he most needed them. 'It's not my curse. I have seen that Fate has decided this punishment for you. These manuscripts are powerful, but they are unforgiving if you disrespect them.' Horokanto died in an accident about thirty years later. That morning, he had fought with Neerumoni and hadn't worshipped the ancient books for the first time in his life.

///////////////

After the army crackdown, everybody in the family began believing Neerumoni's claims about the bark manuscripts. The previous day, rebels had blown up a bridge that connected the village with the National Highway and Guwahati. In the explosion, three Indian soldiers from the battalion stationed in the village were killed. The tall longhaired Punjabi soldier, who always wore a red turban and was respectful towards women (unlike the others), lost his hand in the impact and died of bleeding. The intensity of the explosion caused it to fly and land on the roof of the village fisherman's house. His wife had been sitting in the courtyard having her lunch at the time. A stream of blood fell on her shoulders (some say most of it fell on her rice and face). At first, she thought a bird had shat on her clothes, but the shit was red, and the bird looked like a hand. For a while, she stood staring at her roof where the hand was and then fainted. When her neighbours found her an hour later, sprinkled water on her eyes, and brought her back to her senses, she vomited and started to wail hysterically. Everyone in the village went to see the wailing woman and the clenched fist with five golden rings on its fingers—stones meant to ward off the evil influence of powerful planets. They sucked in sharp breaths through clenched teeth and wished Horokanto was still alive. When Dilipram came, they fell quiet. He was the only sorcerer left in the village now to take care of spirits and snakebites and barrenness in married women. They were convinced that the soul of the Punjabi man was refusing to leave.

The army crackdown happened the next day. Scores of soldiers came in jeeps and surrounded the village. Their boots were loud as they ran towards the hamlets. Someone had started to play the drum in the village prayer hall, and it boomed like the announcement of a war. Neerumoni's neighbour, Bibha, came running to tell her to flee. 'Save yourself and your family members, forget the belongings.' Neerumoni stood frozen for a moment, not knowing how Anju would run with that bulging stomach. Then the two of them hurried along as fast as Anju could manage, hoping it was just a false alarm, hoping that, in the village's central meeting ground, everyone would say, go back, nothing is wrong.

But Neerumoni saw that all the young men were running towards the forests. She saw women, children, girls, and old men running across the fields to get to the next village. They would cross the Tamulidobha River, dry in winter. She, too, ran that way with a heavily pregnant Anju, thinking how Horokanto and she had made love on the banks of this river, in the mud, like two buffaloes, one morning. It was the monsoon, and the river that ran beside the passionately love-making couple flowed with force, creating whirlpools, voluptuous with desire and laughter. Neerumoni heard gunshots. She turned back. Someone said it was Hiren, and someone else said, no, no, no one has been shot. They started to run again.

They returned the next morning, after spending a worried night in Maloybari village across the river. Each and every house had been ransacked. There were boot prints on clothes, white bedsheets were soiled brown and black. Food was strewn around. Beds upturned. Tables broken.

Chairs piled up in front of the courtyard and burnt, both plastic and wooden. Mattresses left out in the rain or set on fire and still smoking. Mud walls broken down. Earthen pots shattered in courtyards. As they were putting their houses back together somehow, the village folk could hear the cries of Prodhan Mahatu, the village milkman. He had forgotten to untie his twenty cows, and the army had shot and killed all of them. Their corpses were lying in the cowshed, stinking of blood and the greenish dung that had come out along with their intestines.

In the haunted house, Neerumoni asked Anil, 'Every single object in this house has been thrown around, but look, the bark manuscripts are where we had left them. They have even thrown away the mustard oil lamp that we lit in front of the manuscripts, so why didn't they try to open this locked wooden chest?' All of them believed that the chest would have been broken and the manuscripts removed, but those were haunted manuscripts, they didn't need legs to return to their original place. They imagined that the soldier who had disrespected the manuscripts was now dying slowly of some strange disease. For the first time, Neerumoni and her family felt safe because of the presence of the bark manuscripts. All these weeks after Horokanto's death, they were petrified, unable to solve the mystery of the sounds. That night, Prodhan Mahatu went to the army camp, stabbed one soldier, and set one of the camps on fire. They shot him dead.

///////////////

Dilipram wasn't a great sorcerer. Now middle-aged, he had learnt most of his charms from Horokanto, even though he was apprenticed to an old sorcerer in Hatimura village, Mayong, for about five years. He lived in the old man's house and worked on his fields in lieu of fees. The sorcerer had given Dilipram the teeth of a male crocodile, the dried hands of a pregnant female

monkey, severed legs of mating lizards, snakeskin, and many other indis-
pensable things required in the art of serious sorcery for the greater common good. When Horokanto was alive, Dilipram would occasionally come
to him with questions: 'Do we use a pregnant bitch's morning urine to
make this potion?' 'I made the potion for cobra bite with khar, but I'm
worried about whether the concentration is strong enough.'

The people in the village had thought Dilipram would inherit the bark
manuscripts. In fact, Neerumoni had offered him the books, but he refused.
She must know, he said, that those manuscripts had a soul, and they always
chose their owner, just as her father had once been chosen. So had
Horokanto—or why would he have fought with his father and gone to stay
in their house to learn sorcery when he belonged to such a rich family? It's
all decided 'above', he told her with conviction, pointing to the sky. 'You
will get signs.' One day, she would have to let go of the manuscripts so that
they reached the rightful owner. That person could even be Anil or one of
her future sons-in-law.

Now, when Anil told him about the strange sounds that shook their
house and robbed them of their sleep, Dilipram suggested that they take
out the manuscripts every Tuesday and Saturday, spread them under the
sun (if there was no sun, the veranda would suffice), light a mustard-oil
lamp, offer some white or red flowers, and pray to the Gods of the ancient
books, requesting them not to trouble the family. 'Try it,' he said calmly.
When Anil stood up to leave, Dilipram told him that, if it didn't work, he
should return on the night of the twenty-second Saturday with a new steel
plate. They would go to the cremation ground. Anil started to walk away.
The breeze lifted the light cotton cloth that covered Dilipram's flabby
body. He turned and told Anil that he had this strange feeling that one of
the trapped souls had become very powerful since they hadn't been controlled by spells for nearly a year now, since Horokanto's death; that soul
might be trying to take corporeal form to fulfil its worldly wishes.

In the deathly silence that followed, Anil felt he could hear ants moving across the courtyard. He broke out in a cold sweat. Dilipram added that the soul could be trying to take birth through Anju, so they would have to kill the child as soon as it was born if the first remedy didn't work. Anil decided that he wouldn't tell his mother about this last part. She would worry unnecessarily.

On the way home, Anil passed Prodhan's house. A strong stench of rotten animals rose from it. He rushed to get ahead of the smell and vomited. Tearing off some leaves from a eucalyptus tree nearby, he inhaled the scent until he felt better. The village would have to do something as soon as possible, he thought, wiping his face with the cotton handkerchief that Anju had woven on the waist loom before she was raped. After Prodhan was shot dead, his wife and two daughters vanished mysteriously. They must have fled to a relative's home. They didn't even wait to receive the body. But that was wise—the army would have killed them, too, had they gone to ask for his body. It was the villagers who received Prodhan's decomposing body. Before that, young men and women from the city had come with pens and tiny notebooks and cameras that made loud sounds. The army had flown them in a helicopter and taken them on a tour of select localities. They would then report that no villagers had been harmed during the operation. Some of them came by car, and the army helped them cross the river on boats.

Anil stopped by the grocery shop to buy some red lentils that his mother had asked for. The shopkeeper wrapped it in an old newspaper. Anil didn't notice the bloody picture that was printed on it.

On reaching home, he apologised to his mother. They should have believed her. He conveyed what Dilipram had told him, except the part about Anju's unborn baby. Neerumoni said, 'Let's wait and see what happens.' They would worship the manuscripts for twenty-one Saturdays and Tuesdays.

She went in to ask Anju if she needed something. But the girl just wept soundlessly, which she did a lot these days. Neerumoni knew why. After she was raped, for a long time, Neerumoni had blamed her for the incident: Didn't I tell you not to roam around with Biren too much? Wasn't I cautioning you for a long time until it finally happened? You destroyed your life and ours, too.

After talking to Anil, Neerumoni shivered. She didn't know if she would raise Anju's child or kill it with the help of other women—as people in the village usually did in such situations. She recalled how Binapani-pehi, an elderly woman in the village who had died in the early nineties, had given birth to a green-eyed, blond-haired baby after she was raped by the British soldiers in the early forties. Neerumoni had been a young girl then. People discussed for years how the village women had shoved fistfuls of salt into that baby's mouth. Two more months left! It was already February. What would happen if she gave birth to twins? No, no, as if one child wasn't enough trouble. . . . Would she be able to stuff a handful of salt into the infant's mouth and take his life? Wouldn't this child be her first grandchild?

When she went to the kitchen and unwrapped the lentils, Neerumoni saw the bloodied face of the slain man printed on the newspaper. She trembled and imagined the blood being mixed with the lentils. Should she wash the lentils again to remove that blood? She felt queasy looking at the blood, the rose-pink lentils. Then she realised it was Prodhan's face: distorted with anger, full of the pain of losing twenty cows that he had reared like his own children—cows that came running to him whenever they saw him, red and brown and white cows that liked to rub their heads on his back, cows that licked their calves' balls and ears, cows that he rebuked if they chewed the clothes hung on the line to dry, cows that had the most beautiful eyes in the world.

She called out to Anil to ask if it was really Prodhan in the photograph. He looked at it and said, yes, that's him. He read the headline out to her.

TOP MILITANT GUNNED DOWN IN TETELIGURI VILLAGE

She threw away the lentils. They didn't have lunch that day.

///////////////

The day Anju spoke a full sentence in her normal tone, Neerumoni couldn't believe her ears. In the nine months since the assault, she'd only heard her daughter cry in agony and impotent rage. Anju was whispering something. At first Neerumoni thought it was the sigh of the rain-bearing wind from the hills. It had been raining hard for a few weeks, an early monsoon. The previous morning, Neerumoni had noticed that the edges of the veranda had disintegrated. Probably the first wave of floods would arrive soon, too.

Neerumoni went to Anju's room and asked what she was saying. Anju said she had seen a child with eyes that shone like flames in her dreams last night. When her mother heard this, she was sure the manuscripts were now troubling her daughter. She looked worried and promised that she would send Anil to Dilipram's house again as soon as he returned. Neerumoni sat beside her daughter. Anju extended her hands and pressed her mother's, wept, and said she didn't want the child. As soon as it was born, she would shove a handful of salt into his mouth.

It was dark outside, as if the sky had covered itself with a black shawl to keep away the chill. Even though it was still early in the day, a soft blanket of darkness settled on the wet roofs, over the rain-drenched trees, paths, stones, and red soil. Neerumoni held her daughter's hands. Through the window, she looked at their dog who was shivering in the sudden chill, curled up on hay in a corner of the cowshed. She noticed that the small wooden chest shook mildly—was it throbbing? moving?—as if someone was trying to escape. She could feel her breaths become heavy, shallow.

Anil didn't return until late afternoon. After serving him lunch, Neerumoni mentioned Anju's dream, and Anil was too stunned to speak for a while. Then, slowly, he told her what Dilipram had cautioned him about—that one of the souls might have become too powerful and could be trying to attain physical shape by possessing Anju's child. Neerumoni whispered: he must have already taken possession of the unborn.

By the time Anil left for Dilipram's house, it was raining harder. He passed the Tamulidobha, suddenly becoming aware of its noisy waters. The hilly tributaries had given her a new life, youthful blood. It was as if she was mocking the village or perhaps trying to wake people from their stupor, warning them of something. He also crossed Prodhan Mahatu's house. Last month, the villagers had cleaned up the mess. They didn't know what to do with his land and property, and they left everything the way they had found it. Even the clothes. One of the men had entered the house and told the villagers that, on the hearth, there was still a container of cooked rice and huge steel pots of milk that had curdled, grown fungi, turned green and yellow and brown, and were letting out another smell that was difficult to describe. Now, Anil noticed, wild creepers had completely covered the house, the huge cowshed, and even the bamboo gate. There was not a glimpse to be had of the mud walls or the wood in the windows.

When he returned home, it was evening. When he told his mother that Dilipram had advised him to relinquish the manuscripts to the flowing waters of a river, she asked him if he was hiding something from her again. He lit a fire, and as he warmed his hands at it, Anil told her that he wasn't. In fact, he should have told her everything the last time, too. A storm had broken out, running through the village like a madwoman. Their thatched hut started to vibrate.

Neerumoni wondered aloud if they would be able to go out. Anju's abdomen was hurting. Anil said that that was even more reason to go, because Dilipram had told them they had to act immediately, even if lighting were to strike down the whole village and the hills. They would have to do it on their own, before Anju gave birth, otherwise the soul would be born in their own house, and no one could predict what it might do.

As they were leaving the house, Anju's water broke. She screamed, but in the wild roar of the dusk thunderstorm, they didn't hear her cries. Anju crawled down from her bed, breathless, lay on the green mattress on the ground, spread her legs, and waited, wondering if she would be able to do it all alone. She lost consciousness.

Anil looked at the betel nut trees moving like drunken men weaving their way down a village street. He wondered if one of them would fall, killing them both. He held the wooden chest firmly with one hand and the umbrella over his mother's head. But they didn't have the umbrella for long. The wind was strong, like the spring storm Bordoisila. People believed the storm was the soul of a newly married woman rushing back to her mother's house with her long hair open, destroying everything in her way: huts, trees, cowsheds, and crops. The storm that evening was as mighty as the impatient Bordoisila. So when they finally heard the wicked laughter of the youthful river, they were relieved.

The riverbank was slippery, and below, the water flowed furiously. Anil saw a wooden chair being carried away. Would they go, really? The souls? It had to be done by Anil's hand, since he was the heir to his father who had died without choosing the rightful owner of the bark manuscripts, who couldn't train someone, who had not given away the knowledge of those books before dying. After they had emptied the box into the tempestuous waters, Neerumoni told him that someone had breathed on her cheeks, and she had heard a sigh. Anil didn't say anything, but she stressed that it had been warm, as warm as it could be in that chilly evening. Then he said it was just the wind, just the sound of the wind moving across the leaves and over the waters. On their way back, they didn't worry about Anju, but only thought about Horokanto—the husband, the lover, the father. Before opening the gate to their compound, Neerumoni said, 'You know, even my father found most of those manuscripts in a wooden box. Things just get repeated.'

'What will happen now?'

'They will travel, maybe even to the sea, in search of another owner.'

Inside the house, Anju was lying unconscious, a newborn between her legs, slick with blood. Neerumoni took a sharp knife and cut the cord. There was absolute silence. She waited; she patted the boy's back. It didn't cry.

Anil wanted to say that it'd be too soon, too good to be true, but he kept quiet. He looked at his sister's face, called to her. He wanted to show her the baby before he buried him.

The soil at the back of their house would be soft like mud now. Digging a deep hole would be easy. Neerumoni sniffed. The air smelled of fresh mud. She wondered why the baby's face reminded her of her dead father who had been hurt because she had eloped with Horokanto.

THE UMRICANS

A month before you move to America, your aunt is admitted to a small hospital in the Northeast Indian town you live in. She needs an eye operation. That year, your mother bought a new Hyundai i10 and hired a driver. He prefers to go by 'pilot'—'driver' is diminishing, but 'pilot' has gravitas, he thinks. He drives you with your mother to the hospital. Your father is away in Delhi on an official tour. He phones regularly.

In the hospital, where the nurses are extra courteous and ward boys are extra helpful, your brother-in-law expresses disbelief at the news that you are moving to America with a scholarship. He is the kind of person who attended a three-week refresher course at Delhi University and tells everyone that he has degrees from there. He is like the driver who thinks he is a pilot. 'We have not haard of this place Minnesota,' he says with a shrug, as if Minnesota is a bad smell, as if speaking in English makes him sound more authoritative about American geography. 'We have haard of New Yok and Los Angles and Sicagoo, but not this place called Minnesota. Are you acsually going to Amerika?' You want to correct his pronunciations, but you don't. Your mother isn't pleased. She starts to say something, but you gently press her hand, and she remains silent. On the way home, she says you should have let her speak. You laugh. 'Oh, Ma, leave it.' Then both of you laugh at your 'Delhi-educated' brother-in-law.

A month later, your parents see you off at Guwahati international airport. It is a small airport and international only because an occasional flight departs for Bhutan. You have travelled to Delhi so many times in the past year for the American visa interview that the guards recognise you. They don't examine your ticket. They wave at you and request that you do not forget them when you reach 'Aameyrika'. You watch your parents' faces and know that they are trying hard not to cry. Later, on the flight out of Delhi, on the flight that is taking you to the US, you wonder if they knew that you, too, were trying hard not to cry. You go to the lavatory and bawl. When the air hostess serves wine, you ask for whisky.

///////////////

At the International Students' Orientation, the staff teaches you how to say 'sorry' and 'thank you'. They say, when someone says they are sick, you should say, 'I am sorry.' The students you sit next to are North Indians. They are the kind of loud and patriotic North Indians you normally wouldn't be caught dead with. You are ashamed that you are laughing with them. 'What other funny things these Umricans are going to teach us?' the handsome Punjabi guy with a beard asks you before switching to Hindi, and you like the way he pronounces 'Americans'. Hindi is not your language. But you don't mind that he assumes you speak and understand it because you are from India. You laugh with the Punjabi guy. A few days later, you are surprised that you are drawn, too, to the Bangladeshi students—the Bangladeshis whom you grew up slightly hating for migrating in thousands to your already over-populated state. You talk about rice and fish curry and Durga Puja and Bhupen Hazarika's songs and feel guilty. You hang out with Shahed—the student from Dhaka—who challenges you to eat a burger without making a mess on your plate. He borrows his friend's car and drives you to Minneapolis where both of you eat at a restaurant called 'The Taste of India' run by Punjabi-speaking Pakistanis. Garlic naan and butter chicken, gulab jamuns for dessert. You both almost weep with joy. When you offer him money for gas, he scolds you, 'Don't be so money-minded like the Umricans.'

A month later, Shubham (the Punjabi guy) and Shahed (the Bangladeshi guy) are your closest friends. When you fall sick in October, they turn up at your apartment instead of sending texts such as 'xoxo', 'get well soon', and 'I am so sorry you are sick'. They make you spicy soup, sleep on your couches, and make lists of girls they want to fuck. A week later, you don't tell your mother about those lists, your bad health, the winter that is coming too soon. Instead, you tell her that there are two seasons in Minnesota: Winter and Preparing to Fight through Winter. She laughs. You think about how she was silent at the eye hospital when you pressed her hand. You are suddenly surprised that she understood your touch. You wonder if she cried as soon as you turned to x-ray your duffel bag at the airport. You hide in the bathroom and cry. You don't tell Shahed. You don't tell Shubham. But they look at your reddish eyes, slap your back, and buy you a beer. They don't leave you alone because you are sad. They force their presence on you, and you like that, and you joke that the Umricans would never do something like that because they are very respectful of your personal space.

//////////////

Mike, your roommate, has an Indian girlfriend called Neelakshi. She often spends the night in your flat, mostly during weekends. He tells you that this year has been amazing for him since he has never shared an apartment with a non-white person before. And how he is thrilled to have more International Experiences with an Indian Girlfriend whom he started dating three months before you arrived. With your permission, Mike changes the apartment's Wi-Fi username to 'Diverse Club'. You are amused and annoyed. He asks you questions that you don't like. He asks whether your hair grows straight up like the African Americans and whether you straighten your hair. He is astonished that you can speak English 'so well'.

Since he is an English major at the university, he corrects your 'fortnightly' to 'every two weeks' and your 'out of station' to 'out of town' and is completely horrified when you use the word 'preponed'. You say, it is Indian English. He asks, 'Does that even exist?' He tells you about the new Pakistani student in his class who doesn't wear a skullcap and expects you to be surprised. He is surprised that you are not.

Mike changes the Wi-Fi username to 'South Asian Station' because he thinks it is more apt. You pretend to find it funny, but you think that he can be insufferable. In December, when his grandmother visits, she asks if you are a Muslim. She is happy to know that you aren't. She gives you a piece of lemon cake and confides in you that she worries Muslims are going to take over America soon. You nod. You don't get annoyed. But you are annoyed when everyone wishes you Merry Christmas on the last working day before Christmas. You rant about it to Shubham and Shahed. It doesn't bother them.

////////////////

Neelakshi moves into the apartment. The good thing is that the three of you now split the rent and power bills. The bad thing is that the frequency of their noisy sex increases to at least four times a week. You are woken up by their moans and gasps, the sounds of their bodies slapping, the creaking bed, and a lot of 'yes-yess-yess' and 'you-like-that-right?'. You are not sure how to broach the matter. You decide you hate American houses. You complain that there is no privacy. Shubham and Shahed find the situation hilarious and ask if the lovemaking gives you a hard on. One morning, you find Mike sleeping on the couch on top of Neelakshi, without his boxers. Later, Shubham says you should have drawn a smiley face on his bum with a black permanent marker. When you call your mother, you don't tell her that you are annoyed with your roommate. You tell her that Mike is good and takes care of you. You make her talk to Shubham and Shahed. She speaks to them in broken Hindi and fluent Bengali. You proudly say that a lot of people from Assam know Bengali—something you would never admit to in India, even though it is a fact.

In April, your mother falls sick. She has hypertension, and your father rushes her to the hospital. She is moved to the intensive care unit. Her blood pressure is unstable for twelve hours. The doctors pierce a gelatin pill and place it under her tongue every three hours. You spend a lot of time on the phone with your father. You feel guilty that he has to manage alone. You are their only son. You look at flights online, though you know you can't afford them. Your father asks you not to come because he knows you can't afford the cost of a flight; after the medical bills, he cannot, either. The pilot helps your father. His wife cooks meals for your parents. He stays in the hospital day and night so that your father can use the car when he needs it. You are the first person your mother wants to talk to when she is out of the ICU. 'I won't die without seeing you,' she chuckles. Your grandmother tells you not to worry, to eat well and return to India as the same 'healthy boy we brought up'. You smile. You wonder if her eyes are welling up like yours are. You remain sad for a long time.

You share your anxieties with Neelakshi and Mike and Shahed and Shubham. Mike asks if the driver will charge your parents overtime, and you want to slap him hard.

You snap, 'It is called goodwill. Everything is not about money like here in America.'

'But you are exploiting the driver; you should pay him overtime!' Mike says hotly.

Neelakshi does a bit of contextualising. 'Why must every act of kindness be returned with money? You can return it instead with kindness.'

Mike is not pleased. He says he doesn't get South Asian Culture. Neelakshi says something funny. She has acquired a risible American accent. She throws her Rs and rolls her tongue a lot. The rumour among the Indian community in the university is that Neelakshi is seducing Mike because she wants an American passport.

Back in India, your mother is brought home. People do such horrible things, she complains to you on the phone. 'Your brother-in-law says that he knows an old couple who live near the airport. They have four children, and all of them have moved to Aameyrika. When the man died, there was no one to cremate him.'

You sense your anger rising quickly. 'Well, Ma, if Delhi-educated people don't know what to do when a person dies, who does?'

'Don't become Aameyrikan like other Indians; please come home when you can. We will arrange the money. Okay?'

You laugh, but you know that your mother is expressing her deepest fears.

In May, Mike sends you an email in bullet points. When a Minnesotan sends an email in bullet points, you should know that they are very mad at you, your friend Amy tells you, and she laughs so much that she almost chokes on her bottle of sparkling water. You decide not to write back but talk. At the apartment, Mike looks through you. When you say, 'We need to talk,' you feel as if you are his boyfriend, broaching a break-up. He turns around and says in a calm voice that he would prefer to be emailed. You say that you would prefer to talk because you have no time to respond to his slanderous allegations by email; you have papers to write. Neelakshi assumes the role of the mediator to save the situation from becoming worse. You debate with her in Hindi and English. Your voice rises many times as Mike hovers. You tell Neelakshi that it is not possible for you to spray antibacterial chemicals every time you use the kitchen and that you will get your own dishes because Mike uses most of the dishes and expects Neelakshi and you to wash them.

In June, you move to a different three-bedroom apartment on Warren Street, sharing it with Shubham and Shahed. You have a nice portico that overlooks a lake. Loons swim in the lake. Their yodels wake you up from your rare siestas and regular power naps, but you don't mind because you like the sight of the large, cheerful duck-like birds. The three of you have gained a lot of weight because your dinners are usually cheesy pizzas at the on-campus café where you wait tables. Bad cheese. Bad bread. They are not bad to eat, though. The three of you join the gym and run for hours on the treadmills because you worry that no girl will sleep with you. But you don't date. You don't even hook up. You want to get good grades. You want to get a good job, and that's why you are working towards a degree in information technology. You want to bring your parents to America and buy them meals at Olive Garden and your favourite, Chipotle Mexican Grill. Soon, you learn how to drive. Every Friday, you borrow a car from a friend and drive to Minneapolis. You have also learnt the bus routes. You don't get lost in the city. Sometimes you go to Dinkytown alone and sip coffee, enjoying the weather and the youthful vibe. You are surprised that you yearn for the sun. Amy says that you have now become a Minnesotan.

During your sophomore year, you visit the website of the Indian American community in Minneapolis. You attend one of their gatherings. They screen a movie called *Pardes* where the actor Amrish Puri sings the line 'I love my India', and you can't stop weeping. You notice that others are weeping, too, and stop feeling like a fool. You want to buy a dinner coupon. It is thirty dollars, much higher than you expected, but you still pay. While having dessert, you meet a family from your state, Assam, who introduces you to other families from Assam, and the other families from Assam invite you home. You find a Little Assam in Shakopee, where several Assamese families have settled. They are from small and big towns. At their parties, women cook food and hang out separately. They are all in their early forties, and the women are all light-skinned and slim. The men are overweight and friendly. You suspect they are all monogamous and boring. You drink whisky with them, and they tell you about relatives they have lost in bomb blasts and skirmishes. They hope the militancy in beautiful Assam will end one day. They share their first experiences in America, and you are startled at how similar the stories of these people in their early forties are to yours. When they get a little drunk, they sing Bollywood songs. They are terrible. Even you sing better, and you are quite bad. Yet, you like hanging out with them, even though in India you wouldn't be caught dead with people who sang so badly.

///////////////////

In your fourth year in America, Neelakshi and Mike get engaged. They had been planning and delaying this for a while due to visa issues that Neelakshi's parents had been facing. They invite you to their engagement party. Your old apartment on James Avenue is now their new rented home. You ask Neelakshi what you can bring. She teases that you have turned into an Umrican and scolds you for asking what you can bring. At the party, Neelakshi, Shubham, and Shahed have to explain repeatedly to Mike's American friends why, in South Asia, it is almost offensive to bring food when someone invites you to their home for a meal. Mike says the Wi-Fi username of the house is still South Asian Station, and Shahed gives you a look that makes you want to hide under the table. Shubham is worried that if Mike's American friends fall sick after eating the spicy chicken curry, they will sue Neelakshi. He says she should send an email listing all the ingredients used so that they know what they are consuming beforehand. Mike laughs and asks him not to worry. He is so happy.

You meet Roshan at Neelakshi's party. He is her friend from Nepal. Roshan is a college dropout and has been living in America illegally for a few years now. He works at the local Korean restaurant for three dollars less an hour than his co-workers. After the party, he gives you a ride back to your apartment on Warren Street. Shubham and Shahed don't join you; they go downtown for more drinks. Roshan wants to discuss how Neelakshi has seduced Mike for an American passport. You avoid the discussion. You are put off by the disdain on his face. And surprised because you know that he, too, wants an American passport, because he, too, wants to become an American. 'Neelakshi sucked his dick for the passport.' You want to scream 'TMI', like the Americans do.

You thank him when he halts the car near Atwood Apartments, where you live. 'Why don't you suck an American dick as well? Don't you want an American passport too?' You slam the door.

Every day, you call your mother. You have saved some money, you tell her. And you could come down that winter. But she asks you to come in summer after your graduation next year because that will be a longer visit and more worthwhile. You want very much to go home, but you see the wisdom in your mother's advice. She will now tell everyone in the neighbourhood that you wanted to come, but she forbade you. It is a chance to show off that you wanted to come and that you have saved money by working. She won't tell them that you wait tables. She will tell them that you assist one of your professors.

///////////////

Six months before your graduation, your mother has a mild heart attack. Your father and the pilot rush her to the hospital. Later, your father tells you that, on the way, she kept pleading with him not to inform you. That upsets you. You want to ask her about it but can't, because you aren't supposed to know. You start keeping the phone in your pocket all the time. At night, you put it on loud mode and leave it next to the pillow because you are worried your father won't be able to reach you. You don't sleep well. You wake up at night to check messages on WhatsApp, to check if there are missed calls. When you cook or read in the library, you check the phone screen frequently. You start to hear false rings and feel false vibrations. You know you are imagining things but don't tell anyone. Nor do you talk to anyone. You don't visit the free counselling service on campus because only Americans go to therapists, not Indians. Because you have friends who come home to take care of you without worrying about germs. And yet, one day, you visit the therapist. You wear a hoodie and cover your face with a scarf because you are so ashamed. 'How does it make you feel?' the therapist asks, looking calmly at you through her thick-rimmed glasses. You are amazed that you think of them as 'glasses' now, not 'spectacles'. You say that to the therapist.

That night, your father tells you that the pilot's family has been very helpful, like a son and a daughter-in-law. They clean and cook for your parents. You feel they are doing things you should be doing. You weep at night. When it is dawn in India, you pick up the phone and call your mother and ask her why she didn't tell you that she had a heart attack. She laughs and says that she won't die without seeing you, because you will have to touch her temple with a flame to set her soul free of the mortal world. You shout at her for speaking rubbish, but she just laughs. It is now March, and you browse MakeMyTrip.com. You use up all your savings to book a round trip for a date in May. You tell her that you are coming home soon. That you found a good deal. How much, she asks. You tell her the amount in rupees.

After the conversation, you walk out to the drawing room. Shahed offers you a cup of tea. You tell him that your worst fear is that you won't be home if something happens. He doesn't ask what you mean by 'if something happens'. He understands. He understands because he is not American. He understands because that is also his worst fear.

When your worst fear comes true just a week before your trip to India, it takes a very long time to sink in. You receive the news during your finals week—two weeks before your graduation. You have exams to write. You have worked hard for this for the last four years. You have waited tables late into the night and then stayed awake until dawn drinking cups of coffee and completing class assignments. When you once received a B minus, you went to the writing centre several times to rework your drafts because you wanted good grades, you wanted to make the best of everything. Your parents are cutting corners to educate you in America so that they might one day come and see snow, see the Statue of Liberty, eat burritos with a lot of sour cream and guacamole.

When you hear the news, you walk out of the library, where you were writing a take-home exam. You clutch your bag hard against your body as if someone will snatch it from you. You are surprised that you are not able to cry and that you are worrying more about graduation, about how you don't have enough money in your Wells Fargo account to book a ticket immediately. You regret that you bought the expensive gown and hat and the tassel so that you could send your mother photos from the graduation day ceremony. Someone calls you from home. You will never remember who it was. Maybe a relative who has taken charge of things. The person talks about preserving the body in a morgue. She will feel cold, you whisper. You feel like you're choking. Like you can't breathe. It is early May. It is still cold in Minnesota. You sit at the cafeteria where people are busy and noisy. You call your father and ask him, what is the meaning of these rituals? What is the point of freezing the body for several days just so you can touch her temple with a flame at the cremation ground? She will feel so cold in the morgue. She hated being cold. Your father weeps. You wonder how he must feel because you are not able to feel anything. You walk out into the cold and sit on a blue plastic chair, shivering. He is still on the phone with you. You tell him you will not come, because there is no point now, and when he hangs up, tears stream down your cheeks, and you mourn the young boy inside who has died along with your mother. You mourn because you have become someone you have always despised. Shubham and Shahed try to take you to the apartment. But you say, like they do here in America, I am fine, can I please have a moment? They notice your steely resolve and say, I am so sorry, I am so sorry, and leave you alone.

HIS FATHER'S DISEASE

The first time Anil brought a man to his room, his mother, Neerumoni, went to the backyard and sat on the stone beside the red hibiscus for a long time. Then she picked up the brass pot and went to the large one-acre pond to take a long bath—swimming from one end to the other, splashing in the water. She didn't want to hear the love-making sounds.

Forgetting to change out of her wet clothes, Neerumoni sat on the banks of the pond and wept. He has acquired his father's disease, she thought, mourning her only son. When she figured it was time for those 'disturbing sounds' to have ceased, she walked back slowly. To her horror, mild moans were still audible from his room. She left the fresh pot of water on the clammy kitchen floor, went to her bedroom, lay down on the bed, and wept.

Those sounds were all too familiar. When Neerumoni was seventeen years old, Anil's father had come to learn sorcery from her father, a high-caste brahmin. Quite surprisingly, her father, known as the stingiest person in the village, appointed Horo as the new caretaker of his farms and agreed to teach him sorcery for free. Later, she had come to know that Horo was close to her younger brother, Nilambor, who had put in a special request to that effect. Much later, after she had settled down with Horo and had one child on her back and another growing in her womb, she came back from the fields one afternoon to hear the sounds of two men heaving and moaning in her bedroom, thickening the silence of the hot summer afternoon. She rushed in, thinking someone was terribly sick. No one was sick inside, but her younger brother and husband were naked on the bed. Their muscular bodies glistened in the dark as they rocked rhythmically. She hadn't gone to the pond to take a long bath and cry that day. That red hibiscus tree was still a sapling, and the stone was a little larger back then. She was too confused and shocked to know what was going on. So, she couldn't cry. She ran back to the fields. A little while later, a very happy Horo was back, his short white gamusa looped between his legs. She noticed red teeth marks on one of his thighs and somehow stopped herself from crying aloud.

Anil was visibly happy, too. She didn't ask him who he was because he could be anyone, and Anil could lie. She hadn't seen him before; Anil must have picked him up somewhere—maybe they studied together or worked together for the 'party'. She didn't care, and when Anil asked her for the third time if she was feeling sick and why she was in bed during the day, she lied that she had a headache. She knew he had expected her to boil some tea because there was a guest. Not with milk necessarily. He had wanted some black tea with sugar—not the usual tea with salt, which was what they had to make do with usually. The boy's voice was deep and sonorous. He said they could have tea another day, perhaps at the Tetelia market on their way to the bus stop.

Her husband's disease had ruined her life. Many nights she had spent burning beside him, sliding her finger between her legs and crying when she climaxed—not out of happiness, but desperation, and hatred for her younger brother, who she had thought was closest to her and not to the man who had married her, saying she was the most beautiful woman he had ever seen. Yes, she had eloped with him. High-caste brahmins were not allowed to marry anyone below their caste, and he belonged to the Koch community, an indigenous community lower down the rung than brahmins.

They had spent several months in the house of one of his aunts in remote Hatimuria village and returned to her village only after Anil was born. That aunt was no more. She had died a year after Anil brought a man to his room for the first time. He was twenty-nine then and hadn't yet graduated even after four attempts. Horo had died in an accident a couple of years ago, and she had already married off two of her three daughters. A little after the counterinsurgency operations started, all the elders in the village advised her that if she didn't get them settled soon, an Indian soldier might 'touch their bodies, and no boy in this world would be ready to marry them'. So, she hastily married them off to men twice their age. When the army raped four girls from their village and a woman six months pregnant, she thanked God she had listened to the elders.

She had noticed then that Anil wanted space and privacy. During meals, he would often say that he did not like to disturb her sleep when 'party meetings happened' in his room. Neerumoni hated those party meetings and so didn't want to release any funds for an extension to the house. She dreaded the meetings that had made him flunk his college exams year after year until he grew such a thick moustache that he began feeling awkward about sitting in a classroom with slim young boys and girls.

One thing she liked about Anil was that he handed over all the earnings from the fields every month and did not keep anything for himself. Every Sunday or Monday morning, he asked her for a few rupees to buy betel nut, tobacco, and cigarettes, and she gave them to him without asking a question. After several months of implicit requests for money to expand the house, when she did not respond, he began to keep a little aside before handing her the rest. That had been the beginning of Anil having a space entirely for himself, she thought.

With the money, to weave the roof, he bought long straws fashioned from seron, which grew like wild grass on riverbanks, and cut fat bholuka bamboos from their backyard, where the red hibiscus bloomed and the shrinking black stone sat. And he built a single-room hut two feet away with a four-hands-high earthen veranda. On the day he was shifting his things from the main house, he kept saying how good the new arrangement would be. He didn't look into her eyes, but spoke of how she would not wake up to the din of debates during party meetings and that she would be able to sleep well and her blood pressure would not rise anymore. He left most of his childhood items—mainly books and some clothes from his younger days—in the main house. Later, when he said he was going to sleep and shut the door, she sat in his old room for a long time. She picked up a pair of old shorts and was filled with wonder at how tiny this man used to be. Then she laughed—of course he was tiny, he had come out from her stomach after all. He was smaller, yes, he was.

No sounds came that night, but the next night she couldn't sleep. She stood near her son's door and listened to the sounds, and in the wee hours of the morning, when the bamboo door creaked, Neerumoni hid herself. Promod's fair skin was glowing; she knew him instantly. He was Nirgun's younger brother, around seven years younger than Anil. Nirgun was the leader of the party that contested elections against Anil's party.

People said, in a few years, Anil would become the village headman, and everything would change for the family: there would be sugar to be had with tea, as many as seven to eight silk dresses and gold ornaments to wear, and meat every day. She only thought of duck meat when the village women said these things about her bright future. And when she thought of the ornaments, she would stare into the mirror, shocked at how she seemed uglier each time. She craved for the reflection she used to see in the village pond during the days when Horo held her hand and said she was the most beautiful woman in the world. Yes, she was. Of course, she was. But after he acquired that disease and started pulling her own brother under his quilt in her absence, he didn't remain the passionate lover he once was. He would hold her desperately, push her petticoat up to her breasts, and enter her. But she didn't like it that way. She liked to be naked in his arms and to laugh and laugh, get tickled. She had wanted him to go down on her the way he used to before their marriage, on the wet sands near the village stream. Later, after their intense and passionate lovemaking, she used to sit naked there, the wet, sharp sand grains pinching her butt, his limp penis stroking the side of her thigh as he dug his nose into her hair, her chest. He had long hair, like suntanned farmers used to in those days. Long hair that gave him a wayward look, like sturdy farmers who smelled like coconut water when they sweated while making love. But she soon came to associate that smell with her younger brother and her husband making love, because that night when she slept beside him, it was the bed that smelled like coconut water.

///////////////

Gurmail Singh, that burly Sikh soldier, was probably the one man Anil loved. And she had seen him care deeply for her son. The army, which had moved out of the village, was back again that winter. A sense of fear spread through the village once again. There was no more sitting around a fire comfortably after dinner. Everyone went to bed early, and young men hid in the granaries, the forests, and the hilly tracks all night.

The army didn't really care; they could kill anyone they found suspicious, and no one would file a case against them. If someone did, their family's fate was sealed. The villagers knew it was better to run before the army began combing the village for separatist rebels. On one of those nights, while Anil and his mother were at dinner, they heard the sound of approaching boots. Their dog barked, and hearing him, all the dogs in the colony struck up a howl. It was eerie. The rest of the neighbourhood locked their doors and hushed their children. The smell of flowers and fresh cow dung floated in the air. Gurmail Singh and several other soldiers stood at their door. He must have been an officer, because the other soldiers stood at attention while he looked relaxed. Was there anyone else in the house, he asked, and when they said no, he didn't scream in Hindi like other officers had done before. He called Neerumoni 'Mother' and asked for some water. While she was getting him a glass of water, she felt him eye Anil suspiciously. Frightened and desperate, she started screaming in Assamese that her son was not a separatist rebel. Gurmail Singh told her to shut up.

He drank the glass of water she had brought him and pushed her son towards the outhouse, asking Anil to show him around and help him find anyone else hiding there. When she tried to go in, the other soldiers pointed the guns at her and asked her not to move. A while later, from the bedroom, she could hear Anil uttering a series of helpless, muffled no-nos and weeping like a child. It was evident from the grunts that he was trying not to scream. After a point, he let out a louder scream and then gradually his whimpers became sparse, before everything became silent. Neerumoni stood there and started to weep. She didn't want to scream and let the whole village know, because if they knew, Anil would turn into an object of ridicule.

Neerumoni didn't have the courage to go in after the soldiers left, but she could hear her son weeping in the silence of the night. When he careened out of the room with a bowed head and walked towards the pond, she rushed in with the kerosene lamp and checked the bed.

The blood looked like a red rose blooming on the white bedsheet, and the room smelled like coconut water. Neerumoni sat there and cried. She wished Anil didn't have that pair of almond eyes with bow-shaped brows that allowed him to play Draupadi. People said he looked exactly like her, and when Anil as Draupadi cried during the public stripping scene in the village production, a lot of women in the audience took out their hankies.

They never spoke about it.

But that Gurmail Singh, who was responsible for the patch of blood on her white bedsheet, soon turned into Anil's love interest. He started to visit every other night, and those same sounds invaded her sleep. She didn't understand how it happened, how her son had ended up liking this hirsute man 'who had committed atrocities upon him'. The smell of coconut water kept chasing her and wouldn't let her sleep. She didn't want to ask him, nor could she tell anyone in the village. The army stayed for two years, and Anil was the happiest man in the village. Every month he went to different places, such as the hill stations Shillong and Haflong and Guwahati city, with Gurmail, and he brought her different gifts. Villagers came to see Gurmail for suggestions. For the first time, they were not scared of some- one who worked for the Indian Army. He was, after all, one of them if he was their prospective village headman's closest friend. Yes, that rumour grew, too—that Anil had great connections in the government through the tall army officer he was friends with, and it would be prudent to vote him to power instead of Nirgun, who was not very honest anyway. When Gurmail left, Anil cried a lot, and so did Neerumoni, and so did several other villagers. The girls who had tied rakhi on his wrist and called him their brother came with beautifully patterned cotton gamusas and gifted them to him. Gurmail cried, too, and three months later, when he visited with his wife and two daughters, the whole village came out to meet him with more gifts, and Anil hosted them.

After staying away from Anil for several years, Promod started to visit again. She didn't know why exactly, but Neerumoni knew that she disliked the boy. Somehow, she couldn't trust him—wasn't it his brother who had dared Anil to stand in the elections, declaring that he might lose his life if he did? Anil hadn't told her about it; she heard of the threat at the women's meeting in the village prayer hall. Leaving the rituals unfinished, Neerumoni rushed back home to wake up a sleeping Anil and ask him. He sounded peeved and rebuked her for being so chickenhearted. She blurted out that he shouldn't be roaming around 'with that effeminate boy who had eaten the head of the beautiful wife he married when she committed suicide a month after their wedding'. Annoyed, Anil left in a huff. Promod would visit him at night and leave early in the morning when even crows were asleep in their nests.

One day, Anil left for the election campaign earlier than usual. They were going to campaign in the Maloybari area. Anil ate leftover rice with fresh green chillies and lime juice and informed her he was leaving. She felt sorry that he was eating such a frugal meal, but before she could say anything, he smiled and said that, once he won the elections, things would change, and they would eat meat every day. He was sure to win. Like any other day, after he left, she pushed open the door of his outhouse to clean it, but to her utter surprise, a stark-naked Promod was sleeping in the bed. Her blood boiled; the smell of coconut water made her crazy. She didn't know why, but she started to beat him with the broom, screaming and shouting 'get out, get out' and asking him if it wasn't enough that he had caused his wife's death. In the golden light of the early morning, the whole village saw a naked Promod running for his life, wheezing and howling. Anil came back late at night. He didn't have dinner. Mother and son had never spoken about what she thought of as his father's disease. So, Promod's matter wasn't discussed, either. In the middle of the night, she heard him crying. She felt sorry for what she had done.

But the damage was done. The whole village started to tease Promod, calling him 'Anil's wife'. Four days later, he was publicly humiliated by a band of men at the Tuesday market. Promod went to his brother's room and swallowed a whole bottle of sleeping pills. In a furious rage, Nirgun went from house to house, telling them that Horo, the father, had suffered from 'that disease', and now the son was destroying the lives of younger men by dragging them to his bed. The village elders agreed. They said he should be taken to the sorcerer who could cure him, but Nirgun said he didn't 'believe in all that'. He would file a case. People should know the real character of the prospective head of the village council. On the fifteenth day after he took the pills, Promod was brought back from the hospital. A police officer took him straight to Anil's house and asked if Anil was the person who had lured Promod into his room for a chat and then forced himself upon Promod.

A bewildered Neerumoni went from pillar to post after the arrest. Lots of reporters came and were talking about something called 'Section 377' that could go in Anil's favour because it had just been repealed. Neerumoni noted down that number diligently on a piece of paper. She phoned Gurmail and told him to make a call on the number '377', because the kind reporter from Guwahati, who had come with a large camera and a strange car with a huge umbrella on top of it and who had coloured her eyelids blue, mentioned that it could be used to save her son. When Gurmail heard this, he began weeping. He wanted to say something but couldn't manage anything beyond the sentence that he would drop everything to come and help her. Things were sorted out when he came. Within two days. He made many calls on his mobile phone and urged Anil to call a village council meeting. Anil did not agree. He said, 'They will kill me.' Finally, Gurmail said he should stop behaving like a madman and assured him that no one was against him or after his life. They thought it was just a disease, so Anil would just have to go and say that he would take good medical care once he became headman. They would then vote for him. Anil said he would withdraw his nomination papers. Nirgun's party was using every means to malign him. Reporters from the many local satellite channels might come back and make him out to be some sort of a demon. Gurmail said he had nothing to worry about, that he was with Anil, and that he should fight the elections.

They ate meat that day. Duck meat. Gurmail had shopped, like in the days when he used to take Anil out for holidays in Shillong or Guwahati and buy him new clothes, the days when he used to call Neerumoni 'Mother'. She slept well that night, even though the sounds invaded her ears and there was that coconut-water smell when she went to clean and arrange Anil's room. Neerumoni had cooked the duck meat with banana flowers and stir fried it with ginger and garlic paste. Gurmail said it tasted like the immortal nectar of the gods, and she had laughed, blushed, laughed, and laughed.

That night, when Anil went to pee in the backyard, someone tried to stab him with a sharp knife, but he raised an alarm, and the knife only mangled the flesh on his arm. The whole village gathered as Neerumoni wailed and cursed, and Gurmail ran out with his gun to find who it was. He was shouting 'come back, coward' in Hindi. An old woman from the village made a paste of marigold leaves and put a layer of it on Anil's wound. Someone found a fresh wad of cotton and tore some clean cloths into strips and bandaged him. The bleeding stopped. But it only made him more miserable.

Day after day, Anil slept. He showed no interest in the election campaigns and avoided repeated calls from senior party leaders in Guwahati. 'They will kill me,' he kept saying. The villagers murmured amongst themselves about what could be done. One evening, they began trickling into his courtyard. When the women saw that their men were going to visit Anil, they were curious. They said to each other, 'Why shouldn't we go, too?' and, 'Who knows, if we explain things to him, he may yet stand for the elections.' So, they nodded at one another, combed their hair, slipped their bangles on, pushed betel nut with thin wads of tobacco into their mouths, and followed their men. When the children started to follow, they said, 'Go away, we will be back soon.' But the children followed anyway. Perhaps they, too, sensed that something was about to happen.

That afternoon, in front of almost the whole village, Anil agreed that he would contest. Just then, a young man from the village came up to him and whispered that Nirgun had come to know about this meeting and that his brother, Promod, was a few metres away, not daring to come closer. 'Promod is crying. He asks if you will ever forgive him. He says, "Ask him to stand for the elections, and I will vote for him."' The man handed over to Anil a crumpled piece of paper on which was written, 'It was my brother who forced me to do all these things. I love you still.'

A strong smell of kerosene and petrol woke Anil up. He wondered why he was dreaming of weird smells when he was in the arms of the man he loved most. Anil brought the naked body of Gurmail closer and dug his nose deeper into his chest. He put his arms around Gurmail's waist. They had made love passionately after a long time, and he was feeling happy-tired. The bed was wet with their sweat, and he took a deep breath, taking it all into his lungs, and once again he smelled kerosene and petrol.

'Anil!' Gurmail was screaming at the top of his voice. He was pulling his pyjamas up and asking Anil to run. Anil didn't know what to do, and Gurmail only said, 'Just run! Get out!'

The house was on fire: the newspapers that had been collecting ever since he moved to the outhouse, the clothes, the almirah, and the old wooden furniture—everything was on fire. Someone flung the door open. Anil had wrapped the bedsheet around his waist by then. It was his mother.

'They are trying to kill you,' she screamed. 'Someone set the house on fire and locked this door.'

He stood there, not knowing what to do, and it suddenly struck him that this could have killed his lover and his mother, and that it was all because of him. In the courtyard, he howled and cried, and Gurmail said, 'Shut up, it's not because of you. I am going to find who did it.' Neerumoni hugged Anil and cried. He clung to her and said that it was all because of him, that he shouldn't have agreed to contest the elections. He should have instead gone to the forest with Gurmail and never come back.

That was the first time he spoke to her about it, and they both looked at each other. His mother's back was to the house. It was burning down. He turned his eyes to the flames engulfing what had been home, for he couldn't look into her eyes anymore. He had built that house to carve a space of his own. It had implicitly told his mother what his 'male needs' were. And now, in front of the burning house, he was telling her that he loved Gurmail.

The fire had spread to the whole house now, and his mother was howling, saying something he didn't understand. He released himself from Neerumoni's arms in a fleeting second and started running towards it. 'Leave it, leave! Life is bigger than the things you are trying to get!' Instinctively, she cautioned him, but when he went in and latched the door from inside, she knew that he hadn't gone in to bring anything back. She wailed and clawed at the ground. Gurmail came back too late. He had gone in search of the person who had set fire to Anil's home. By this time, the whole neighbourhood had woken up to an unusual smell—of burnt human flesh, the smell of burnt human flesh.

LIKE THE THREAD IN A GARLAND

What Nishad suspected about Rubul before his wedding:
November 2016

My best friend, Rubul—who is thirty-nine and still a virgin—married Anuradha on the fifth of November 2016. For a long time, I wondered whether he was gay. But, after close assessment over eighteen years, I have concluded that he is not. That's why, when people gossip about his sexuality, I am the one who denies it most vehemently. However, since our friendship is legendary, and his first girlfriend even spread the rumour that we were lovers, few believe me.

'He is not, I know him very well, he has been my best friend since we were kids.'

'Oh really,' they say.

We were seventeen when he was with his first girlfriend. I don't know why, but he froze when she grabbed him the night she came to stay over at his place. He sent her to sleep in his sister's room, and two days later she broke up with him. He was so depressed.

Anyway.

Those things happened almost two decades ago. There is another problem to tackle now. Rubul has now been married for four days, and they haven't had sex because of his lack of initiative. He hasn't even kissed her. He held her hands several times. Squeezed them twice. Once, she walked in on him changing. He smiled awkwardly and turned his back to her.

Anuradha is very upset. On the first night—the wedding night on the flower-bedecked bed, like in the movies—Anuradha pretended to be the coy bride. She had read in an Assamese women's magazine that men are aroused when women are shy and show mild resistance. But Rubul took her pretence seriously and froze. My guess is that he didn't want to be the guy who had only sex on his mind on the wedding night. So, when she gently removed his hand from her arm, Rubul wondered if she was tired. Because he was exhausted. The wedding rituals were draining. And he had fasted all day. He was allowed to eat only fruits and palm sugar with water for dinner. He wasn't sure what the rituals for women were like, but he was sure that it was much more arduous for them. So, he sat still for a few minutes and then said, 'We should sleep.' He switched off the lights and went to sleep without changing. In the middle of the night, he went to the bathroom, stayed there for a very long time, and returned wearing his shorts and a half-sleeved thermal T-shirt. In the light-blue hue of the night light, she observed his legs. When he was climbing onto the bed, she hoped he would make a move, maybe climb on top of her, too. She took a deep breath and prepared herself for the moment. But he just turned onto his side, away from her, and fell asleep immediately. Anuradha wanted to slide her hands around his waist and then slip her right hand down to the band of his shorts. But she was worried that Rubul, who was such a good boy, wouldn't approve of her behaviour. She didn't get any sleep.

Since she didn't sleep well, Anuradha woke up with a headache that made her hate everyone in her new home, including the family dog, Khekarkhaiti. The next day was horribly long. She was dressed up by Rubul's mother and Subho, her sister-in-law, forced to wear make-up, lipstick, and heavy jewellery, and she had to sit in the living room where people came to 'see the new daughter-in-law'. She didn't want to wear make-up. In her job as a small-time TV actor, she had to wear it for as long as fourteen hours a day and had since developed a deep aversion to applying anything on her face. She also didn't want to wear any more silk. Or jewellery. She had played a dutiful daughter-in-law in the TV series, wearing gaudy outfits even while shooting kitchen scenes. She wanted to wear shorts and her black T-shirt that said 'I AM NOT PAID TO BE NICE TO YOU' and watch soap operas that didn't make any sense. The day was long because she had to touch the feet of at least 52 people and smile at 192 people as part of post-wedding rituals. She decided whose feet to touch or not based on how much grey hair they had. A number of people asked her if she would complete her master's degree, advised her to be patient, and ninety-nine people whispered in her ears about having a baby soon because 'post-twenty-five pregnancies were hard and wouldn't be good for the baby'. At a certain point, she felt that the silly role she played in the Assamese mega-serial wasn't entirely fictional. It was based on her life.

At the end of the day, she decided Rubul was the root of all her misery. At least she ought to have had good sex before that ordeal. She had been waiting for the wedding night for so long. Why had she gone through that painful bikini wax if her new husband had no interest in her? After the marriage was fixed in May 2016, they often met alone in her house or in parks, where the possibility of making out was high. But he didn't make a pass. Occasionally, he held her hand, and that sent ripples through her body because he was so handsome and smelled so good. Like, manly. Manly without cologne. She thought, oh, he respects me and doesn't want me to feel like I am just a piece of ass, so he isn't staring at my boobs or placing his hand strategically on my thighs or letting his hand 'accidentally' slip from the waist to my ass. Those were the signs of a good boy—at least in Anuradha's referential universe. So, she was convinced that, after they were married, he wouldn't sleep around with his co-workers. She didn't even consider the possibility that he might be gay. In her universe, gay men were effeminate and worked as choreographers, fashion designers, and make-up artists. So, five months after their wedding was arranged, she married him without having had sex even once. And in the lead up to it, she spent her days imagining how he would rearrange her bones on the first night and how they would leave the bedroom like the scene of a battle.

Rubul hasn't told me any of that. And honestly, I really don't want to know. I know this because Anuradha is friends with Rishav: THE BOY I MET AT A PARTY AND MADE OUT WITH. But later I started dating his sister, Pooja, and am in a relationship with her now. And Rishav is very upset about that. But since he is still not out, he can't tell his sister about our episode. He remains in touch with me through rude messages that sound like banter but is not. Rishav is unhappy that I am dating his sister and not him. He dislikes me, and he wants attention from me. Anyway, it is too late for that now. Pooja has met my parents, and we are kind of semi-serious and partly monogamous.

Rishav texts, 'You are such an asshole, just like your best friend Rubul, who has destroyed Anuradha's life.'

I write back, 'It is not conclusively proven that Rubul is queer.'

'He doesn't fuck a beautiful girl like Anuradha, and you are saying he is not queer?'

'I need you to grow up. I can't be part of this conversation. We will talk again in ten years, when you are thirty-four. Bye.'

He will message me again in a few weeks, and we will have a similarly rude conversation. His sister, Pooja, is four years younger than me, but she's over thirty, and we can talk like adults.

Rishav is pissed. Really pissed.

Anyway, I was talking about Rubul. Anuradha is very annoyed right now. She would take a sledgehammer and break down a mountain if she could. She complains about her sexless marriage to Rishav all the time. Rishav, who is damn gossipy, tells Pooja everything. Poor Rubul's entire life is now stored in the form of encrypted messages on WhatsApp and gleefully shared screenshots. Rubul has never spoken about his sex life with me. And he won't, either, unless it becomes a serious problem. I know that. But a week after the wedding, Rubul called me on FaceTime audio.

'I need to discuss something serious with you. When are you coming to Assam?'

'What? About your marriage?'

'Yes, how did you know?'

'Hahaha.' That was my way of ignoring the question.

'How did you know?'

'Hahaha.'

'Nishad, it is important.'

'Tell me what you want to discuss with me.'

'I have to meet you for that, but you are in Delhi, and I am two thousand miles away in Assam. You told me some things before the wedding. I should have listened to you.'

I sighed. 'You know I was just cautioning you! And I never wished for those things to come true.'

Rubul said something like yes-I-know. My heart sank. Once, when we were nineteen, and Rubul and I were lying on the edge of a pond after a long day of fishing, he had rolled over to me and pressed his lips against mine, sucking on them. I froze. I had not expected him to do that. We never talked about it because I did not kiss him back. When he was done, I said, 'We should get home.' The sky was bright blue. The crickets were singing relentlessly.

A week after that conversation with Rubul (two weeks since his wedding), I rang him. 'Guess what? I got promoted.' He was overjoyed and made some muffled excited sounds since he was still at work.

'I want to throw a small party during the last week of December at my new apartment. It will be a sort of housewarming, too. This means we can talk. How are things between you and Anuradha? Are they better?'

'When you visit, I will talk to you.' Rubul's tone had changed.

'Rubul, you aren't postponing dealing with a serious problem, right?'

I think he sensed the urgency in my low voice. I don't lower my voice usually. Nor do I speak that slowly. He could hear caution and worry in my tone, and if I was worried enough, he knew I would have a chat with his mother. Though we are exactly the same age, I was always the big brother, approving things, sorting stuff out for him. He knew that. I would find out later that he didn't want it. That he was postponing dealing with a serious problem.

But that day, he just said, 'I won't do anything without telling you. See you soon.'

'That means you are planning to do something.'

'Yes.'

God, is he going to come out? I started to sweat at the thought of it.

What Nishad told Rubul Before Getting Married:
May 2016

First, you really need to know more about this girl. That she lives in Azara, has a degree in history, and respects elders is not enough information on which you can decide to get married to someone . . . Rubul, you don't get married because it will bring joy to the family. You get married because you want to get married. So what if she is chosen by your mother? Does your mother know you drink nowadays? That you have graduated from rum to whisky during social occasions, and that you have also eaten pork and betrayed your brahmin caste? So what if she is chosen by your mother? With all due respect to Babita Aunty, she doesn't know what you want. You want a partner, Rubul. You want someone with whom you can sit down and discuss your favourite movie, favourite novel. After you write a scene for one of those stupid television serials, you want someone who knows you well enough to comment on it and push you to work harder. . . . Wait, you misunderstand me. I am not asking you not to marry Anuradha. I mean, she sounds lovely, and from that photograph you showed me, I see she is pretty. But that's not enough reason to marry a girl. You marry because you want to marry this person and no one else. I mean, just tell your mother that you don't want to commit to a wedding now, and at least hang out with her for the next six months before you decide to marry her.

Wait, what? What do you mean, she isn't that type of girl? Which world do you live in? I am not even asking you to have sex with her. Just go out. What? Is her family putting pressure? But she is only, like, what, twenty-five? There is something fishy here. Can you find out why they are pressing your family to decide within a week? Does she know that you come home very late at night? That you work for twelve hours, fourteen hours? Your mother, sister, father may stand for it. But why would she tolerate that? You will have to now return home early. You will have to make sure her needs are met. You can't just return home at two in the morning, ask for dinner to be heated, and then go sleep. You will have to chat with her, make love to her. Marriage is a responsibility. She will be waiting for you all day. Especially because she doesn't have a job right now.

What are you going to do? In your own words, this is something you can't change about yourself. Have you told her? Okay, you haven't. Why haven't you told her? When you are marrying her, you are taking responsibility for her. You can't expect her to tolerate everything that you do like your mother and sister. Can you?

OMG, she has a boyfriend who is threatening her and telling her not to marry you? Okay, this is serious! If you don't tell Aunty, I will call her. What if he harms you? What if he tries to attack you? I am terrified of these surrendered insurgents. If he is a former militant, he must be, like, fifty? Okay, fine, forty. So what? They still roam around the state with a gun, and they don't think before using it. They have lots of money, ya. I am terrified. Of course, I am! Will you go argue with someone who is carrying a gun? You know how it is! You know that no one can actually control former militants. And seriously, and this is my final point, what if she votes for Modi?

What Babita told Nishad after the wedding date was decided: June 2016

Nishad, the first thing Anuradha did when she entered our house was to look at Rubul's grandfather's garlanded photo—my father-in-law, who was a freedom fighter and such a wonderful person. Then she joined her hands in salutation to him, and it was at that moment that I knew I had made the right choice. Also, you know, that morning, I went inside the prayer room, lit a ghee lamp, shut my eyes, and prayed, 'God, the girl is stepping into this house for the first time today since the wedding date was fixed. I have sprinkled holy water everywhere and have also asked the maid to mop the entire house with salt water to neutralise the power of evil spirits, but now it is in your hands. You have to show me a sign. You have to.' Then, you know what happened, Nishad? I felt a gust of wind. I felt as if someone entered the prayer room! One of the red hibiscus flowers tucked into the hands of the statue fell on my lap. I was worried that the wind had put out the lamp, but when I opened my eyes, the wick was burning bright, the flame was strong, and the room felt warm. It was a very strong flame.

Tell me, Nishad, do togor flowers bloom in June? We have that large togor flower in the courtyard, remember? When it blooms in April, the smell travels almost to the main road. Everyone talks about our togor flower. On very rare occasions, it blooms in May, too. But that morning, I saw a lonely togor flower. It was surreal. But I knew it was a message. I knew I had chosen the right girl for my son, that it is the ideal match.

You are family, so there's nothing to hide from you. You know that Rubul's sister will now move to the top floor since he is getting married? I mean, we middle-class people plan everything, don't we? She wasn't in my plan. I didn't plan to build a top floor. The foundation of this house is for four floors, but I thought, later, when Rubul earns, he will build as per his requirements. But his sister's marriage didn't work. She had to return to us. Now, when Rubul's bride comes home, there will be space constraints. I mean, we will manage, but there will be some discomfort, right? So, I have asked Subho to move upstairs. She will put a part of that floor on rent and live alone with her two children. Cook on her own. Live independently. I don't want the two girls to have tussles. When Anuradha heard that, she became so sad. She asked, can't she stay downstairs, with us? Note that she said 'with us'. She held Subho's hand and said, 'Please don't go. People in the colony will think I am a horrible person who made sure her sister-in-law was driven out of the first floor even before she stepped into the house as a bride. What will they say about me?' You know, Nishad, this cemented my belief: this is the kind of girl I want for my son, and she is just like the character she plays in the serial. This is why, though she is a supporting actress, people love her. In the serial, she is like the moral core of the story that is full of horrible, scheming mothers-in-law and sisters-in-law. But in reality, too, she is pure like water from the Ganga. And in our house, too, she will be the moral and ethical core. She will come and keep the house together like a thread in a garland. She won't let things fall apart. She will be the foundation of the house. She will be like a lamp and spread light in the house.

What happened when Nishad invited Rubul and his family to lunch: December 2016

I had thrown the lunch party to celebrate my promotion, but it was also a sort of housewarming since I had bought this apartment six months ago and done nothing to mark its possession. All the guests were invited to come by 1 p.m., but I had asked Rubul and his family to arrive by noon. I knew Rubul would delay by an hour—that was standard. So, I lied to Rubul, 'I have asked all the guests to be here by noon, so you can come no later than 1.' I knew Rubul knew that I was lying. 'And listen, we will find a spot to talk about your problem.'

'Don't worry about it. I was getting fed up. So, I took care of it, and now things should be fine.' Rubul sighed. It wasn't really a sigh of relief, so I was surprised and still curious.

'Are you sure? What did you do?'

'No one can be sure. I will tell you everything when we meet. Do you remember Vikas from our batch?'

'Vikas Surana? The doctor? Yes, I do. I didn't know you were friends with him. He used to bully everyone.'

'Yes, but now he doesn't bully anyone. He helped me.'

Vikas was an oncologist. He wasn't a psychiatrist. My mind raced. Was Rubul suffering from erectile dysfunction, did Vikas prescribe drugs? I couldn't wait to meet him the next day and take him aside for a proper chat. He should see an expert. Not a friend who was a doctor.

At three in the afternoon, Rubul and his family still hadn't turned up. Bina-pehi, my aunt, who was supervising the caterers, asked me what to do. The caterers were anxious to leave; they had more or less packed up, and Rubul's family were the only guests still to arrive.

I looked outside; the weak winter sun would probably set in less than an hour. I suggested that we could store whatever was left in casseroles, including Rubul's favourite, the chicken liver.

At four, I called Rubul for the third time, and it went unanswered. Finally, I called Babita Aunty.

She said, 'I guess you know it is not my fault.'

'Yes, I know. Rubul hasn't turned up to pick you guys up, right?'

'Yes. I am still dressed. The new bride is watching TV. We are all waiting.'

'How surprising.'

'Subho is pissed and won't talk to him, so I am calling every half an hour like a maniac, and your best friend won't even receive my calls.' She was clearly very annoyed.

'Well, Subho's resolve won't last long, will it?' I heard her sigh at the other end. 'Did you tell your new daughter in-law that this is standard behaviour for Rubul?'

'Don't ask. What can I say? We could have rented a cab, but he said he would come on time to pick us up.'

'Well, the poor girl must be dying of hunger.'

'I think I will just steam some rice, and we will have it with leftover dal right now. We didn't cook lunch today because we were to eat at your place. We will still come, baba. We will come. Maybe we will turn up in an hour and have an early dinner.'

I rang again, an hour later. My apartment was now empty. The guests and the caterers had left. My parents had also left for their own house on the outskirts of the city. Bina-pehi decided to stay back, so she could help me just in case Rubul & Co. made a late-night appearance.

Rubul's mother said, 'He is still stuck somewhere. So, no early dinner. We will have proper dinner with you. Heat up the leftovers, and we will have them at dinner time. Subho ate some fruits and cornflakes. Anuradha and I, we just ate some rice with dal. The poor girl was all dressed up. She has changed into sweatpants now.'

We both laughed. 'If your son doesn't change his ways, your new bride will go running back to her mother's house, you know that, right? And no god can stop her.'

'I know.' She sighed. 'I thought he would change after marriage.'

I hung up and looked at the orange sky, the homecoming birds. From the fourth floor, you couldn't see the dirt, the manhole, the mud puddles on the road. From the fourth floor, you could see the round shape of the mosque clearly and the parking lot of this apartment complex. At night, halogen lights lit up the area. Rubul wouldn't change, I knew. I also knew that this would cost him his marriage.

They turned up at 11 p.m. I was watching something on Netflix, trying hard to stay awake.

'We are heeeerrreee!' Rubul screamed from the parking lot. It was too cheerful and very annoying. I walked slowly to the balcony and saw him waving at me. Babita Aunty, Anuradha, and Subho looked sullen.

'We are on time for *linner*!!' he announced as he stepped out of the elevator.

That was hardly likely to bring anyone cheer. But Subho managed a smile at me as she handed me a box of cashew sweets. Anuradha looked exhausted when she greeted me.

'We are on time for linner!' Rubul repeated in the same cheerful tone, since no one had responded to his announcement.

'Rubul, don't try to be funny,' I said.

'Do you even know what "linner" means? I invented the word yester-day. It is short for Late Dinner.' He looked at everyone, as if for an applause.

'Rubul, don't try to be funny,' Subho said and walked into the apartment. She saw Bina-pehi and, even before hugging her, started to complain about her brother.

'My family loves bitching about me,' Rubul said with a grin on his face.

'They have every reason to,' I replied.

'Exactly, Nishad-da,' Anuradha said.

Rubul just grinned.

I was sleepy, tired, and angry, but I felt sorry for Anuradha—it had been a frustrating marriage for her. She had bought a new mekhela-sador for this occasion. She had also been looking forward to meeting my parents for the first time since the wedding and had also bought gifts for them. During dinner, she was mostly quiet.

The apartment complex was quiet, and with no one around but the guards on duty outside, it was unbearably silent. I put on some music by Zubeen Garg: 'Mayabini Ratir Bukut'.

'I will just have plain rice with dal,' Anuradha said when my aunt started to serve her.

On the table, there were brinjal fritters, chicken cooked with cashew paste, fish in a tomato curry soured with a lemon, goat rogan josh, sautéed cauliflower and potatoes, and palm jaggery kheer and shiny light-brown lalmohans for dessert. So, of course Bina-pehi's eyes popped in horror.

'Why? Why don't you want to eat? You think we don't cook well?'

'No, no, not at all.' Anuradha shook her head vigorously.

'Do you think our kitchen is dirty? No, no, what are you saying?' she gasped. 'I have no doubt your mother cooks better than this, but does that mean you will go hungry in our house? I am sad.'

'No, no, please don't be sad.' Anuradha looked like she would burst into tears.

'We've known the caterers for a very long time. They are clean, and they make healthy food, Anuradha.' My aunt continued to hurl missiles at the poor girl.

This was the tactic the host used to guilt-trip guests into overeating: nine pieces of chicken instead of three, an extra bowl of kheer, four slices of cake instead of one, and of course, a lot of rice—like, a lot. That the new bride, who was visiting for the first time, would eat only rice and dal was an alarming situation for my aunt. That was why she pulled out her most powerful weapons at the very beginning.

Anuradha, who had been speaking softly so far, protested loudly, 'No, no, that's not the case.' She looked towards me for support, for reasons I will never know. 'I have heartburn,' she muttered.

'It is okay.' I came to her rescue. 'Let her eat what she wants. She ate a late lunch today, why wouldn't she have indigestion and heartburn?'

Subho praised the chicken. 'The chicken is just amazing. Anuradha, you sure you don't want a little?'

'I am sure.'

My aunt continued to lament. 'You are the chief guest of today's lunch, Anuradha! You have to eat something. I will be so sad if you don't eat. Are you alright? Can I get you some Pudin Hara or Hajmola for your heartburn? I also have trifala—when we had heartburn, Ma used to feed us trifala. Now I am worried about you, my dear.' Bina-pehi's voice grew louder with every sentence.

I was sure Anuradha was fine. And that she didn't have heartburn, or if she did, it wasn't serious. She was launching a passive resistance against her irresponsible new husband turning up eleven hours late for a meal they had been invited to.

'I am fine. I don't want anyone to worry about me,' she repeated, staring at her plate.

Rubul also knew what was going on. And perhaps his mother and Subho, too. He took the ladle, picked up a leg piece with a generous helping of cashew gravy. 'We will worry about you. And I will, of course, worry about you.' Then he poured it over her rice.

Anuradha was startled. She hadn't been prepared for that. She paused. Then she slowly pushed her unfinished plate of food towards the centre of the table—just a few inches. I was surprised she didn't raise her voice or push her plate away with more force.

'I am done.'

'You won't eat the chicken I served you?' Rubul asked. As if rejecting the chicken piece he had served meant that she was rejecting him.

She looked straight into his eyes and said coldly, 'No. I said I have heartburn.'

He looked at her for a few seconds. It was so awkward. Then he looked down at his plate and took a spoonful of rice and meat to his mouth. I knew he would do something stupid, but I didn't know he would do something so stupid. I saw his eyes turning red. Suddenly, he pushed his plate away to the centre of the table. It collided with a glass of water that fell on the table and spilt over onto Anuradha's clothes. Then he stormed out of the dining room. 'No need, no need to eat.' First, he said that in a muffled tone, and when he had taken about four steps more, he said it loudly. 'NO NEED, NO NEED TO EAT.'

Anuradha started to shed tears. 'How is any of this my fault? I said I won't eat chicken, and he is forcing me to eat.'

I looked at everyone and said, 'I am not going to talk to Rubul. He is misbehaving.'

'No, you should give him two tight slaps,' Babita Aunty said.

Five minutes later, I was thrusting a plate of fried chicken liver at him. We were standing on the balcony. It wasn't too cold. We both wore light sweaters. I asked him what was wrong with him, and he said he had work to do. What did he want to talk to me about a month ago, I asked, and he said this wasn't the best time. I told him he couldn't be eleven hours late, and he couldn't stall people who were waiting for him by assuring them that he would be there to pick them up in an hour, in two hours, in half an hour. They could have taken an Uber if he had let them leave the house, but he had stalled them for eleven hours. That wasn't acceptable. He said, no one understood him, and I laughed. I ate the chicken liver fry, laughed, and said that there was nothing to understand, that he was being an asshole.

He looked into my eyes and said, 'You have no idea what I am going through, Nishad.'

'What do you mean? You said you took care of the problem.'

'I thought I did, but I don't think I will be able to solve the problem. It is not under my control.'

'And Vikas? You said he helped you.'

'He did, but he can't make the problem go away.'

I could come up with a list of therapists I trusted, but it would take a lot of effort to persuade someone like Rubul to visit one. Still, I would have to do it. Rubul would start with 'I am not mad, I don't need a therapist', and I was ready to talk him out of those misconceptions.

So, I said, 'Listen, what is it? Let me help you.'

'I don't want to trouble you or put you in any danger.'

'Danger? What kind of danger?'

It seemed to me Rubul wanted to avoid the topic, and I wanted to say, there was no danger. If he wanted to get out of the marriage even now, I would help him, talk to everyone. One didn't have to remain trapped in a loveless, sexless marriage.

'You have to tell me now. What danger?'

Rubul covered his face with his hands. 'I should have listened to you, Nishad. You always had a sense. You always knew better. You know me better than me. And your gut feeling about people and situations is usually correct.'

'You are scaring me now.'

'I will come tomorrow morning. I need to discuss this problem with you. I can't start here. I don't want Ma and Anuradha to know.'

'Of course. Come for breakfast tomorrow,' I said.

Inside, the atmosphere had turned cheerful. Anuradha was not weeping anymore. She was talking about recipes with Bina-pehi, and Subho was switching channels and commenting on dresses and make-up. Babita Aunty gave Rubul a look, but I gestured to say 'not now'.

A little later, Rubul cracked terrible jokes, at which only Anuradha laughed. Subho pretended to laugh, his mother didn't laugh, and a totally unresponsive Bina-pehi looked confused and sleepy—as if she was joke-proof. A couple of hours later, I watched them walk to the car from the fourth-floor balcony. I wanted to go downstairs to see them off, but they all insisted I stay home since it was cold and quite late. But it was cold on the balcony, too. I watched Anuradha holding Babita Aunty's hand, helping her get to the car though she didn't need any help; Subho still yawning, chattering; and Rubul walking towards the car to unlock the doors. Just then, a tall, bearded man in a black leather jacket appeared as if from nowhere and punched Rubul. He was holding a gun. Before Rubul could make sense of what was going on, the man pressed the pistol against his temple.

///////////////

Was it a revolver? Was it a pistol? What was it? I had no idea! For a few seconds, I froze. I had grown up in Assam during the worst years of violence; I grew up reading all those reports about people getting killed, civilians being armed, the killings between rival groups, former insurgents killing underground ones. But I had never actually seen any of it. Despite growing up in a state full of violent insurgent movements, I had never touched a gun. So, I just froze; it was like I was watching a film.

The bearded man was drunk, perhaps. Still holding the gun to Rubul's head, he said something. Rubul appeared to reply, fear writ large on his face. He looked different without his spectacles, which had been knocked off his face. The man looked angry and was shouting. He was broad, had a large head, and his unzipped jacket revealed a blood-red T-shirt. He wore a gold chain that shone in the light of the halogen bulbs. And then it really became like a movie, like one of those Hindi movies. Anuradha pushed Rubul aside, pounced on the man, snatched his gun, and held it to her own forehead, just between her thick bow-shaped eyebrows. In the quiet night, I heard her voice loud and clear, 'If you don't leave right away, I will shoot myself.'

The man started to shake his head. Perhaps he was saying, no, no. Still shaking his head, he crumpled to the ground and started to cry, 'Don't do that.' His voice was loud and pierced through the silence of the night.

It was then that I came back to my senses, grabbed my phone, and went downstairs. I guessed that Anuradha knew the man from before. They were close. Very close.

When I reached the parking lot, Babita Aunty was throwing up, and Rubul was trying to make her drink some water. I wanted to say something but couldn't think what.

The bearded man was gone.

Anuradha screamed, the gun still in her hands, 'We have to leave. He may come back with his friends. He is crazy.'

'What? Why didn't you say that earlier?' Babita Aunty screamed as she sprung up and slid into the car. 'Kill me-o! Just kill me here-o!' she cried.

Rubul was dazed and shocked and in no condition to drive. I pushed him inside the car and asked Anuradha to sit next to me. 'We can't go home. He knows Rubul's address,' she said, pointing the gun towards the road.

'I know where to go. Give me the keys,' I said.

'Kill me-o! What are you showing me, God? Anuradha, why are you still holding the gun? What if—'

'Don't worry, Ma, I know how to use a gun.'

Suddenly, there was an awkward silence. We stared at Anuradha for a few seconds, slightly scared.

Babita Aunty broke that silence. 'Oh god, my daughter-in-law knows how to use a gun, and I thought those hands would nurture everyone and everything in my house. My gun-wielding daughter-in-law! My son hasn't seen a gun in his life! Even I haven't touched a gun in my life, and I have a daughter-in-law who knows how to use a gun.'

'Ma, please shut up,' Rubul snapped.

'Kill me, kill me now,' Babita Aunty said, looking at Anuradha.

'Drive! Now!' Anuradha said to me, calmly, the gun still in her hand.

At that point, I wanted to talk to Babita Aunty about some flower that had bloomed out of season and given her a sign, about flowers that had fallen on her lap, about the perils of hurriedly arranging a wedding, about pushing her own son and family down the slippery slope of a forced marriage. But I didn't say any of that because I was suddenly full of admiration for Anuradha's courage. How she had taken stock of the situation, like a lifeguard on a beach! How she was giving me directions in a calm, resolute voice! When I told her that we would take refuge in my parents' house, she said she knew another way. She knew secret roads to my own parents' house that I didn't know. The house where I had grown up, the house where Rubul and I had spent a good part of our childhood! The road she took was dark, potholed, and narrow but safe. She said the bearded man's large Scorpio would avoid such roads. Anuradha clearly knew this man well. She knew the model of his car, could predict his behaviour, knew how to use his gun, and knew the roads he would avoid because he loved his car. What else did she know about him? His business enterprises? The length of his beard? The smell of his breath? Which molar caused him pain if he ate ice cream? The length of his penis? She knew him too well, and it didn't bode well for her.

But I didn't care because, in less than half an hour, the secret road she had taken would land us at my parents' place, and they would be shocked to see us. Babita Aunty and my mother would cry thinking about what could have happened. Rubul could have been shot. I could have been shot. Everyone could have been shot. That same night, at some point, Rubul's mother would go up to Anuradha, still holding the gun, and slap her hard. 'I thought you would light up my house, but you are all set to burn it down!' She would tell Anuradha to pack up and leave the next day, and for the first time in his life, Rubul would disobey his mother. He would say that she had saved his life and that she wasn't going anywhere. Anuradha would weep silently, rubbing her face with her free hand, and Babita Aunty would hold my mother's hands and wail, 'The witch has already started to control my son.' I would give each of them a pack of tissues. Cry, cry your heart out, I would murmur. In a bit, everyone would stop crying. We would take action to ensure everyone's safety. At dawn, we would call Vikas Surana's father, a high-ranking police officer, because Vikas Surana, the school bully, the oncologist, had given Rubul his father's personal mobile number a few weeks ago. Mr Surana would assure Rubul that the man would be arrested. Anuradha would take the phone and provide every detail of the bearded man: his two residences, four phone numbers, names of his aides, his best friends and their numbers and addresses, possible hiding places, etc. 'Mr Surana, I have his gun as proof—yes, it is a .22 calibre revolver. Yes, he is a former militant,' she would add before placing the phone on the cradle. 'The witch knows everything, she might as well be married to him,' Babita

Aunty would tell my mother, and my mother would look confused and ask her to hush.

But those things would happen later at night, between now and dawn. At this point, while driving the car, I was just full of admiration for Anuradha. She would be a good partner. Like the thread in a garland, she could stitch things together.

/////////////////

It is dawn.

I wake up Ramen-da, the help, and ask him to make tea for everyone. When the tea is brought out with a tray of Britannia thin arrowroot biscuits, Rubul picks up a cup and asks me to follow him upstairs. I am still processing the incidents of the night before. I am wondering what will happen to Rubul's marriage now. I am still full of admiration for Anuradha— her deft handling of the situation, the ability to decide on the spot. . . . When I make no move to follow, Rubul moves towards the stairs and asks again, 'Are you coming?'

He knows this house well. My room is upstairs. There are several photos of the two of us together framed and hung on the walls of that room. Photos from my birthday celebrations. Photos from the last day of our higher secondary with pineapple pastry smeared on our faces. We are in school uniforms. Grey pants. Red sweaters. Stork-white shirts.

'I think you should talk to Anuradha,' I tell him.

'I want to talk to you. NOW,' Rubul bellows.

Anuradha looks up at him. She is drinking tea, sitting a little away from Babita Aunty.

I have rarely seen Rubul this assertive. I realise he is very serious. I follow quietly.

'Shut the door.'

I do as asked and sit on the bed. 'Tell me. But I think you should be talking to Anuradha. She is in a very difficult situation.'

'Fuck you, Nishad.'

'Fuck you.'

There is an awkward pause.

'This was the fucking problem I wanted to discuss with you. I have been receiving threats from her ex ever since the wedding date was fixed. I haven't told Anuradha about it. I didn't want to scare her.' Rubul is staring at the floor. 'I am so stressed that nothing has happened between us till now—you know what I mean?'

'Yes, I do.' I add with a smirk, 'You don't have to elaborate.'

'Fuck you.'

I sit next to him. 'She is your life partner. This is a decision both of you have taken together—to be together. You need to discuss everything with her. And after today, I have to tell you that she seems like someone who can really take charge. She might be younger than us, but she is damn smart. If you want to be with her, stop treating her like a child. She is your equal.'

'Yeah—I figured. Our honeymoon is next month. Maybe it will be a fresh start.'

I look at Rubul for a few seconds and say, 'Yes, don't return a virgin from your honeymoon.'

Rubul covers his face and laughs. He asks if he can confess something, then pauses, a smile on his lips. He shrugs and then says that he doesn't like my new apartment. He likes this room, this house; it has character. I feel a strange sense of calm. I am not upset that Rubul doesn't like my new apartment. Perhaps I knew it already. So, I agree. I tell him that I, too, miss this house. Rubul asks if that mango tree is still there, the one he climbed once to pluck mangoes and fell from, fracturing his left hand. Yes, that mango tree is still around. It continues to produce lots of fruits every summer. I miss this house, Rubul murmurs, his eyes shut. In a few seconds, he is in a deep sleep.

I throw a light blanket on him and step out of the room. As I walk down the stairs, I hear Babita Aunty yelling at Anuradha. I hurry down. Rubul's door is shut. He won't wake up for a while.

AFTER ANTHROPOLOGY

A day before they left for Matt's father's house in Sioux Falls, Raj cheated on Matt with a colleague. It was nothing more than a fleeting thing. But he thought it was important to tell Matt. He didn't cheat on Matt just to confess, but once he decided he would ask Matt for a break in the relationship, Raj was filled with guilt and a strange sense of relief.

So, when Matt returned from work that night, Raj opened the door and looked at him pleadingly. 'I got a blowjob today,' he said, after Matt had taken a shower and changed and then come to the kitchen to get a drink of water. Matt looked so bright and fresh. His hair was still wet. He didn't choke on the bottle of water, like you see in television soaps. He stopped drinking, placed the bottle on the kitchen counter, and said, 'What the—?'

'Yes,' Raj said, turning his back to Matt, his heart beating fast.

Matt sat down on the couch, near Raj, and switched on the television. He lowered the volume. 'Who was it?' He was calm. His voice was lower than the lowered volume of the television, not the voice of a man whose partner had just told him that he had cheated on him.

'Jim works with me at the restaurant. He's a waiter.'

'Is he hot? I've never seen him,' Matt said. They prepared dinner in silence. Raj wanted to cook rajma (Matt called them kidney beans) with ginger-garlic paste but did not have the energy for it. He thought Matt's reaction was strange.

They had been together for four years, and this was the first time something like this had happened. In the early weeks and months of their relationship, when Matt checked out guys in malls, restaurants, on the sidewalks, Raj would be offended. He would ask Matt to 'rein your eyes' and walk around swollen-faced. Matt would smile indulgently, ask him not to worry, tell him that no one would snatch him away. Sometimes, he would run a finger along Raj's arm, from elbow to wrist, arousing him. But those were the early days.

'You're not angry?' Raj asked, breaking the silence. He hadn't eaten much.

'I'm glad you got a blowjob. Blowjobs are great.'

Raj looked at Matt with glassy eyes. He wondered why Matt had used the word twice, if not to stress on it.

'You're being sarcastic. I thought I should tell you. I like honesty.'

'So do I. I appreciate you telling me.'

Raj didn't understand how Matt could use the word 'appreciate' in this context. Matt appreciated many things: a lift to the grocery store, if someone brought him a new client, the recommendation of a good doctor or the friend who pet-sat when Matt and Raj were away in India for their holiday. But was it appropriate to use that same expression when your boyfriend told you that he had gotten a blowjob from someone else? After a while, when Raj was tossing the dishes into the dishwasher, Matt hugged him from behind, pressed his body against his, and said, 'I love you. It's okay. I'm not one of those husbands who would throw a ft. You made a mistake. You're sorry, that's why you told me. Let's forget about it.'

Raj wanted to say that he hadn't yet said sorry, and it was preposterous of Matt to assume it.

'I am not sure if I would react the same way if you fucked someone.'

'I know. And that is why I would never do it, baby.'

Raj didn't like the sound of 'baby' in Matt's voice that night. He felt as if Matt was mocking him. The high moral ground that Matt always took annoyed Raj. He was annoyed by how Matt laid stress on the 'I' in 'I would never do that, baby'.

So, he asked, 'What are you trying to say, really? Something happened today. I just didn't have control over what I wanted.' Raj was surprised that he wanted to scream at Matt, he wanted to ask: why are you being so nice, are you trying to make me feel worse?

'No, baby,' Matt said, irritating Raj further. 'I am trying to say that I know you love me and only me, and nothing will change that. This encounter had no meaning. I'm not pleased with what happened, but it's okay. It happens. We should look at the larger picture.'

Matt had this theory: the Larger Picture Theory. He always looked at the larger picture and encouraged others to do it as well. He framed his larger-picture funda in such a manner that everyone else sounded foolish and short-sighted. He was the one who could look ahead. Had foresight. Was more tolerant. Accepting. The one who forgave all. And Raj felt he was always the guilty one, the foolish one, the smaller one, the less loving one. Matt's righteousness burnt through Raj.

That night, they slept far apart on their large bed. Raj wanted Matt to get angry. He thought about the hours of guilt he had suffered after the incident in the restroom and felt foolish. And he wondered whether Matt didn't pick a fight about it because he loved Raj less intensely now or because they were planning to meet Matt's father for the first time. Minnesota had just passed the Marriage Equality Act after a bitter fight against the 'Vote No' campaign, and they had married in a small ceremony that some of their friends and none of their family attended. Matt's mother had died long ago, and his sister, Kristine, had left the house when she was fourteen. Raj's parents had stopped receiving his calls after he told them he was marrying a man. Over the past few years, Matt and his father had renewed their relationship. 'After all, he's my father,' Matt said. 'My biological father.' I understand, Raj had said. Bloodline, family—words no one could understand better than an Indian. Indians were obsessed with those things. In fact, when Tony emailed two months ago, when Raj wasn't even thinking about the possibility of taking a break, it was Raj who had suggested that Matt accept the invite. Though Tony had thrown Matt out of the house after finding him blowing the jumpsuit-clad plumber, he was still Matt's father, Raj said. Establishing an easy equation with his father could only liberate him, Raj added, deftly exploiting Matt's 'Larger Picture Theory'. But it was also true that Matt wanted his father's love and approval—not unusual for someone who had lost his mother when he was five. Secretly (and Raj knew this), Matt was grateful that his father had never married again and had made Matt his priority—until he found out his son was gay in the least ideal way ever. In short, it was a complicated relationship with layers of love and hate; you got a bit or more of both, irrespective of wherever you dug.

Later at night, Raj felt Matt's right hand on his shoulder. '—wake?' he muttered. Raj didn't reply. He pretended he was asleep, though he knew that Matt always knew whenever he was still awake. He wished Matt was a little petty and wondered if he was being so kind and generous and correct because Raj was different, came from a different country, different culture. But they had planned the trip to Sioux Falls two months ago, and it would now be terrible if he backed out. Maybe they could take a break from the relationship after the trip, he thought, before falling asleep.

On their way to Sioux Falls, they stopped at a small restaurant by the freeway to eat lunch. Matt ordered his salad with a lot of lettuce, and Raj had a chicken burrito with a lot of sour cream. They ate in silence.

'Is something wrong?'

For a few seconds, Raj was silent, and then he decided to speak up, 'You know, okay, I'll just say it—I thought you were unnecessarily crabby this morning. Is it because of what I told you?'

Matt threw his hands up, exasperated. 'What is wrrrooooong with you? You're still thinking about it?'

'Then what is it?' Raj raised his voice but quickly realised he was creating a scene.

They ate the rest of their lunch quietly. Raj wanted to ask Matt why he had been so angry in the morning that the phones were not charged and the power banks not packed. They could charge their phones in the car, and they would make their way to his father's house without a GPS just fine. Raj had dated Matt in the 'pre-smartphone days' and was good with routes. He didn't say this, though, because he knew what Matt would say: 'When my phone dies, it drives me nuts.' Among the many things Raj had not figured out yet about Matt was what drove him 'nuts' and what didn't. Matt had a long of list of things that drove him nuts: a bad day at work, saltless steak, salad without lettuce, a dead phone, poor connectivity while travelling, unwashed underwear, used towels, flattened toothpaste tubes, too much snow in winter, too little snow in winter, salad with too much lettuce, internet outage, and much else. Raj wanted to list it all, but he kept quiet. He didn't want to escalate the matter.

'There's something I need to tell you,' Matt said about an hour later, as he drove.

'You got a blowjob? Then we are even.' Raj was immediately ashamed about the sarcasm. In this way, their relationship would turn into an emotionally abusive one. 'Alright, tell me. I am sorry.'

'My father is a bit strange.'

'I guess he is. He disowned you and then owned you back when you became a lawyer. Very convenient.'

'No, I mean, he watches Fox News all day and drinks beer and eats only steak, and of course, he votes for the Republican Party. You might find it difficult to deal with him. And I think he is a bit racist.'

Raj laughed for the first time in three days. 'I'm sure it will be fine. I've dealt with many racist people in this country! I don't care what he eats or who he votes for, but it is a bit worrying that he watches Fox News!'

'I'm serious . . . I'm a little worried, Raj.'

'It will be fine.'

'I'm going to meet my conservative father with my husband, and my conservative father is introducing me to his fiancée. I mean, all those years after Mom died, he didn't bring a single woman home. For a long time, I thought he was asexual or gay.'

They both laughed. After a while, Raj said again, 'Now you're worrying me. You guys won't get into a fight, right?'

'Arrrreyy, don't worry, just chill—I'll show you the place where I first had sex with a plumber!'

Raj laughed, not because of the possibility of visiting the site of Matt's chequered erotic life, but because he wanted Matt to continue saying arreys in this sweet manner, with the extra stress on the Rs. Raj extended his left hand and slid it between Matt's thighs. Matt said he was sure they were never going to reach Sioux Falls in one piece with so much distraction. Raj hoped Matt wasn't too anxious about introducing his homophobic father to his brown husband. He didn't want to think about the break he wanted from the relationship. He wanted to think about the prospect of making love to Matt in the house where he had grown up.

Raj disliked Tony immediately, and it wasn't because he was a large man who welcomed them with a massive can of beer in his right hand. It wasn't because, as Matt had warned, Fox News was playing on the huge fifty-five-inch wall-mounted TV so loudly that it was like walking into a movie theatre several minutes after the film had started. It wasn't even the fact that Tony had treated Matt badly once upon a time. Raj couldn't put his finger on what exactly it was about the man that put him off. But he didn't let his dislike show. He smiled at Tony, and Tony smiled back at him. Matt didn't hug his father, didn't shake his hand. He entered the house with a trying-hard-to-be-enthusiastic 'Hey, Dad' and a smile that was exactly like the one Tony had flashed at Raj, the kind of smile that indicates someone is in pain or constipated.

Raj greeted the lady who came up to them, her earrings swaying vigorously.

'This is Irene,' Tony said.

'Hello, Irene,' Raj said.

Tony added in an enthusiastic voice, 'She's been cooking all day. She learnt some new recipes from girlfriends at her church. It's all burgers and chicken and steak and some salad, though. No kaboobs for Raj, sorry.'

Raj smiled. He didn't point out that they were kebabs, not kaboobs, and was grateful the option of Indian food had been considered to make him feel comfortable. 'That's alright, it sounds delicious.' Then, after a pause, because he thought Tony and Irene would appreciate it, he added, 'I'm very excited.'

Matt gave him a strange look, and Raj knew why—he wasn't the kind of person who liberally sprinkled his sentences with 'amazing', 'excited', and 'cool'. In fact, he often cribbed about the American tendency to use those words. He ignored Matt's puzzled look and continued to wonder what it was about Tony. Was it because of the volume Fox News was playing at that made it almost impossible for them to have a conversation? Irene suggested that they turn it off, and Tony reluctantly agreed, only to switch it back on and play it on mute. I should be able to accept Tony as he is; I was, after all, warned adequately, Raj thought.

'I've always wanted to visit India, you know—my church made a trip to Calcutta last year,' Irene said during dinner. 'I'm sure it's a beautiful country.'

She had a singsong manner of speaking that Raj found both irritating and amusing. Raj didn't want to disappoint her by telling the truth—that most big cities in India were dust bowls and so overpopulated that they had almost turned him into a misanthrope.

He said instead, 'In parts, yes, it is beautiful. And it is a very large country. You won't find the cities beautiful, I am sure.' He paused and then added without really meaning it, 'You must come. I would love to show you around.'

Matt gave him that same look again.

'Maybe Tony and I could go for our honeymoon to see the Taj Mahal,' she said, rubbing Tony's hands, her voice now thin, high-pitched. Raj was a little annoyed because she wasn't pronouncing 'Taj Mahal' properly. With the extra stress on the N, she wasn't even saying 'India' properly.

Tony had a loud voice and sounded as if he was suffering from a cold. 'We'll see. I'm not sure, we will have to apply for visas and all. Are there lots of Muslims in India? I've heard there are.'

Matt and Raj exchanged glances. Raj wasn't offended, but he knew Matt would get angry. He was the kind of person who wore his liberalism on his sleeve and suffered from what Raj referred to as 'liberal guilt'. Raj often asked him to get over it. In fact, when they first met, Raj had called him a 'Political Bottom', and Matt had paused for a bit and then said, 'Only a super cute guy like you could get away with calling someone that'. Even after they began dating in earnest, Raj often told him that while he did need to be aware of race, Matt couldn't keep apologising for being white in a country where race relations were fucked up.

For the moment, Raj decided to focus on the baked chicken and served himself some more of the tasty beans-and-broccoli salad. He wanted to eat light. After he had confessed to Matt about the blowjob affair, they hadn't made love—and he felt like making love that day. Raj had heard numerous stories about that house—Matt's fetish for hooking up with blue-collar straight or straight-acting workers and how his English setter dog would often bark relentlessly at the man who fucked Matt. It was in this house that Raj wanted to make love to Matt.

During dinner, Tony gulped down litres of beer, some of it dribbling down his chin. He interrupted Irene all the time and dominated the entire conversation with talk about cars and health care and how the government was taking his money away through taxes and how lazy people who didn't work were rewarded with food stamps. These were things that bothered Matt, not Raj.

'So, where are you guys staying tonight?' Tony asked Matt, digging into his bowl of apple crumble topped with whipped cream.

Matt looked surprised. 'Oh, I thought we would just sleep in my room—is that okay?'

Raj wondered why Matt needed to add 'is that okay'. This was his house. The house he had grown up in. On their way in, after they had eaten at the restaurant by the freeway, Matt had spoken of how excited he was about sleeping in his own bed, in this house, after such a long time. Raj wondered if 'is that okay' was a reflection of how hurt he was.

Raj braced himself for an altercation, an unpleasant situation where he would have to take control and defuse the situation in case Matt flipped. He looked at Irene, who seemed so unsuspecting and so pleased with every-thing that it bored him. Eating slowly, he concentrated on the conversation, all set to defuse it, if required. Tony's civil (not warm, not loving) behaviour had given him the courage to do that. Otherwise, he had decided he would remain quiet most of the time and let the father and son speak.

Tony took a few seconds to think. 'No, it's fine. You can take your room. It's clean. Find the sheets in the storage bed.'

'Alright, thanks, Dad. You sure?'

'Yes, I just wasn't sure if you wanted to stay here. That's why I asked. You should always ask, right?'

Though he didn't look at Irene or ask her, she said, 'Yes, how wonderful that you guys—'

As usual, he didn't let her finish and added that he would have asked the housekeeper to make the bed for them if Matt had told him earlier.

Raj spoke, with a tone of caution in his pace and voice, 'Tony, if it's a problem, we can book the American Inn, you know. It's just across the street.'

'Don't worry about it,' Tony said, looking at Raj. 'Stay here. You don't need to make that Patel any richer.' Matt thanked his dad and paused for a few heavy moments, adding that Mr Patel was a very hard worker. Tony didn't respond. Instead, he asked Matt if he would join him outside for a smoke.

////////////////

In the kitchen, Raj rinsed the dishes and placed them in the dishwasher, and Irene protested repeatedly. She said he was a sweetie. Though he was chatting with her, telling her how he had met Matt for the first time at a gay bar in Minneapolis, all he could think about was Matt's body, and he was feeling hornier and more conscious of his erection in front of Irene. He didn't dare check if it was showing, and he couldn't stop smiling at the possibility of passionate lovemaking in the same bed that Matt had grown up sleeping in. That bed magnified the importance of the act for him—as if it would somehow make him a part of Matt's childhood, part of the special experience of the man he loved. Then, the thought of taking a break returned, and he turned soft and felt drained of energy. It would be difficult to broach the topic with Matt. Suddenly, Raj realised: three days ago, it had been just a thought, and now it had morphed into a decision.

Raj thought of the times he and Matt had travelled together, the way airport security would often take Raj aside to check his hands for gunpowder residue while Matt hovered nearby, talking, sometimes even trying to hold Raj's hands. Though they never talked about it, it was understood that Matt would remain close by at every domestic airport. When they had travelled to India, Raj's nervousness about travel vanished like camphor blending with air—as if the moment he stepped on to the Air India flight, he became a full person: less vigilant, less careful, less apologetic. In the US, when he was frisked by TSA, was stopped and asked questions, he felt smaller and smaller, as if he wasn't a whole person, as if he needed Matt to make him whole, validate his existence as a real human. Matt's calm after the cheating incident made him cringe: why did he always need to be so good? Why did he have to be so righteous. If they took a break, Raj would be on his own, out from under Matt's suffocating protection. The dishwasher was now making the familiar sounds of water mixing with soap and splashing on the dishes.

'I hope they don't end up having an argument,' Irene said, mopping the granite kitchen slab with an orange cotton dishcloth and asking him if he would like some coffee. 'I bought some really good coffee.'

'Oh, I won't mind some coffee. Thanks, Irene.'

'Do you think they'll argue?' Irene asked, looking a bit anxious.

'Don't worry, Irene, I think they both just want to forget the past. They are sort of determined to wave the white flag.'

Irene chuckled, 'That's a nice way to put it.' Though she chuckled, she then added that she had been a little worried about Tony all day and how he would act over dinner.

Raj asked if he had said something to her.

'No, I mean—I am sure Matt knooows this,' she said, looking straight into his eyes in a way that meant she was saying something extremely obvious. 'Tony gets a bit anxious when there are guests. Every time you went to use the restroom, he kept asking where you were, wanted us to go and check on you. He just likes to be in—you know—full control. It took him a while to let me stay over, too.'

'Relationships are complicated.'

'I agree, but not always—look at YOU TWO,' she said cheerfully, loudly, rubbing her hands together. Raj wondered if she was nervous. 'But you're right,' she added in a matter-of-fact tone with a shrug, 'relationships are complicated. My son hasn't seen me in six years. I don't even know if he's okay.'

Raj asked, 'Why? I'm sorry—I don't mean to pry, but that's a little upsetting.' He paused before saying the phrase 'little upsetting', and between 'little' and 'upsetting', he paused again—a breath or two.

She now burst out into a shy giggle. Then she came closer, flung the towel onto the kitchen slab, and whispered, 'I slapped his wife.'

'Oh my god . . . you don't look like the slapping kind!' Raj was laughing now.

'Oh, yes, I can do that. She called me a bitch. And I said, you want to know what a real bitch looks like? Take this!'

And when both of them had burst into a loud laughter, Matt and Tony joined them in the kitchen. In between the laughter, Irene told Tony that she'd told Raj about slapping her daughter-in-law, and Tony grumbled that only a stupid bitch would call a lovely woman like Irene a bitch.

Raj and Matt kissed each other passionately, first on the couch and then while climbing up the stairs. Matt sat down on the carpeted stairs and let Raj nibble on his chest, around his neck, grab his ass. 'We should go up,' he mumbled, and Raj said that he couldn't wait to, but Matt would have to show the way because Raj didn't know the house. They sort of crawled up the stairs, rolled on the carpeted floor, and entered a room that Matt pushed open with one hand while he kept his other hand busy between Raj's legs. It was a medium-sized room: dark, with enough light streaming in from the street to show them the window, the queen-sized bed, the table with a lamp that Matt extended a hand to switch on. There was now enough light for them to navigate the space even through the passionate intimacy without stumbling into or colliding with anything.

'Do you want to find fresh sheets?' Raj asked as he was pulling up Matt's T-shirt, but Matt said he didn't care, his hands still inside Raj's zipper, caressing him into hardness. He picked up Raj and placed him gently on the bed. Against his bare buttocks, Raj felt something hard, sharp. Not sharp enough to cut through his skin but sharp. As if he were sitting on a bed of pencils and twigs. And the thing creaked. In the dim light, as Matt went down on him, he turned around to look, screamed at the top of his voice, and sprang up from the bed, knocking Matt's nose with a thud. When Matt switched on the lights, Raj was on the floor, leaning against the wall on the opposite side of the bed, shocked, breathing fast. Matt was holding his nose.

'Raj!' Matt rushed towards him. But Raj pushed him away, pointing to the bed, and saying, fuck-fuck-fuck, what the fuck is that. Then, the door flung open, and Irene and Tony walked in and saw Raj—shirtless, pants and briefs pulled to his thighs, with an erect penis, breathing fast, and saying what the fuck is that.

Raj wanted to die. Irene gasped, and Tony screamed, 'What the—'

'Dad!'

No one said a thing.

'Dad, what the hell is this? What's this doing here?' Matt asked, pained, pointing to the bed.

Raj was standing now, his pants back on his waist, his hands folded, face twisted in fear and disgust. 'I need some air, Matt.'

'Raj, please wait.'

'I'll see you downstairs. I'm sorry, I can't be in this room.'

He didn't say 'excuse me' before Irene moved aside. He sat on the large couch downstairs, still panting, still embarrassed. The house was quiet, and from where he sat, he could hear them talking. Not bits and pieces, but all of it. Agitated voices.

'What do you mean, why did I do this? I did nothing!' Tony's voice.

'You did nothing? You did nothing? Then what is this? What is this nasty, dirty thing doing here on my bed? Shouldn't it be in the basement? How many hundreds of years old is it?'

'I did nothing,' Tony repeated.

'Dad, please, you went upstairs after we smoked. What were you doing upstairs?'

'I was checking—'

Irene started to complain, 'Honey, I have told you so many times to just throw these things away, but you just hoard them. I mean, you just hoard—'

'Oh, shut up, Irene.'

Irene didn't stop speaking, 'How scared I was when I came across it one day. Oh god, that boy, he is scared, he is such a sweetie.'

'It's fake—just a Halloween thing.' Tony's tone was dismissive. 'Your boyfriend is overreacting!'

Raj was breathing normally now. He was full of guilt and shame. He covered his face with his hands and tried to recollect what had just happened. More than his fear at discovering the skull, he was ashamed that two new people had discovered him in that state: helpless, panting, his pants down; he couldn't bear to face them anymore. It would be a little cold outside, not much. He put on a jacket, his socks, his shoes, his red silk scarf. He took out his smartphone and confirmed whether the hotel across the street was open.

'Raj!' Matt was coming down the stairs. 'Raj, where are you?'

Tony screamed behind him, 'Hey, I told you that the room hadn't been used in a while.'

Raj gathered his suitcase. He was calm, a bit too calm, when he spoke. He didn't raise his voice. He wasn't agitated. He apologised for waking them up so late, and for freaking out about the fake skeleton, and said that it had looked so real when he first saw it in the hazy light, and that he was a bit tired and would rather book a room at the American Inn.

'Oh,' Tony said.

'Oh,' Irene added. 'Are you sure, sweetie?'

'Yes, please don't worry. I'll see you all for breakfast, or maybe you guys can join me there.'

It was Matt who screamed, it was Matt who lost his temper, 'What do you mean "join you for breakfast"?'

'Matt! Stop screaming.' Raj was cold and calm. 'It's fine. You stay here. I'll see you in the morning.'

'I'm coming with you.'

It was cold outside. Matt followed Raj, who walked out without any further words. The road was empty and quiet. There was no wind. The cold fall night hid the multicoloured leaves.

He turned around and looked at Matt and almost whispered, 'You want to work things out with your father. You stay.'

Afterwards, in the hotel room, holding the free coffee that he had poured himself at the reception of (hardworking, rich) Mr Patel's American Inn, he wondered what Matt might be doing. Was he arguing with his father? Was he sitting in one corner and still figuring out what had just happened? It always took a while for Matt to figure out such things. He would go for a smoke and think. Now, holding the free coffee, in Mr Patel's American Inn, Raj wondered what there was to figure out, why Matt would need more time before he stormed out of the house and joined him in the inn, where Raj had not invited him.

Raj decided he had overreacted. He'd been scared, but if Irene hadn't seen him half-naked, if Tony hadn't seen his erect penis, maybe he would have stayed. Or maybe he wouldn't have. But it was over now. As soon as Matt had given him that puzzled expression outside the house, in that nippy fall night, he knew it was over between them. He switched on the TV and changed channels until he found CNN.

Raj realised he didn't like Tony because he looked so like Matt, they were almost carbon copies. He was worried Matt would grow old to look like that, and the list of things that drove him nuts would grow longer and longer, and he would always justify everything with his Larger Picture Theory. And in that tattered and old carbon copy of a face that was so uncomfortable to have Raj in the house, he saw an aged, unhappy, frustrated, and frightened Matt.

There was a knock on the door an hour later.

'I'm sorry,' Matt said.

Raj felt something snap inside his chest, like an artery. He wept and said that, no, he was sorry. He was sorry that he overreacted.

'You shouldn't be apologising; he did it. He put it there on purpose.'

'It doesn't matter, Matt. You should have stayed back—your bond with your father is important to you. But I am so glad you are here. I thought—'

Matt stopped him, held his hand. 'Don't go there.'

He unzipped his duffel bag and took out a fresh towel—he didn't like using towels in hotels. Then he spoke in a low, regretful voice, 'You know what? I screamed at him.'

'Oh.' Raj gasped and covered his face. 'I am so sorry, I shouldn't have reacted like that. This is all my fault.'

'Raj! Don't say that. I would have probably had a heart attack if I had seen that skeleton. And I didn't scream at him for putting it there because there was no way I could have proven that. I screamed at him because . . .' Matt paused and looked away. 'You might find this odd, but I was ready to stay there for another couple of hours and talk to him, teach him. But he kept saying "your boyfriend" when he talked about you. "Your boyfriend is overreacting", "your boyfriend shouldn't have left like that", and I couldn't take it anymore. I screamed at him. I said, Dad, he is my husband, I married him, I took vows to live with him forever.'

Raj hugged Matt so tight that he might well have broken a few bones. He didn't want to think about the break that he had wanted to take even a few hours ago; he didn't want to think about whether he would have wanted to grow old with Matt if Matt had only turned up in the morning.

BECAUSE A MOTHER-IN-LAW WAS ONCE A DAUGHTER-IN-LAW, TOO

What Anuradha Told Her Therapist
Session One: 14 January 2017

First things first, okay? I am here because my mother thinks I should visit a therapist. I am not here because I am dying to meet a therapist. So, I am just happy to not talk at all for one hour, and you can just do your own work. Yes, yes, I know this is your work. Aren't you supposed to satisfy your client? I don't care about ethics, Dr Gohain. If you feel guilty about taking money from me without doing the work, we can just talk. I can consult someone who will just listen to me and not try to blame me.

What do you mean by 'don't blame yourself'?

Of course, I blame myself. I am sad and depressed because my marriage didn't survive a week after my Ex-Lover tried to kill my New Husband. He asked me multiple times about my past, but I lied to him. It was my fault. I should have never hidden from him that I once dated a dangerous man. And I knew . . . I knew that my Ex-Lover was capable of this. Now, you tell me—no, no, just tell me honestly—am I not the one who is to blame here? Why should I blame my New Husband? He is an honest man. In fact, he wanted me to stay; he stood up to his mother. His mother was all over me; she didn't understand what I was going through, you know? And to think of it, once upon a time, even she had been a daughter-in-law just like me: clueless, scared, like a fish out of water in a new house full of new relatives and the many guests who stayed back after the wedding. Assamese weddings are huge, full of drama, like soap operas, no?

After my Ex-Lover tried to kill my New Husband, my mother-in-law wasn't ready to live under the same roof as me. So, I decided to leave. I mean, tell me, tell me honestly: why should I make the life of my New Husband more difficult because of a mistake I made? He already has that Jomodogni-type mother! What? Arrey, Jomodogni, the mythical saint who was known for his horrible anger, you don't know?

[*Drinks water. Wipes tears from her eyes.*]

I mean, I don't even want to talk to you. But since I am here, if you don't mind, can I just talk about my life? I think—and I know it is difficult to believe this—I think things would never have come to pass if I hadn't decided to become an actress.

It was not what I wanted. Ever. I wanted to study hard and become a sociologist. During my high school years, my mother used to tell me that there was an excellent women's college called Kamala Nehru College, and if I could secure a seat there, she would let me go to Delhi. I didn't want to go to Delhi, but my mother wanted me to pursue a career outside the state.

It is 2016 now. I am separated from my husband. I don't really know if I love him, but I wouldn't mind trying out my life with him because he is a nice guy. He really is. Unlike other guys, he doesn't think with his penis—I mean, I would have liked him to think with his penis once or twice during our short married life—but after separating from him, I have realised he isn't like other guys. He respected me. He thought I was tired and didn't touch me during our Wedding Night when we slept on a bed of flowers.

How could I be so sure? I don't know. I just know. I guess, I am tied to him in some way: those rituals, those vows, vedic chants, they must have some supernatural power, isn't it, that bonds two unknown people forever, for the next seven births? Or it must be the power of the mantras. I still remember the smell of turmeric and black-lentil paste on my body from the day of the wedding. It's like it happened yesterday. Sorry, I am a bit traditional. Yes, I am an actress. Yes, I have sixty-thousand Twitter followers, and I write Facebook posts about women's rights, but honestly, I am a traditional Indian girl at heart, you know? Don't judge me, please.

By the way, I have more followers on Facebook: about two hundred thousand.

[*A long pause.*]

How I have reached this dismal situation is another story. I will tell you about that later, but I was talking about 2011, when peace had returned to the state after the long insurgency, but we didn't really know if it would stay for long, and I had to make a decision: leave to study in Delhi or stay and study here, pursue a career here. You know, peace in this state is like weather. Really unpredictable. That's why my mother was adamant about sending me off to Delhi, but I really didn't care to go. I was so happy here. I was at the cusp of making another decision that would change my life forever.

But Delhi. That was my mother's first choice. She had strange ideas about the education climates of different cities in India. According to her, Bangalore was full of private colleges, and you could get admission there by paying a large sum in the form of a donation in something called the 'Management Quota', and she had little respect for anyone who didn't go to

Stella Marris or Madras Christian College or Mount Carmel. What? Stella Marris is in Chennai and not in Bangalore?

And Madras Christian College?

Oh, yes, of course, *Madras* Christian College.

Sorry, you know what I mean. You get the essence of what I am saying, right?

So, according to my mother, Bombay was not good for girls because the casting couch—she had read in a widely circulated Assamese women's magazine about this mafia—lured young, pretty girls and exploited them. 'Exploited' is a euphemism for sexual slavery. My mother wouldn't use words such as 'sex', hence 'exploited'. At the most, she would say, 'Bad things. They would make girls do bad things.'

Anyway, what was I talking about? Oh yes, Delhi admissions. So, during my higher secondary, she gathered information in whatever way she could about colleges in Delhi. A woman she trusted, an elderly woman in our colony whose son had gone to Cambridge University for higher studies after completing an undergraduate degree in Delhi University, told her about Kamala Nehru College. I told her there were many other good women's colleges and also co-educational colleges in Delhi, but my mother was sure that KMC was the college for me. It was later attested by the achievement of our neighbour's elder daughter who went to Delhi to find a seat in a college called Lady Shri Ram, but returned with an admission offer from KMC. My mother was convinced of her brilliance. So, months before my class twelve exams, it was decided that I would go to study at KMC. That was my ticket to success and to a lucrative life out of state.

But didn't I say already that my life is full of twists and turns, just like the daily mega-serial I used to work for? They might as well make a serial on my life. Oh, do you have some tissues . . . I am sorry. I am sorry for crying and wasting your time.

Session Two: 21 January 2017

I am fine, thank you—Magh Bihu celebrations were fine last week. I love eating, so why wouldn't it be fine! Haha! I am really looking forward to talking today. I mean, I really enjoyed my first session last week. It is nice to be able to talk with no one to interrupt me. I will pay you to only listen to me. You don't have to say anything. Hahaha!

I mean, I must tell you how I became an actress before I get to how my marriage broke up (if I ever want to tell you about how my marriage broke up).

The stories are all interconnected. It would make more sense for you to know my past before I share the problems of my present, wouldn't it?

[*A deep breath.*]

My life started to change when, a few months after I was promoted to class twelve, our school principal called me to her office. Of course, I was scared. I thought she must have noticed that I was bringing a mobile phone to school secretly. Then I thought, how would she know? Did she even know of my existence? Some terrible person must have complained to her, and she was going to expel me. I wondered if Punyaprabha Madam had done it because I refused to take Assamese tuitions with her. Who needs extra classes in Assamese? I always did so well! In class ten, I earned letter marks in Assamese. Eighty-plus, you know?

I was really stupid then, and I always assumed the worst. Honestly, now I don't. I don't have any problems with my life. I mean, it was in many ways my fault that my marriage didn't work out—I will tell you about it later—but I have had a good life. Isn't it? I am talking about now, which is 2016. . . . How many people get mobbed when they go to the mall and get requests for selfies? I started acting without any plans, and see where I am? You know what I have learnt from all my experience? One shouldn't be controlling. Just do the work and let go. Because, honestly, do we really have control? You tell me. After all, we are all little entities who live on a very small piece of rock that is floating in a dark space. Why are we floating? Why are we on this earth? No one knows. So, why bother about anything? Everything in the universe is proceeding according to the ways of the universe. But this mind, this fucking mind, is the root of all problems. So, after this marriage debacle, I am just going with the flow.

Oh, yes—sorry about the digression.

The principal's office was really scary. It was so large. And it was the only room in the entire school that had an air conditioner, which added to the steeliness of the space. She was writing something on a notepad. The air conditioner made a persistent whirring sound—like a large dragonfly trapped in a plastic bottle, trying to escape. When I walked in after asking for permission, she said nothing. Then I concluded that she must have seen me kissing the boy from Don Bosco. Would she call my father?

I hoped she would call my father. He would say something like, if you want to kiss a boy, bring him home and kiss him in your room, why do it in front of everyone in the marketplace?

But my mother would kill me. She would literally take a gun and shoot me.

'I heard about your skit in class.'

'Madam?'

'Hoosna Madam says it was good.'

'Madam,' I gasped. 'Thank you. Thank you.' I don't know why I thanked her twice. Perhaps I was relieved that the meeting was not about the mobile phone or my sexual exploits.

'Do you remember the judge? She is a film producer. She liked your performance and has requested that I ask you to give her a call. She is planning to launch a television serial. The pay is good. It will be a mega-serial. Talk to her.'

'But, Madam, I don't want to act.'

'Just talk to her. I am not asking you to do anything. She asked me to convey the message. I am doing her a favour. You talk to her, okay? Then you do whatever you feel like—of course, with your father's permission.'

She didn't know my father would let me do anything.

That evening, I called the Producer Lady who had judged our skit. She said she wanted to meet me. I covered the receiver of the landline telephone and asked my mother if it was okay.

We were the kind of middle-class people who wouldn't refuse anyone who offered to visit us. So, we invited her home. She was so cheerful. She talked about my acting talents, and I talked about my plans to study at KMC. She was wearing a beautiful printed blouse and a long skirt that looked great on her tall frame.

'KMC?' The producer looked surprised. 'KMC is a good college, but she should also apply to other colleges such as LSR and IP and, of course, Hindu and St Stephen's. There are so many colleges in Delhi University. Why would you apply to just one?'

'No, no,' my mother interrupted her. 'She will study only at KMC. That is her aim in life.'

'That's not my aim in life, Ma. I want to become a sociologist.' I was offended.

'That only I was telling, na.' My mother responded in English to my English, and I was so embarrassed by her strong accent. Why did she have to use 'na' at the end of every sentence when she spoke English?

I was already regretting inviting the Producer Lady home. It was out of sheer politeness that we had let her come home, and it was out of sheer politeness that I went for a screen test. The Producer Lady said I shouldn't worry. If I failed, I would at least have nice high-resolution photos to upload on Facebook. I didn't have a smartphone at the time, and anyway, smartphones used to take grainy pics then. In some ways, that was a truly lucrative offer.

Session Three: 1 February 2017

The Producer Lady was also the director of the soap opera. She had directed several thirteen-episode family drama serials for Doordarshan before satellite TV came to India. Her voice was loud, clear, and optimistic: 'Listen, we aren't making another *Because the Mother-in-Law Was Once a Daughter-in-Law* kind of soap opera. Our mega-serial is different. This is the situation. You have made dal. By mistake, you have put a lot of salt. Your mother-in-law is scolding you in front of everyone. As in, scolding you really badly. She is even humiliating your mother, your grandmother, your aunts, your sister, your father, and you are silently listening, with a stern expression on your face, but also wiping off tears occasionally. But when she scolds your husband for marrying you, you have to just look straight into her face and say this dialogue: "Ma, scold anyone you like. Scold me as much as you like. But if you scold my husband [take a step forward, and the mother-in-law takes a step backward], I will bring the kerosene from home and . . ." You pause here.'

She, too, paused and looked at the cast, the spot boys, the cameraman, as if she was trying to gauge the suspense.

I also looked around. I mean, I was really curious. We were in the middle of a beautiful set with bright drapery, huge sofas, bright lamps with lampshades that had ornate prints, and chandeliers that were so bright that they felt like the sun. Everything was pretty. Everything was excessively bright. A lot of red and orange and bright blue. The walls were painted dark pink and had replicas of Raja Ravi Varma's paintings of voluptuous, pretty women. All framed in wood. There was the smell of lemongrass essential oil in the air, though I doubt it was natural.

The spot boys, the cameramen, the ADs, the make-up artists, everyone looked really tense. As if they were all wondering what the character would do with a can of kerosene. The Producer Lady surveyed everyone. I was wearing a silk mekhela-sador for the audition and had a thick layer of make-up on. I wanted to scratch my face. Perhaps the make-up was some fucking cheap stuff. I worried that the next morning I would wake up with pimples all over. All I wanted to do was flee, just do everything wrong and get out of there, go back to my studies, prepare to go to Delhi University.

'Okayeh!' she said and straightened her back. She scratched her forehead, caressed her long hair, and said, 'Anuradha, this is your first scene with the mother-in-law. This is your third day in the house. You have made dal. In many ways, this is like a test for you. If you don't make good dal, it is not only a defeat for you, but also a defeat and a matter of severe embarrassment for your mother. Your aunt, who has come to stay with you, is still there. She has already hidden her face under the end of her sador because you haven't been able to make good dal. But that's not the point here. You are a different kind of daughter-in-law. Okayeh, say that with me?'

'I am a different kind of daughter-in-law.'

'Once again!'

'I am a different kind of daughter-in-law.'

She raised her voice. 'I am a different kind of daughter-in-law. I can wear jeans to a party, ride a bike if I need to, and wear a sari or mekhela-sador with the veil on my head when I go to temple or am with my elders. I am a different kind of daughter-in-law.'

I repeated after her, 'I can wear jeans to a party, ride a bike if I need to, and wear a sari or mekhela-sador with the veil on my head when I go to temple or am with my elders. I am a different kind of daughter-in-law.'

It seemed to make her happy and boost her morale. She raised a fist to the sky. 'Okayeh, guys! Let's say it together again: "We aren't making another *Because the Mother-in-Law Was Once a Daughter-in-Law* kind of soap opera."'

Everyone chorused her line, but with less enthusiasm. They sounded tired and exhausted and unconvinced. 'We aren't making another *Because the Mother-in-Law Was Once a Daughter-in-Law* kind of soap opera.'

'We are trying to create a different kind of character here—a rebellious character. We are a bit tired of dutiful, docile daughters-in-law, you know? So, you pause. Let the audience think for a few seconds that you are going to threaten the mother-in-law. Then flare your eyes and say loudly, firmly, assertively: "I will bring a can of kerosene, pour it all over my body in the living room, and light a match. Don't you dare touch my husband. He may be your son, but he is my husband now. How dare you insult my husband's choice?" Okay? Will you be able to do this, Anuradha? Take as much time and as much glycerine as you need.'

'Yes, I will be able to do it. What if the glycerine smudges my eyeliner?'

She looked extremely irritated. 'You don't have to worry about that. And your eyeliner must be waterproof.' She turned around to the assistant directors. There were two of them. 'When she delivers her dialogue, you guys play the chants. Okay? The chants that talk about the power of the Mother Goddess.'

One of them, a short guy with light skin and long hair and confused looks, said, 'Those aren't ready yet. We have some chants, but we aren't using them as background music when the show goes on air.'

'You guys are just worthless. Play them to me right now.' Producer Madam looked very angry.

When they played the chants, I wanted to burst out laughing. They were basically from another silly Hindi soap opera. I know a bit of Sanskrit, you know, and growing up in Assam, you do know the meaning of those Sanskrit slokas in praise of Durga, the Mother Goddess. Basically, they meant: Oh Mother, give me joy, give me wins, give me wealth, give me beauty. Anyway, they used them during my audition scene.

Fortunately or unfortunately, I passed the screen test. They offered me the role. I refused immediately. I hated those long-running family saga soap operas. So what if this one was one of the first mega-serials made in Assamese? And so what if I passed the screen test?

My mother and I were sure: I wasn't going to act. I was going to Delhi for further studies and to study at KMC. That's what I told the Producer Lady, too. 'Baideo, I don't like this role. I don't know anyone who would scold me like that for making dal that is a bit too salty. I don't think I am the right fit for this role.'

Sometimes I wish my father had barred me from acting. My life would have been different, you know? That day, I transferred all the photos to a flash drive and left the studio.

'You should apply to more colleges,' the Producer Lady shouted at me from behind. 'Don't throw your life away like this. You are so talented.'

She was looking so hassled. As if I had caused her a great loss.

But, as I said, my life is like that soap opera I eventually acted in—full of twists and turns. It wasn't because of the Producer Lady that I joined the film industry. I joined the film industry because of a stalker.

Session Four: 7 February 2017

Bipasha always played pranks with me. Like that one time during a school picnic on the banks of Chandubi Lake. People say that Chandubi Lake was formed during the earthquake in 1897. It was such a massive quake that the entire forest sank to become a lake, taking with it several neighbouring villages. I get goosebumps when I listen to the story. I mean, would we find skeletons at the bottom of the lake? Household items such as cast-iron cooking utensils? Spades and axes? That's why some people say that the lake is haunted.

Anyway, the bank of the lake had this bloom of tiny yellow flowers, and thousands of multicoloured dragonflies were hovering over it. I had never seen such a wide variety of dragonflies and in such large numbers. Some of them had bright blue, pink, red, and green tails. Honestly, they looked so wonderful. Some young kids from the neighbouring village were chasing them. It bothered me. So, I asked them what they would do with those dragonflies. They said they would put them in glass jars or used Coca-Cola bottles, keep them alive by feeding them dew and insects, and display them in their living rooms.

I was horrified and was trying to convince them not to do that when Bipasha came over and asked me to hold an envelope. A white one.

I asked, 'What is it?'

She said, 'Just hold it.'

All our friends had gathered at that spot by then. Suddenly, something made a buzzing, whirring sound from inside the envelope. I screamed and threw it away.

Bipasha was quick to pick it up. 'What are you doing?' she said with a mischievous smile in her eyes. 'I just asked you to hold it carefully.'

All our friends were laughing.

'What is trapped inside? What is inside the envelope?' When she said it was a large, beautiful dragonfly, I almost cried, 'Free it, let it go, please let it go . . .'

I threw a fit, and the little village kids laughed at me. My friends, especially those horrible guys, were also laughing at me. I snatched the envelope from her hand. It was just a steel coin with a rubber band tied around it in such a way that, when there was no pressure on the coin, it unwound, making a whirring, buzzing sound. From outside, it felt as if an insect were trapped inside. She was just pulling my leg. I was mad.

So, when Bipasha told me that someone was stalking me, I was stern: 'This isn't one of your pranks, right? I really don't like your pranks.'

But, to be honest, I am often oblivious to what's happening around me, so I was a bit worried. Even though, at first, I didn't believe her.

When she showed me the stalker, my first stalker, I was sort of disappointed, you know. I mean, why couldn't a hot, handsome young man stalk me and give me a heart-shaped card and a teddy bear that opens its eyes every morning and says, 'You're beautiful'? Oh, such teddy bears used to exist back then. One guy who was madly in love with Bipasha gifted her one. It was very expensive. When she said she already had a boyfriend (she was lying), the guy went back to his motorbike, took out a lighter, and burnt the toy. Bipasha thought it was sort of hot, but I told her she had just saved herself from a lunatic. 'If this gift can't be yours, it can't be anyone else's.' The guy pointed a finger at her before leaving, as if it was her fault that she wasn't single. Much later, though I thought it was creepy and scary, I wished someone loved me madly. I wished someone was possessive over me. It was stupid. As I said, I was so stupid.

Bipasha told me to remain alert. We saw the Stalker Woman another day, when we were eating momos at a restaurant, and ignored her. 'She must be looking for a daughter-in-law for her son,' Bipasha teased me. But things became more serious when I saw her in a black SUV parked outside our house.

It was a Sunday. I was sitting on the veranda and sipping a cup of tea when I saw that a woman was taking pictures of me from the street. She was holding a professional-looking camera.

I told my mother. I mean, how could I not? My mother wanted to pick a fight with the woman, but my father cautioned her: what if she was armed?

That was also an important point, hoyn-noy? Our help said that she had seen the car parked in front of our street for one week, and that it always left when I went to school.

And I thought, wonderful. I have a stalker. It is not a hot, young man. Not even a young man . . . my stalker is a middle-aged woman with salt-and-pepper hair.

My mother did something really smart. She picked up the telephone and called all the ladies of her Mohila Committee. You know those women's organisations that used to exist during those years? They sold beauty products to one another and gathered every month at one house or another with food and bitched about people in the neighbourhood or discussed logistics for the 'Best Mother Contests' for the local Bihu Organising Committee. My mother was also in one of those. No, no, not a branch of the Women Writers' Association. My mother's organisation didn't do intellectual stuff.

Anyway, after my mother's call, members from the women's organisation started circling the car. My mother and I watched from a window. Finally, when a group of around fifty women had gathered around the car, a petrified-looking middle-aged woman emerged from it. I walked up to her, my mother holding me tight.

'Is something wrong?' she asked nervously, looking like a scared, wet cat.

'You tell me. Why are you stalking my daughter? If you don't speak up immediately, all of us are going to take out our footwear and flatten your face.'

'Your nose and face will be of the same level after about half an hour,' Barua Aunty said. 'Like a flat-screen TV.'

I added some ghee to the already burning oil: 'She was following me in the mall, taking my pictures with that large camera.'

The moment I said 'camera', Barua Aunty swooped like a kite towards the car. In a few seconds, the camera was broken to pieces by the collective might of the assembled women.

Inside, my father was rubbing ice on his forehead. A few other men, whose wives were also out surrounding the woman, were trying to console him. They were worried that their wives might get themselves arrested, but the women had given them strict instructions not to interfere.

'She must be a gang leader of some human-trafficking organisation. She thinks our Anuradha is pretty and wants to kidnap her and then sell her somewhere. Do you think she has no one? Someone please call the police and the news channels.'

'We should beat her up,' my mother suggested.

'No, no, let the news channels come. They are always looking for this kind of news. They should record it and air it so that no one dares to come to our colony and do such things again. If we beat her up now, we would have to beat her up twice. Once now and once again for the news channels to record it. If they don't have a video recording of the beating, they won't air the news. Even if they do, they won't present it during the 7 p.m. prime-time news. We will make the beating look spontaneous.' Barua Aunty was shouting now.

The Stalker Woman quickly introduced herself as Nirmali Begum, the casting head of the mega-serial I had turned down. She collapsed on the ground, hands joined, and started to howl, 'Please don't kill me-o, I have two daughters-o. I was just doing my job.'

A few minutes of awkward silence. Sound of a neighbour's Doberman barking. The milkman passed by, staring at us.

We apologised to her for breaking the camera and brought her home, and Barua Aunty, along with six other ladies from the neighbourhood, accompanied us to ensure our safety. One lady even checked her for fire-arms. Nirmali Begum stopped crying and explained to us that, after my screen test, a different girl from Jorhat had been brought in to play the main lead, but they hadn't been able to finalise the second lead, also a woman's character, the main character's bestie.

The storyline had changed a bit since I auditioned, and now the story was about two best friends who were unknowingly in a relationship with the same guy. For the first six months (the first season), they were going to focus on how tight the friendship of the two girls were and how they would save each other from different kinds of girl problems. For the next six months, they were going to focus on how they fell in love with the same horrible guy. For the third season, they were going to focus on how the guy would marry both of them, and both the girls would be in different households, with different sets of problems, and how they would discover slowly that they were married to the same guy and decide to take revenge.

Nirmali Begum didn't know what would happen after that, but they had managed funding for two years. 'Please don't tell anyone I divulged the plot. I will lose my job,' she begged.

My mother served her orange squash, but Nirmali Begum didn't take a sip. She looked around. 'Aren't you all drinking, too?'

'Don't worry, it isn't poisoned,' Barua Aunty quipped.

'No, no, I really didn't mean that. I mean . . .'

'We had breakfast while you were busy stalking our girl. You must be the one who is thirsty,' Barua Aunty added. I nudged her with my right knuckle. In response, she looked at Nirmali Begum and said, 'Hehehe, I was joking. Please drink.'

Nirmali Begum took a small sip from the glass. 'Oh, I am diabetic, I can't drink this.'

'Oh,' Barua Aunty said.

'Oh, we didn't know, sorry,' I said.

'We told you we aren't interested,' my mother said. 'My daughter wants to study. Why is that Producer Lady asking you to stalk her?'

'The entire team thinks you are the best person for this character—the second lead. Since you refused, she wanted to make a pitch to the Board of Directors for a higher remuneration and see if you would join us. But the BOD said that they wanted more photos of you, and this was the only way, and you know, natural, without make-up, you still look so good. So, we thought—'

'So, you thought it is okay to stalk a woman. Have some shame!' Barua Aunty didn't let her finish.

'We don't even know what the current salary is,' my mother said. 'What are you even talking about? This isn't about money. My daughter wants to be an academic.'

The pay was two thousand rupees per episode. So, monthly, I would earn around forty thousand rupees. We all went quiet. That was a lot of money!

I think that was the moment it was decided that I was going to work as an actor.

Would you believe me if I say what I was thinking about then? That silent moment when everyone was turning over the idea that I would be earning forty thousand rupees per month for an indefinite amount of time? I was thinking about the whirring sound of the air conditioner in my principal's office. Standing in the living room, I started to sweat, wondering if a large dragonfly had been trapped inside that machine. The sound had become so much louder in my mind.

Nirmali Begum said, 'She will be okay. Trust me, she will be okay. I will always be with her. Also, the channel has unlimited money. It is funded by former insurgents. The show will air on Channel Rohedoi but is part of Rising Sun Media Group. They run the second-largest newspaper in the state and also Rising Sun News, which has the second highest TRP among all the news channels.'

'I will do it.' I sat down on the couch and said, 'I will do it. I want to earn money.'

Eventually, it was my decision to enter this world. I signed up for something that would turn me into a dragonfly trapped in an envelope.

But I was so young! I wished someone had stopped me, held my hand, and said, no, don't do this, you want to be a sociologist, you want to go to Delhi University, then abroad for doctoral studies.

But perhaps it was written in my fate. Because it was on the sets of this television soap opera that I met my ex-boyfriend. He was hot and handsome. Tall, dark, and muscular. He carried a gun always because he was a former insurgent and had concealed carry permits. I had an affair with him. He was part of the Board of Directors and jointly owned the channel.

No, no, I didn't want to marry him! I mean, I was in my early twenties, and he was already in his forties—it was just an affair. But he didn't see it that way. So, when I secretly got married, he started threatening my New Husband. But I really didn't think this would happen. . . . One day, he turned up at a dinner party and held a gun to my New Husband's head. His entire family was upset, but his mother made my life hell. He told her, it is okay, everyone has a past, it doesn't define them. But his mother wasn't able to reconcile herself to the fact that I had been in a relationship before—and that, too, with a former insurgent.

But she is right, isn't she? Who would want to rub a strange weed on their face in a forest? Who would want to touch a strange fruit, let alone eat it? These surrendered rebels not only have government protection, but are like proxy governments. People are scared of them. Who isn't scared of people who roam around with live firearms even after leaving the rebel organisation? So, I left their house. It was difficult for me to stay. I tried staying, respecting my good New Husband's wish, my good father-in-law's wish, but his mother wouldn't forgive me. She had forgotten that, once upon a time, she had been a daughter-in-law, too.

THE WAY YOU WANT TO BE LOVED

1.

It is almost midnight. You have laid the table with enough food for six people though there are just the two of you. Two minutes ago, you told the man who is sitting next to you that you love him and want to spend your life with him. You have known him for four years. He is your friend, but you are too close. So close that your other friends call you the 'bromosexuals'. You already know his answer, because he is staring at the steamed white rice on his plate. For two whole minutes, he holds a piece of carrot and stares at his rice. He doesn't touch the cauliflower that has been sauteed with mango powder and cumin—his favourite. Your world is coming to an end. If you don't handle this situation well, you will never be able to face him again. So, you keep quiet. It is so hard to breathe.

He is the first one to speak. 'Utpol, this is awkward . . .'

You are whispering, 'I am sorry, I am so sorry.'

'No, don't be. I knew. I have been wondering . . . see, you are one of my closest friends, and we have been friends for four years,' Rudra says. 'But I can't love you the way you want me to. It is not possible.'

The two of you are having dinner at your apartment. You have cooked his favourite chicken curry. There is a red candle on the table and, in the corner of the room, a stone aroma dispenser. A tealight heats up the lavender oil and water in the little bowl.

'I understand,' you say, but your gut is about to come pouring out. 'I needed to tell you that I have feelings for you. I needed to be honest with you. I am so sorry.'

That is true. You want to be honest with him. You need to tell him before the untold stories churn your stomach, demolishing its walls. But you had also thought he would feel the same way because he cuddles with you and watches movies with you under the same blanket. Every weekend, when he comes to spend time with you, he leaves after planting a kiss on your cheek. For about three and a half years, these signs of affection didn't bother you, but you don't know what happened around three months ago. You woke up one day and realised Rudra is the man you want to spend your life with. You needed to tell him that, be honest with him, give it a shot.

'Please don't be sorry . . .' Rudra says. He doesn't finish his dinner. Leaves early. He tries to hang around, but as he said, everything is awkward now. You are burning with guilt. Once he leaves, you throw away the food: the cauliflower, chicken curry, split pigeon peas, potato-and-carrot fry, cucumber-tomato salad in unprocessed mustard oil. You spent six hours cooking these. You press your face into your pillow and cry, trying hard not to make sounds. You live alone. You don't know why you want to cry silently.

After the heartbreak, you join dating apps so that you can sleep around and forget him. You are angry with Rudra, and since you can't say hurtful things to him, you distribute yourself in the arms of nameless men. After sex, the bed is as cold as night stones. You find yourself in unknown homes in random corners of the city. In the mornings, if you are lucky, you can hear the din of trucks and other large automobiles carrying perishable and non-perishable goods outside. Otherwise, a heavy silence broken only by the sound of ceiling fans nearly chokes you. If you are lucky, your date is still sleeping, and you can pad out quietly like a cat, because you know you will never meet him again. If you are lucky, you won't end up bawling in the cab back home or on the Metro Rail, feeling guilty for sprinkling parts of yourself across this city that rarely gives back. This is a brutal city. There are brutal people here. You want to get out of here, but you find yourself in the same restaurants, the same neighbourhoods under the shadow of gulmohar and peepal and banyan and neem.

It has been two months since you told Rudra that you don't want to talk to him. It has been two months since Rudra said to you that he doesn't accept your decision to not speak to him because *you* fell in love with him and *you* jeopardised the friendship. He is not ready to lose a friend. He calls you every week, and because you can't resist, you receive the calls.

You don't see how he is wrong. You are in love. He is right, it is your fault. You feel so lost so often that you find corners in your office to shed tears. You can't bawl in your office. You continue to talk to Rudra, but only when he calls. Yet, there are some days when you call him because you just want to hear his voice. Once, you hear the voice of another man in the background. Rudra always receives your calls, even if it is in the middle of the night. Two months ago, you were the best of friends.

'Who is that, Rudra?' you ask in a quivering voice.

He pauses. Then he says, 'I know this is going to hurt you—I brought someone home. But you should know the truth. You deserve to know the truth.'

'Okay,' you say.

Rudra is silent.

'Okay, I will call you later.' You hang up and rush to the sink to throw up.

It has been two months, and you feel like a malnourished, yellowed patch of grass under a brick. You stop calling him, not because you dislike him now, but because you don't want to throw up or spend any more nights sleepless. After a point, you start keeping to yourself. You go to work, edit copies on your desk. You edit good news and bad news. Celebrity gossip and classified pages. Your silence is frightening. Your colleagues want to talk to you, but they notice your red eyes, your dark circles, your stern face, the Melancholy Look, and the Stay-the-Hell-Away-from-Me Look. One of your colleagues, who cares about you most, who is almost a friend but not yet a friend, calls Tara—your closest friend who lives in South Delhi.

Tara saves you from this mess. She always saves people from messes. Actually, it is her profession, like, literally! For the last two months, she has been busy with her new NGO that works for queer rights. She also heads a small legal team that fights for LGBTQ+ rights in Delhi. They have filed a case against the colonial law that criminalises gay sex. Gay men, lesbian women, trans people all over Delhi know her phone number. When women contact her, complaining about families forcibly trying to marry them away, she calls important people in those cities. Those important people send the police to save those women and bring them to Delhi, and Tara ensures they find shelter in the Kasturba Gandhi Memorial State Home for Homeless Women. When trans men experience body dysmorphia, they call Tara's office on the hotline. When Delhi police arrest men for holding hands in public, when they beat up men for kissing in public, when dirty cops arrest hapless gay men because they want to have some quick fun on the job—'If you don't have sex with us, we will arrest you under the Section 377'—they call Tara's number for SOS help. Tara's phone is never silent. Tara and her work partner, who are both co-founders of the organisation, are lawyers. They are always speaking about 'article this' and 'section that'. You have

heard that Tara is especially gutsy, that one must see her at the police station. You wonder if you ever want to see that side of her. You admire her
immensely.

At first, Tara texts you. When you don't answer her texts for a week,
she comes to meet you at the office. She brings homemade food and always
turns up at lunchtime. One day, she drives to your apartment and tells you
that she is here to take you to her house where she is organising a big party
the next day. 'Only handsome single men will be invited. You will pick one
of them, but you will not attend crazy parties to get drunk.'

You sit on the sofa and stare at her as if she is talking about UFOs.
There is a yellow light with a bamboo lampshade hanging from the ceiling.
The bookshelf on your left is full of novels that you have grown up reading
and loving. The forty-two-inch television is playing on low volume because
you fell asleep on the couch while watching. You shouldn't have slept on the
couch. Your neck hurts, and you still feel sleepy.

It is early morning. She has brought your favourite South Indian coffee. She pours you a cup from the drip. There is freshly squeezed orange
juice and poached eggs on the table. The ceramics collide against each
other, and the sound is music to your ears. You realise it is not the ceramic,
the smell of coffee, or the orange hue of the juice, but it is Tara. Her reassuring presence. Also, the sounds tell you that there is music in everything. You
just have to know how to listen.

For the last two weeks, every morning, you have woken up and eaten
yogurt with frozen fruit. Or bacon. Or put cheese on a slice of bread to grill
in the microwave. Now, the fresh peaches feel lovely in your mouth.

'Thank you,' you say.

'Come with me, please, come with me. For how long are you going to
mourn this?'

You are silent.

'Alright, mourn, but at my place. You play with my dog. My cats. You have a job to handle. You have a life ahead of you. You are the only son of a single mother.'

Your heart is aching, and yet you laugh with her. You are a patch of grass under a heavy brick, but Tara lifts it. You don't even know when you agree, when you pack bags, when you are on the road from one end of the city to another. You realise that you have accepted Tara's offer only when you register that you are stuck in a massive traffic jam.

'How long have we been here?' You look around and see that you are under a flyover. You are somewhere in Central Delhi. On both sides of the road, fruit and juice vendors are trying to attract customers. The fruits are so colourful. You see that a tandoori chicken vendor has dressed a whole chicken in the red tandoori spice paste and hung it upside down. A man next to him fries egg rolls. The air is so polluted and dusty that you can see it moving. Almost everyone is roaming around with surgical masks. There is a large advertisement of a mask ahead of you on the left side of the road. It claims to have two layers that filter every small particle. There are no insects. They are all dead because of pollution. At least that is a good thing, you think.

'We are all slowly dying.'

'What? Yes, very slow—half an hour, tops. Don't worry, we will be home soon.' She looks straight ahead as the car moves an inch. 'If you need to sleep, just doze off.'

You want to sleep, but you want to talk to her so that she doesn't feel bored. It will take another two and a half hours to get to her place in this traffic. Without traffic, one hour and forty minutes.

'No, I am sorry I have been quiet. How are things with you?'

'The usual—hey, sisterfucker!' She rolls down the window and shouts at a guy who cuts past her.

2.

On the day of the party, you make hummus from the chickpeas soaked overnight, and she makes kheer from the basmati rice soaked for an hour. You cook the cauliflower-and-potato stir-fry with a hint of mango powder, and she simmers the fried fish with tomatoes and lemon juice.

You call your mother and chat using the hands-free. 'Are you doing okay? Have you had dinner?'

'It is good to hear your voice. Your cheerful voice. Babu, these things happen. . . . I told you about Irfan. I was head over heels in love with him. I thought, this is it. He had such dreamy eyes.'

You burst out laughing. 'Don't! Don't tell me, it is weird! And you know, I have heard that story so many times!'

She is happy that you are happy. 'Alright, so what's going on at the party later?'

You tell her pretty men are coming to the party, and she wishes you good luck. She lives alone in a faraway city where she works and won't move to Delhi to live with you.

The truth is, you aren't looking forward to meeting anyone. The truth is, Tara is only half-serious about finding you a date from the party. She just wants you to enjoy yourself and ensure that you don't descend into depression. You appreciate that, and that's why you are here, cooking food, laughing, cracking jokes, listening to stories about the clients she has taken on pro bono. As she lays the table and chops the salad, she talks about the trans person in Jaipur thrown out of her house for wearing a sari instead of trousers; about the lesbian in Asansol subjected to corrective rape; the gay man forced by his family at gunpoint to marry and how she helped him escape to Sweden. The truth is, all you want to do is watch a movie with Rudra because he likes to cuddle during movies. But you also don't want him to cuddle because it stirs your body and churns your emotions, and you also don't have the energy to say that you don't want him to cuddle. You miss cuddling with him. It may be asexual cuddling for him, but not for you.

This, Tara thinks, is a problem, and you have just made the mistake of telling her about the 'asexual cuddling' (Rudra's phrase, not yours!).

'If he can't take off his pants in front of you, why is he cuddling with you?' she says, adding yogurt to the chicken curry. 'Why does he want to keep talking to you? Why does he tell you about his hook-ups? Can't he give you a break?'

Good questions. These questions have bothered you, too. But you end up feebly defending him.

'Don't you dare defend him. You have suffered for two months now. I won't let him do this to you. Either he is terribly confused, or he is just leading you on.'

You just burst out laughing. 'Oh, Tara, I love you.'

3.

Even ceramics can make music. You tune in once again to the sound of people starting to eat, when they serve themselves more whisky, more wine. Tara complains to everyone who brings something, 'Why, why have you all become so Westernised? You aren't supposed to bring anything. I have cooked so much food!' She is mixing Hindi and English. Her Hindi sounds like Assamese.

'Hahaha, how can we come empty-handed?' her guests say.

'Well, in this country, we bring sweets. There was no need to cook something. We all know how to imitate the bad things from America, not the good things!'

'What are the good things in America?' Danielle, who is American, says and pours herself some more wine. She grew up in rural Alabama. 'At least women can go to a clinic and get an abortion here. But I agree with Tara on one thing: you guys didn't need to import Halloween from us! As if you don't have fourteen festivals a year already!'

Since she is the only American in the room, and none of you have been to America, you all laugh, agree with her. Later, you tell Danielle, 'You know, no one has never never been to America here?'

'Did you say "never never"? Am I drunk, or you are drunk?' Danielle bursts out laughing and drinks more. She picks up the peanut bowl.

The calling bell rings. Someone rushes to open the door.

'You are drunk, I am not, and you heard it correctly. Yes,' I said, 'no one has never never been to America in India. You pause after the first "never", and the meaning will be clear.' Danielle stares as if you are speaking in Greek. 'I mean to say that there is so much of America in this country anyway. If you live in South Delhi and shop in some of the areas, you are bound to bump into American expats. But the expat community is a recent addition. My generation grew up watching Hollywood and . . . I mean, *Titanic* was my movie. I came of age watching Leonardo DiCaprio's ass!'

'And this man came of age watching Kabir Bedi in a bikini in *Khoon Bhari Maang*.' Tara is loud, cheerful. You look up and see a handsome man with stubble. You feel self-conscious. The man blushes, nudges Tara. He looks at you for a second and then looks around the room with a smile on his face.

'This is my friend, I told you about him,' Tara says to you. Is that supposed to mean something? She has never spoken about any friend who is supposed to be at the party. You shake hands with the man. He says hi and finds himself a seat.

Tara's friend is a quiet man in his forties. He wears a teal-blue blazer and dress pants—overdressed for a party where everyone is supposed to relax and bitch about the current government which wants to ban beef-eating because it is 'anti-national' and arrests students who tweet criticisms of government policies. According to this government, students, women, tribals, queers are all anti-nationals. So, when someone brings a Malayali beef fry from a restaurant in Saket, everyone shouts, 'Anti-national dish! Anti-national party!' But the man in the teal suit just sits in a corner. He grins, raises his glass in support, but doesn't leave his couch. You watch him and wonder: this isn't a crowded Delhi metro where someone will occupy your seat if you move your ass for one second. Since you steal glances at him several times, he comes up to you and says that he has never met you at Tara's house before. You are leaning against Tara's table, occasionally petting her cat. You are proud of how well you have masked that you find him attractive.

'That means you rarely come here. I visit her every weekend.' You smile smugly, not mentioning the past few weeks when you couldn't even leave your house.

You don't know why you are being snarky with him, but you like the attention. He flattens your cockiness by saying, 'Actually, I live next door, and we meet almost every evening for tea. I mean, only during weekdays. I am Sunil, Sonali's cousin.'

'I see.'

Sonali is Tara's long-time partner of twelve years. They bought this apartment together and have joint bank accounts. Everyone wants to be them. They are beyond damn serious. They are monogamous.

'So, what has Tara told me about you?' Both of you are now standing in a corner. The balcony is close by. He gestures that you take a step towards it. 'It is cool outside.'

You lean on the railing and look at the high-rises. Despite the dust, the noise, the dirt, the garbage, Delhi's skyline seems very beautiful at night. As if thousands of fireflies have glued themselves to the sky for a night-long meeting.

'Nothing—Tara has said nothing about you. Honestly, I know nothing about you.' Perhaps, you add the last line because you want to continue to be cocky. You nod and add, 'She must have got it mixed up. She is so busy and meets so many people, you know? But I am happy to meet you.'

He observes you, as if judging whether you are fucking with him. You feel an intense desire to rip his shirt off. You have missed sex with someone you find attractive. Someone who is gentle and nice and funny and says smart things to arouse you. You suspect he is all that: gentle, nice, funny, smart. And yet you are surprised when he says something witty, 'But I know a lot about you now. I know how to turn you on.'

You laugh, nearly choke. 'What?'

'Are you okay?' he steps forward. He is so close now that you can smell his cologne. You like the smell. Soft, fruity, musky. He gently taps your hand. 'Okay?'

'What do you mean by that? We just met, and you know what turns me on?'

'Oh, I heard you like Leonardo DiCaprio's ass.'

You know your face is red. Hurriedly, you cover your mouth as if that would hide your blush and say, 'Oh, excuse me, I need to get a glass of water.'

You know he is grinning and watching you. So, your back is a bit stiff, and you don't look back. You really don't know why you maintain a stiff back just because the man you want to sleep with is watching you. When you return, he is inside the house. Everyone is eating. The sliding door to the balcony is shut. He asks Sonali who cooked which dish. He only praises the dishes you prepared. Your cheeks flush, and your ears are hot.

4.

The mornings have been hard. But today you are grateful to still be at Tara's.
Sunil turns up in the evening. You answer the door, and he smiles at you. He
walks in with boxes of food. The living room is filled with the smell of
chicken fried in soy and oyster sauces.

'Tara said you like Chinese. I do, too.'

You watch him unpack, unable to say anything. You feel strange. You
feel loved. Does he really like you, or is he just messing with you? This
attention is not new to you. Rudra is like that. Caring. But you messed it up
by falling in love with him. What does this man want from you? Adopt
you as his younger brother? No, you don't need an elder brother. Have
you as his friend? No, you don't need any more friends. You are fine. You are
just fine.

It is quiet in the living room. You don't speak much as you eat. You
thank him again and again, and when he says, in a slightly irritated tone,
that you don't have to thank him over and over, you say, 'Then what should
I do?' You snap, even though you know he is a bit surprised by your cold
behaviour, this formality, this mostly quiet dinner where you just keep
thanking him.

'Just eat.' He spreads his hands over the food. 'If you don't want to talk,
it is okay, but let me know. I won't try to make small talk.'

You bring him a Coke with ice. 'I am sorry.'

He stares at the Coke for a few seconds and then takes several quick
sips. 'I don't drink Coke. I drank it because you brought it.'

Suddenly, you are grateful he is there, sitting in front of you. You feel
grateful for this Chinese, that he is drinking your Coke, that he is irritated
with your steely behaviour, that he is not storming out.

You think about the previous night when the room was filled with
food and people and gossip and single men. Now, it is just the two of you,

because Tara is in her bedroom much earlier than usual. You want him. You want him to hold your hands and gently ask you to guide him to the bedroom. Instead, when he holds your hand, you crawl close to him, dig your nose into his chest, wrap your hands around his firm body, and weep. You didn't plan to weep. You had planned to kiss him on his neck. But you weep because you suddenly miss Rudra. What surprises you is that he doesn't ask you why you're crying. He smooths your hair and says, 'It is going to be okay,' and repeats that every few seconds. 'It is going to be okay.' He says it in different tones until you stop crying. Later, when you are about to fall asleep, you wonder if he used to be an actor; how does he know such a wide range of voice modulations?

When you wake up, it is dawn. Someone has taken off your shoes, spread a blanket over you, and your head rests on a pillow taken from the guest bedroom. Tara is still sleeping. You sit there for a couple of hours, holding the blanket around your body like a shawl. It is cold. You text photos from the party to your mother. She writes back, 'LOL.' She thinks LOL means 'lots of love' and has been using it for years. You find it so heart-achingly sweet that you have not corrected her ever. You make coffee and wake Tara up. Sonali left at four in the morning for a business meeting in Singapore.

She strokes her cat for a while and then rubs her eyes. 'I hope you guys had sex. I have never retired to my bedroom so early.'

'We didn't.'

Tara's mouth is wide open. 'What? Such a fool you are.'

'Does he know anything about me? Did you tell him that I had a heartbreak recently?'

Tara confirms that he doesn't know anything about you. Not about your recent heartbreak. Not about your pretty home in the beautiful hill station of Shillong or about your mother who lives alone. He doesn't even know that, for the last few years, you have been toying with the idea of moving abroad for graduate studies, even though you love your job as a copy-editor at *The Indian Express*, and you haven't come around to the applications because you don't want to live abroad. You like it here. There is good and bad and ugly, and yet you like it here. You feel there is nothing waiting for you in another country. From faraway Shillong, you have made your life in Delhi.

'Then why did he tell me it is going to be okay? It felt like he just knew everything.'

'Experience. Sunil is forty-two. He has gone through a lot, Utpol. He came out after his son was born. It was a messy divorce. His son is now in college and hates him. He understands pain; he just keeps himself busy with his work—some real estate business. He knows time is the best balm.'

Your heart softens. You plan to call Sunil that evening and ask him out for coffee, but you don't get a chance to do that because your neighbours call you in the afternoon to say that your mother has had a stroke. She was found in the bathroom, unconscious. They don't know how long she had been lying there.

5.

On the fourth day at the hospital, you start realising that you haven't shaved, bathed, eaten properly, or slept adequately. Your mother is in a cabin, taken care of by nurses. Though there is an extra bed in the cabin, the attendant has to run around a lot. It is the best hospital in the city. Perhaps the best in South Asia. But it is also very crowded. There are people from the Middle East and America and Africa who come here for surgeries. Every floor has at least two 'May I Help You' desks, but the people sitting there give you unfriendly, unhelpful looks. The elevator is always crowded, and you have to wait for at least ten minutes to get in. This delays things and frustrates everyone, but it is no one's fault because there are four elevators on each floor.

To make matters worse, you go to the men's restroom and discover it is a cruising spot. Men proposition you there. They are all stressed. They all have relatives and loved ones suffering. Once, you find a very handsome young man, who looks inexperienced, staring at you. When you are washing your hands, he comes up and says, 'Good weather, isn't it?' He speaks crisp English.

'I am not interested.' You stand next to the dryer, spreading your hands.

'Do you know dryers have more bacteria? One should always use a tissue.'

'Use of paper napkins contributes to climate change.' You sound grim.

The young boy is cocky. He is so eager to impress. 'Wow, you know stuff. But oceanographers say we are past the due date to make a change.'

Outside, at the food court, you both share a Coke. He tells you his name: Anshul. You ask him to join a dating app. OkCupid. Grindr. Tinder. Don't do this, you tell him. It is not safe. Date. Go out. Take your time. Before leaving, Anshul asks if you would like to share your number. No, sorry, you say, feeling merciless. Later, you just walk around the food court aimlessly. You should have found a spot with that young man. Why did you need to mentor him?

After an hour, you are in the queue at the pharmacy when a firm hand touches your shoulders.

Tara and Sunil.

'Give that prescription to me. You go with Sunil and get some rest.'

'What are you guys . . .' You are so shocked.

Sunil is wearing some nice aftershave. A pink shirt fits his body. The pants are slim fit, and you feel ugly around him. They say that they are here to take care of you. They won't let you run around alone anymore. Sonali is back, Sunil has taken leave from work.

He drives you to a nearby hotel. There is food on the table. Your favourite Chinese dishes from your favourite restaurant in North Delhi: tofu-vegetable soup with chunks of pork, steamed chicken momos, kung pao chicken, and garlic noodles. This means he drove all the way to North Delhi just to go to that restaurant. He stands near the door and asks you what you want to do first: shower or eat or sleep? There are two beds and a couch in the room. He hands you a towel and a soap bar, some moisturiser and shampoo.

'You didn't have to do this . . .'

He chuckles. 'Who says I am doing anything? This was Tara's plan.'

You know he is lying.

'Stop being annoying. At least you can be honest.'

He grins, looking incredibly handsome. You take off your shoes and unbutton your shirt.

You are wearing a white vest. He sits comfortably on the couch, legs folded, and flips a magazine.

You stand in the middle of the room. The sunlight is bright and warm and nice on this winter afternoon. It is the fifteenth floor or something. You can see the whole city. The view is breathtaking.

From here, it is difficult to gauge how polluted Delhi is. Even the haze that covers the city for weeks in the winter looks lovely, like mist over hills. Everything is romantic about this situation, and you realise you are no longer a patch of grass under the brick. You are turning green in slow motion, but you find it hard to believe, and perhaps that's why you almost ruin it.

'Sunil, what do you want from me?'

Shocked, he folds the *Outlook* magazine. 'Are you always so rude? Or is it because you are stressed?'

'I am sorry; everything is confusing.' You sit down on the sofa.

He paces the room.

After a few minutes, you say, 'You are upset with me. I was rude.' You make it sound like a statement, but it is a question.

'Yes, I am, but you are going through a lot now. Right now, it is not about me.' He folds his hands and sits down in front of you on the ottoman. 'Listen, get some rest. You will feel better.'

Immediately, you walk into the hot shower. His patience astonishes you. Your lousy behaviour amazes you.

You let the water flow over your skin. The real world creeps in. You are worried about the long path to recovery after brain surgery. What if the operation is not successful? The doctors aren't giving you hopeful responses. They say they are trying their best and that you shouldn't worry. What does that even mean? The operation will take at least six hours. You want to de-stress, and you start to cry at the thought of the pain your mother must be in. There is a knock on the bathroom door. When you turn off the shower, he asks if you are okay. You are embarrassed. You say you are fine, and he tells you that he is heating up the food in the microwave for you. You take your time, patting yourself dry. When you are outside, he is standing with his back to you, laying the plates on the small coffee table. He has a perfectly round ass.

'Ah, there you are.' He sounds happy. 'I can't wait to eat. Get dressed quickly, and I will then leave you here to take a nap.'

'I want sex.'

He stares at you. He is confused. 'Utpol, I am not trying to trade anything here, you know that, right?' He sounds wounded.

'I know. But you are also not interested in adopting me as your brother, right?'

He just laughs and stares at you, then laughs again and comes close to you. Holding your face in his palms, he laughs again. 'Oh, Utpol, you are . . .'

His lovemaking is gentle and firm, quick and slow; like a massage set to music. He kneads you. It is like being in a spa. You are in a dreamlike state.

The sun is so bright outside. Everything is beautiful: the bed, the sex, the room, the view, and Sunil. You feel valued and important and desired. You feel as if someone has transfused your blood. This new blood is bright and blue and magical. It makes you feel wonderful. The shocks of pleasure are quick, like bolts of lightning, and you are surprised that he knows what he wants: he lets you do what you want to do, puts you in charge. Your face on his face. Your chest on his chest. His right leg spread around your waist and the left one on your shoulder. When you are inside him, he doesn't flinch. He stares at you, straight into your eyes, his face flushed red, and he asks, gasping, do-you-like-it? You moan loudly in joy, though you didn't mean to, and you have never seen him happier.

Yet, in the end, you feel guilty. For seeking pleasure when your mother is in pain. You wet his chest with your tears once again and apologise profusely.

'It is going to be okay,' he says again and again. 'It is going to be okay, Utpol.'

6.

Hospitals are so cold. Even hundreds of smiling nurses, prayer nooks, and cheerful posters can't make it warm.

The doctor says that there is no point in waiting in the cabin and driving yourself crazy for the next six hours. You should get out. Get some air. Relax. And eat, please. You nod and think, they must say this to all the attendants whose loved ones undergo life-threatening surgery; in case, the patient doesn't make it, the attendant can't fall sick. So: 'Go, eat well.' The attendant will have to be stern and strong, have the courage to walk from counter to counter, clearing the dues without mourning. Because there will be no time to grieve. The bed needs to be cleared. Many people are waiting for treatment. If one patient dies, it is just a number for them. Thousands are waiting to get in. Some will make it, and some won't.

'Don't be silly,' Sunil says when you express these fears to him. You sit in the hospital cafeteria and try to have dinner. But you can't eat because your mother hasn't eaten anything all day. You don't eat because, when she was taken inside the operation theatre, you kissed her first on both her cheeks and then her forehead and told her you would be right outside, waiting for her, that you won't leave for a minute. The warm feeling of her skin is still on your skin, and you want to preserve that. If you eat, it will go away. If you don't eat, the warm feeling will stay. The warm feeling is essential. It has to stay, right here, on your lips.

'I will be fine, Babu,' she said.

'Can we go for a walk, please?'

What you like about Sunil is that he doesn't ask any other questions. Outside, there is a deer park. Along the lines of the deer park, there are clubs and bars that only people with deep pockets go to. You like the bars and eateries here. But on a day like this, you would like to go to the park. It is late, there will not be many people strolling. It is supposed to be a safe location. Sunil laughs and says that, when he was a young undergraduate student at Delhi University, he used to come here for quickies because there were no dating apps then, no websites. This was before Yahoo! chat rooms and Planet Romeo, he chuckles. 'I am talking about the mid-nineties, man.'

'You are that old?' you chuckle. This is the first time you are chuckling, smiling, after several days.

He punches you affectionately and gazes at you. You are sitting on a wooden bench. There is a lake in front of you. During the day, the lake looks green with its moss cover. Now it seems like a mirror image of the night sky, but the night sky has stars, and the night pond has no stars, is just black. He kisses you. It is a deep, passionate kiss. At first, you don't kiss him back. You just feel his kiss on your lips, his lips pushing yours open. You take it slow because you have found a new connection with him. You think you have known him forever. More importantly, you feel safe with him. Things are okay when he is around. You believe nothing can go wrong when he is around. The trees rustle. There are monkeys sleeping on the branches. You have never kissed someone in a public place, let alone a deer park bench where old men and women come for morning walks and gay men come to cruise in the evening. But it is late at night now. The park is quiet. You let his tongue roll inside your mouth. You let him suck the air from your lungs because you know that he is going to give back the air he sucks, along with his own oxygen, and you will emerge stronger and brighter. So, you let him. You don't know how long you have been kissing when suddenly someone taps on your shoulder with a stick.

Two policemen are standing there. 'Having fun? It is a cold night.' They laugh loudly, speaking in Hindi.

Sunil's face is frozen. You start to breathe harder.

'Sir-ji . . .' Sunil tries to say something, but a loud 'shut up' silences him.

'We have seen everything,' one of the policemen says.

'Listen, you take what you want and let us go . . . please.'

It is as if he has said something absolutely shocking and offensive. You don't realise what is going on until they start dragging the two of you out of the park.

You scream, 'What is happening?'

One of them slaps you. 'Don't show off your English.'

You figure you have lost the language to speak with Sunil. You don't know how to speak Hindi well. You stammer and stutter. Sunil is from Delhi. He is local. He tries to negotiate, but the policemen keep saying, 'Article 377—you are going in for good.'

They push you into the white patrolling van. You have seen this van so many times in this brutal and lonely city before. In movies, criminals and convicts are shoved into this van, and now you are pushed in just like one of them—a pickpocket or a rapist or a thief. It doesn't take you long to realise what kind of a mess you are in. If you can't get out of this mess in the next few hours, you will have to become one of Tara's clients. The van starts to move through the streets of Delhi, taking you away from the hospital where your mother is. You feel a lump in your throat.

Inside the van, it is dark. There are two benches at the back, running parallel to the glass windows that are beyond the iron grills. Sunil asks them something, but they don't reply. A guard who doesn't have a gun sits on the bench in front of you, next to a young man with scruffy hair, his hands tied with a jute rope. He stares at you. Then he nudges the guard sitting next to him and asks, 'They are both well-dressed. What did they do? They don't look like pickpockets?'

'Hey, shut up,' the guard says, 'Shall I give you one on your cheek?'

'Oh, hahaha, I get it—you guys must have been doing something.' He winks at you. 'To each other?'

'Hey, shut up, motherfucker!' The guard slaps the man.

Outside the station, you ask for a lawyer in your broken Hindi, and this enrages them. 'You want a lawyer? Shall we file the charge sheet? Come, let's go to the police station.'

That much you know. They will arrest you but won't file the charge sheet for hours. Maybe for ten hours. You just wait in the lock-up, but you don't have that much time. It is the fifth hour. The surgery will be over any minute. Your mother will regain consciousness, and she will want to see you, and you should be at the door of the operation theatre because that's what you have promised her. She will panic if you are not there. She will not know whom to call when you are not there. Though Sunil is trying to nego-tiate a payoff, you start crying. At a certain point, Sunil asks them to let you go because 'his mother is in the hospital'.

They laugh at Sunil. 'What will we do with you? You are too old for us.'

Something churns in your stomach, and you puke. One of the policemen hits your head with his hand and scolds you in his broken English,
'Drinking when your mother is dying? No shame?'

Something shifts in you. You start to scream, 'She is not dying, she is
not dying.'

You are not able to control yourself because you think of the many cases
that Tara has told you about. The man who went on a Grindr date and found
a cop posing as his date and had to pay him off to not get thrown in jail. The
young boy in East Delhi who was asked to go down on the cops because he
couldn't pay. Sunil comes and hugs you, and you immediately become quiet.

'Utpol, I will take care of this, trust me. It will be okay,' he says in his
it-will-be-okay voice.

It calms you down. You wipe your eyes.

First he calls Tara, then Sonali, then Tara's colleague who helps run the
NGO. No answer on any of the numbers. You are shaking now. Tara's
phone is never silent. Sunil tells you that it is not on silent mode, it is just
not reachable. She must be in a place where there is poor network.

'Do you think they want money, Sunil?'

'Yes, of course,' he whispers. 'They are not going to touch us. They
know we can give them money.'

I hold the bars of the lock-up and watch the two policemen. They are
normal men. They have wives and children and nephews and sisters and
nieces and old parents. They are called in by haughty principals when their
children don't do homework or get into a fight with the other students.
Before Diwali and the new year, they worry about what to gift their wives.
Every morning, they take the Metro to work because that is all they can
afford with their government jobs.

Sunil is not able to reach anyone. Why is Tara's phone not reachable?
She said she would be home. She would meet him at the hospital in a few
hours. Is she already at the hospital? The reception is terrible there.

Sunil gestures to the arresting officers. They walk up to him.

'Are you going to hold us here like this or talk to me? It has been two hours now. Let us talk in private.'

The policeman has a beard. He hasn't shaved for many days. He looks wild. His red eyes show signs of tiredness. 'Depends on how much you have.'

Sunil looks straight at his eyes, 'How much do you want?'

The man's Adam's apple goes down, and he takes a step back. He looks at the other officer who writes a number in the air with his index finger. 'Fifteen,' he says. 'Not a rupee less, I am telling you.'

'Sure. Open the locks right now and drive both of us to an ATM and then to the hospital.'

'So, your mother is really sick?' He smiles, looking at you. 'Don't do any minding to me, okay?' He attempts English.

Sunil's voice is like a whiplash. 'Don't talk to him. Open the locks now.'

Hospitals are chaotic spaces. People are always running. No one is happy. No one comes here because they are happy—except perhaps people who have babies. The energy here is of stress and anxiety and unhappiness. The kind of unhappiness you were immersed in before Sunil entered your life.

When you finally reach the hospital, Tara is standing near the operation theatre, crying on Sonali's shoulder. She is stressed for some reason. Everything is fine. Nothing is wrong. All is well, you tell yourself, but when you look at Sunil, he is saying that to you, too. These are things you say to each other and to yourself when things are wrong. These are things you tell each other so that you don't fall over the edge. You run towards Tara, and you feel that is the edge of the cliff, and yet you run towards her, breathing quick. Your eyes are smarting. Your nose feels itchy, and you don't feel your legs, and yet you run towards Tara, knowing you may fall.

'Where were you? Where were you?' Tara is angry and upset.

'What happened?'

'Just go in, right now,' Sonali screams. You walk ahead when you hear Tara saying, 'No, we can't let him go in there alone. Someone should escort him.'

You freeze where you are. 'What are you talking about?' You are not able to feel your legs, and your body feels light. If you move, you may fall, or faint, or just die. 'Why can't I go alone? Why does someone need to accompany me? Answer me,' you say, without turning back. Something tells you that you shouldn't look back, and if you look back, all your fears will come true. If you look back, you will know why Tara is crying. You try to take a step ahead, but you just collapse on the floor. 'Why? Why can't I go alone?' You start to weep, you turn back. Tara is weeping. 'Tara, why does someone need to escort me? I know I can make it there alone. I have been looking after her on my own before you guys came to help me. What makes you think I need an escort? Tell me, otherwise I am not going in.'

Tara's cheeks are wet. 'She wanted to see you. She just came back to her senses for a few minutes. The doctor couldn't find you. Your cell was off. So, they called me. She is gone, Utpol. She is gone.'

'What?'

'Utpol, she is gone.' Tara is crying.

She comes forward to hug you, but she is scared to embrace you. She is standing in front of you with her hands outstretched.

'Tara, tell me the truth.'

She doesn't say anything. No one speaks. She looks at Sunil, who kneels down next to you but doesn't try to hug you. He just says, 'Utpol, get up, let's sit somewhere?' You don't say anything. Your mother's voice echoes in your mind. She said she would be fine. What a betrayal. You feel angry. With her, with the world, with the hospital, with everyone. With the policemen. Yes, the policemen. You will burn the police station today. You feel Sunil's hand on your shoulder.

'Don't touch me.' You push him away. 'It is because of you. You are the unlucky one. You seduced me and made me do things that brought this upon me. You made me think about my own happiness and pleasure when she was suffering, and that's why she left.'

Sunil has tears in his eyes. He doesn't say anything. He just stares at you as if he has lost the ability to speak. His forehead creases, and his Adam's apple moves up, moves down, up and down, up and down, up-down-up-down, and you run inside where your mother is waiting for you. They are all liars. She is awake and fine, and she will talk to you. You are sure about that.

7.

It is evening. You decide to walk from the train station because you want things to make sense. Usually, you rent a manual cycle rickshaw from the Delhi Metro station to your colony, but today you decide to walk like your undergraduate days. In ten minutes, you are tired. The footpaths are crowded. Cycle-rickshaw pullers ring their bells to attract your attention. Sometimes they call, 'You name the price, we take you to your destination.'

It is evening, so people are returning from work. They stop at one of the vendors under the large neem trees and buy bread pakoras and tea. The smell of tea boiled for too long floats in the air. The air is damp, so there is no dust.

It is winter. One month has passed, and you have not been able to forgive yourself for taking care of yourself. You suddenly crave tea. The maid must be home. She has an extra set of keys because she comes in around 5 p.m. to make your dinner. It is six and getting dark. The smell of tea boiled with cardamom, ginger, and cinnamon distracts you, but you want your tea in a certain way. She knows more or less how to make tea but often makes it a bit too sweet.

It is alright, you tell yourself, climbing up the stairs to your house. She can place the milk, sugar, and crushed spices in a saucepan with water. You will stand next to it until it boils and add sugar before pouring. But you are so exhausted when you get home that, after giving her the instructions, you walk to your room and surrender to the bed. The bed is arranged.

Sunil must have come in since she doesn't make your bed. You have told him not to come, but he comes in to check on you every day. You don't like his presence in the house, but he is adamant about being in your life. You have not let him touch you in the last month, and he seems to be okay with that. He lets himself in with his extra set of keys when you aren't home and makes your bed, cleans your house, makes your food, even though the maid is there to do all of it. You are resolute about not renewing the relationship. You don't know why. You also don't know why you gave him your extra set of keys. As if you are punishing yourself for your mother's death. As if being with him makes you feel guilty. You sought out pleasure when her brain was cut open. You don't deserve happiness.

'Bhaiyya.' Malti wakes you up. 'Chai. Snacks laun?'

'Nahin.' You shake your head. You take a sip of the tea. 'My god, Malti, it is amazing.'

She hesitates. 'Bhaiyya, I didn't make it. Sunil-ji is here.'

You want to stop drinking, but you don't want to create any drama. You wait for Malti to prepare the meal. Sunil instructs her to cook some dishes. From the bedroom, you hear them. Those are things you like: split pigeon pea dal, banana stem brought from Chittaranjan Park Market One, fried pointed gourd. He asks Tara what you want and shops for those things. He still lives next to Tara's apartment, one hour and forty minutes away from yours, but he makes sure he stops by once a day to check on you.

Sonali and Rudra and your colleagues also take turns to stay back at your home at night so that you aren't alone. You have no feelings for Rudra anymore. You are convinced you don't love anyone.

They think you will do something silly. You have told them you won't hurt yourself. But they don't listen. Your relatives come and go. Even Tara and Sonali disappear for a day or two because they have work, but Sunil comes every day, talks to the guests, arranges things in the house, and instructs Malti so that it is vacuumed and mopped. Ensures that the laundry is done and there is food in the fridge. Yet, you don't speak to him. You avoid him. On certain days, he spends the night on the living room couch.

You step out of your room to place the teacup in the sink. Sunil is in his pyjamas and reading on his iPad. This means he is going to stay back tonight. Malti takes her leave.

'See you tomorrow,' you say.

Then she talks to Sunil. Something. You don't hear. The truth is, Sunil has been handling everything. Even the power and water bills. And yet, you don't speak to him. You look at him and feel sorry. For yourself—since you can't appreciate what you have and have decided to remain unhappy. For him, too—since he is doing everything for a stupid young man who has a skewed and stubborn sense of logic.

He watches you, puts the iPad aside.

You watch Malti go, lock the door, and walk to the living room. 'Sunil, I have said this before. You don't have to do anything for me.'

'Please let me do what I feel like. I will stop coming if you change the locks.'

You sit down on the couch. This is your favourite spot in the living room. Once, when your mother was visiting, it became her favourite spot, too. She sat there every day, and you tried to pull her out of that spot. Both of you fought like kids for it. From there, you have the best view of the room, the best view of the large-screen television. Things make sense from this spot. 'I haven't thrown you out because I just want to be polite.'

'Why are you speaking to me today?'

'I was quite desperate for a cup of tea. And you made it exactly the way I like it.' You are trying to smile. 'My mother would have liked me to thank you. If someone gives you something when you are tired, especially food, it shows that they care.'

Sunil shakes his head and laughs soundlessly. As if he is very hurt. 'Care? That's all? Do you know how much I love you?'

'I know you love me,' you reply in a deadpan tone, like a doctor's voice when they can't save someone.

'And yet you won't speak to me.' Sunil's voice is now agitated, shaking. 'I know I am guilty. I should have known better.' The yellow light through the bamboo lampshade is giving his face a bright hue.

You get up, rush to him, and sit down on the carpet. You are now next to him. He is on the sofa. You are on the rug. This is the closest you have been to him since that night.

'No, Sunil, I am not angry with you, but I am also so angry. I just don't know who I am angry with. When I look at you, I think about that day, I regret going out with you. I regret that we kissed. I can't blame you for any of that, but all I can think about is those two lost hours. I cannot forget it, I just can't. You remind me of that.'

'Why are you telling me all this today?'

'My mother would have liked me to tell you these things. My mother would have told me to tell you that you should move on.'

His eyes are moist. 'I don't do move-ons. I will only move on if you don't love me, if you don't want me. Tell me that categorically, convincingly, and I will stop. But you have never thrown me out of this house. You have eaten silent meals with me. You have exchanged pleasantries with me and never said, don't you dare come tomorrow. All you have said is: you don't have to do this, leave me alone, leave me alone.' His eyes are welling up, and soon, tears roll down. It hurts your head, your chest, your throat. You have never seen him like this. He is like a rock; the kind of rock that forms foundations. He knows everything about everything. He can solve everything. That day, he had solved things at the police station with his wits and composure. You wouldn't have been able to get out for the next two days if he hadn't been there.

'I am sorry,' he whispers and smiles. More tears stream down. 'I am so sorry that I remind you of that night.'

'But it is not your fault.' You look at the large picture of your mother hanging on the wall. It is garlanded. The flowers are fresh. Sunil changes the garland every day.

'Let me,' he chokes as he speaks, 'let me remain present in your life. Tell me what to do. How to love you. And I will. I will love you the way you want me to love you.'

You notice for the first time that the flowers on your mother's photo are khorikajai flowers. They are difficult to find in Delhi. You told Tara once that your mother liked khorikajai flowers because their lovely smell travels a long distance. Also, it keeps a very long time. Sunil has been able to find these flowers in Delhi—in this city of dust and haze and car exhaust and traffic jams. You aren't sure about anything anymore. You aren't sure how much longer you can remain aloof. Give him the silent treatment and keep him at bay. If he brings your mother's favourite flowers for her garland, he deserves to be forgiven, and yet, you can't forgive him, because you haven't forgiven yourself.

So, you just cry. You stare and stare at his face and then crumble in his arms again. You wet his chest again. You present dark, damp spots on his red shirt, but this time, it is not a cry of despair. It is a strange kind of relief and happiness. You know that your mother would have been happy to have met this man.

NAFISA ALI'S LIFE, LOVE, AND FRIENDSHIPS BEFORE AND AFTER THE MUSLIM BAN

Nafisa:

It would be unkind to say that Nafisa's life is boring. 'Staid' would be more appropriate. Nafisa lives alone in a rented apartment. She works at a lab, where she is a scientist. She is new in town. Though she has seen brown people at the grocery stores, she isn't able to guess if they are Bangladeshis or Pakistanis or Sri Lankans. So, she doesn't smile at them. When she gets done with work, her husband, Adil, is still asleep since it is dawn in India. She doesn't call him but leaves a text saying, 'Hey, I am home', so he doesn't wonder upon waking up if she has reached home safely. Adil worries because she doesn't have a car and usually walks to her lab. To take the bus, she has to walk almost a mile to the stop. Adil worries about her a lot, and his irrational worry is the most exciting thing in Nafisa's life. She often complains to Adil that it is dull here. She wishes aloud on the phone for something interesting to happen. Nafisa's wishes will soon come true. There will soon be some unnecessary drama in her life, and she will regret complaining that she was bored with her regular, everyday life.

Nafisa doesn't have the courage to drive in America. She failed the learner's permit test twice, and the women at the local DMV are so rude and so loud, and they ask so many questions and want so many documents that she doesn't want to ever go there again. Despite the boredom and her commute, Nafisa doesn't want to leave this town. She wants to work hard, rise to hold senior positions at the lab, and get fancy grants from wealthy corporations to conduct research on gene editing to cure cancer. She is on a work visa, and when students who are on a student visa meet her, they give her both admiring and envious looks. They always ask, 'My god, how did you get a work visa?' Because I am brilliant, she says in her mind, but aloud she says, 'Oh, I was just lucky.'

She doesn't tell anyone, but she has decided to apply for a green card and eventually become an American citizen. When Adil enters the country, they will make a baby. The baby will go to India with an American passport because he will be born here. It will be a boy. She is sure about that. She is confident about her plans, too. She knows they are foolproof. She will do everything by the book. She will follow all the laws. She will never get a DUI because she doesn't drink, has never been to a bar even to dance with friends. In fact, she has never broken any laws in her life, not even home curfews or love laws that tell us who should date or marry whom. When it was time to date, she found a good Muslim boy, also an Assamese speaker. Born and brought up in Bangalore, he took a keen interest in her when they met in college. She was the only Assamese speaker in the entire college.

Sometimes, she doesn't text Adil after reaching home. He panics and calls her repeatedly, asks her in a hoarse morning voice if she is all right. She watches her phone's screen and realises she perversely enjoys his fear. She likes it. She finds his groggy, broken voice sexy, and though she is okay, she lies and says that she is sad. He talks to her for a while to make her feel better.

As days go by, she creates different kinds of fictitious situations: 'Adil, stay with me please till the bus arrives, I guess I am going to faint. The bus will take me home directly.' Adil says endearing things to her, and she sniffs his fear, which makes her feel safe. After reaching home one day, she lies to him that she has a fever. He asks her to take a Tylenol. 'I just don't have the energy to get up; you just talk to me.' He is watching a movie with his friends. She likes it when he comes out of the theatre for fifteen minutes, encouraging her to go to the kitchen to take a tablet. That night, she sleeps better because she feels secure. The loneliness of the city doesn't bother her. This continues, the only drama in her life, until the real drama happens. We will come to that in a bit.

Nafisa and Annie:

The second most exciting thing in Nafisa's life are the conversations with her neighbour Annie. It's not that she actually likes Annie or enjoys talking to her. But she likes that someone notices her, accosts her, and talks to her. It is a reconfirmation of the fact that Nafisa is a human being, made of flesh and blood, and visible to others. Otherwise, after stepping out of her white lab coat for the day, she doesn't have anyone to talk to. Annie has black hair and wears pretty, printed shorts that Nafisa wants to steal. She wants to wear such shorts one day and sit on Adil's lap at a park and run her finger along the back of his neck. She knows she will feel him growing.

Annie quarrels a lot with her boyfriend, who lives with her. Max calls her a 'bitch' and shouts 'oh, fuck you'. She also screams, 'Fuck you, bastard.' They also have a lot of noisy sex. One night, when she hears a woman's moans, Nafisa worries and wonders if she should call 911 because the characters in *Law & Order* do that. She peeps out from her second-floor apartment. She sees Annie grabbing a portico pillar, Max behind her. He is clutching her stomach, and his chin is digging into her hair. They are having sex outside in the dark, with some light from the streetlamp falling onto them. Nafisa is aroused and ashamed for being excited. Her cheeks grow hot. She could never imagine herself having sex in public.

Annie talks non-stop when she accosts Nafisa. She doesn't have a job, and Nafisa wonders how she can live without responsibilities. Sometimes, Nafisa misses her bus in the morning because Annie doesn't stop talking about her cat that died six months ago, how Max is a veteran, their damaged car that Max rammed into a tree, what their health insurance covers and does not cover because Max has had PTSD since serving in Iran, and her chronic back pain from a car accident in Chicago that also partly injured Max who was driving. Max was already on a disability cheque; after the crash, even she filed for disability. Now they both live on these cheques and his military pension. Nafisa doesn't want to know any of this, but she is patient and polite and listens quietly. Annie often forgets what she told her a few days ago and repeats her stories: the cat that died six months ago, disability cheques, cars ramming into trees, military pension, etc.

Annie likes Indian food. She says that Nafisa's cooking smells good. Nafisa isn't sure if she should invite them to her house for a meal because she isn't sure if she can stand Annie talking on for several hours. The longest she has spent with her is forty-five minutes when Annie perhaps said four hundred thousand words and Nafisa literally said these four words: 'oh', 'really', 'that', and 'okay'.

But Nafisa feels sorry for Annie and especially sorry for Max. She has seen him on his manic days. He goes under the car with a toolbox and comes out after many hours. Occasionally, he crawls out of the car and walks around the parking lot. Nafisa can see all of this from her dining table or if she stands near the fridge. Max is usually bare-bodied, wearing only boxers, when he works on the car. When he bends forward, she can see part of his buttocks—they are really tiny shorts, like the ones that are trendy among undergraduate freshman girls. Nafisa can't even imagine wearing them to bed. Actually, she watches him because she waits for a glimpse of his ass. This is something Nafisa does not acknowledge even to herself. So often, after getting a glimpse of what she has been waiting for, she walks away from the window and murmurs, 'Ya Allah, why did I waste all my time watching Max?' Then she does some housework or cooks.

Nafisa and Adil:

On the days when she doesn't want Adil's attention, she types that she is fine and keeps her phone aside. She doesn't even watch an episode of *Law & Order*. Instead, she sits at the dining table with a cup of tea and observes the parking lot through the window on her right. She buys her tea leaves from India because that is where you get the best Assam tea. Assam tea is stronger and brisker than any other kind of tea she has drank anywhere else. She prefers tea to coffee. But with the electric coffee-maker, coffee-making is so much more convenient that she ends up drinking coffee in the morning. That's why she makes tea after work. The milk is boiled with cardamom and tea leaves over a low flame while she changes and wipes off her make-up with a wet tissue. She likes her teatime. She finds it relaxing and luxurious. But somehow, today, she feels a little sad. She feels lonely. She wants Adil to be with her. She wishes he didn't have to postpone his arrival for another six months to be present for his mother's hysterectomy; Adil is her only son. She reminds herself that she is here as a researcher, and the immigration authorities will issue him a dependent visa. He will look for a job once he arrives, and when he gets a job, he will get a new visa. They will have a baby boy. They will have a house with a large green lawn. They will live happily ever after.

When she thinks about Adil's arrival, her mood changes, and the evening becomes slightly bearable, but her sadness doesn't end. Though everyone in this small town is out running on the streets, she feels as if the whole world is asleep and only she is awake, watching the world like a jobless night owl, with no excitement in her life.

That's going to change soon.

Nafisa and her mother:

Adil thinks Nafisa has a lot of drama in her life already because of her mother. Nafisa left home for further studies in 2002, and since then, she has owned a cell phone to remain in constant contact with her mother. In 2002, it was costly to call between Indian cities, so she would send a missed call. One missed call meant, 'I have reached home safely', and two missed calls meant, 'Please call me back'.

These days, after coming home from her lab, Nafisa sends a text to her mother, too. When she is cooking dinner, she posts photos to her mother via WhatsApp and rings her before sleeping. Her mother never keeps her phone on silent. Nafisa is her only child. Since her retirement, her life revolves around Nafisa who suspects that her mother lives according to US time. They have two clocks in their bedroom: a blue clock set to Atlanta time, a black clock set to Indian Standard Time. She suspects her mother only follows the blue clock. The black clock is made of granite and is more expensive. The blue clock is cheap, bought online. On certain nights in India, Nafisa's mother wakes up and starts calling her if she hasn't texted, 'I am home'. If she is with colleagues, especially during late nights, her mother will call her every two hours to check in. It has started to become embarrassing, but she hasn't been able to convey this to her mother.

It is Friday. Late night here and late morning in India. Nafisa is standing in front of a restaurant on the east side of town. Though it is just 10 p.m., it feels as if it is one in the morning in this small city. Her friends have already left. They offered her rides, but she was sure she would find an Uber. She hasn't yet. They are all forty minutes away. Uber is also on surge, and they are charging her sixty dollars for a ride that should cost her only fifteen. Soon, her phone dies. Eventually, when Nafisa reaches home in a local cab booked by the waiter, her phone comes back to life. It screams with a ton of notifications, both from Adil and her mother. Her father receives her call. Nafisa learns that her mother had a panic attack after Nafisa's phone died. Her mother threw up and then sat under the water tap, letting the cold water drench her whole body. When her mother hears Nafisa's voice, she regains normalcy.

Adil complains that Nafisa's mother called him around fifty times during the hour when Nafisa's phone wasn't reachable. She wanted Adil to call his friend in Michigan to ask if he could reach Nafisa.

'It doesn't make sense, so dramatic.'

Nafisa understands why Adil is irritated. But she doesn't take it well when he calls her mother dramatic. Her mother has always been like this, since childhood. 'Adil, you don't know what it means to grow up during an insurgency,' she says in a cold, steely voice. Adil doesn't argue, but Nafisa feels terrible about her mother. She vows to keep her phone on and orders a power bank.

Nafisa and Max:

After talking to her parents and Adil, she is exhausted. She pours herself some peppermint tea, adds a few drops of honey, turns off the light, and sits in a chair. The fridge is behind her. The window on her right has the blinds pulled up. It is shut, but the sound of cars on the road is still loud in her room. Because of the streetlamps, she can see an occasional loner—usually a student—hurrying home.

She thinks how different her life would have been without the insurgency. If her childhood hadn't been mottled with news of bomb blasts and skirmishes and rapes and gun battles between the security forces and rebels. She thinks about her mother and forgives her because, sitting here, watching the cars in the parking lot and staring at the damaged bonnet of Annie and Max's car, she isn't able to imagine what it must have meant for her mother to send her to school all the way across the city every day, knowing that her child may not return home if violence erupted. The fear of death was so normal, but it didn't mean that the experience was bearable. That's why she had forced Nafisa to leave the state. And now she is far away from home in a small, predominantly white town where the cab drivers are more than surprised to learn that she is a scientist: 'Wow, you must be a brilliant lady if they hired you all the way from India.' She knows that it is not a compliment.

She stands up and looks at the road and slides the window open. The sound of cars becomes louder. A gust of cold wind. The smell of crushed leaves. She is bored. Nothing happens in her life. Standing there, she imagines herself at fifty. She will be an old woman who has done nothing adventurous, who has done everything by the book, every expected thing, and never something surprising. Does she want to get into trouble? No, she doesn't, but she wants to do something exciting. Suddenly, she recalls the forty-minute car ride from the restaurant to her house when her phone was dead. Those blissful forty minutes! Watching the quiet night outside, she felt free, something she has not felt in a very long time. She felt single! Yes, Nafisa gasps, stamping one of her legs—she felt single and free and liberated. And now, with the phone in her hand again, after making those calls, telling her mother she is okay, talking to Adil and promising him that she will carry a power bank the next time, she feels trapped. I wish I was single—not answerable to anyone's worries. She gasps, surprised she feels this way.

It is 12 a.m., and that's why she is startled when she hears Max. 'Hey, how are you?' She is almost scared to death. 'What a lovely day! So bright!'

Bright? She wonders if he is drunk. What is he doing out in the parking lot this late, in his shorts, in this cold? The streetlight bathes him. She notices that his body is glistening with sweat.

'Yes,' she says, a little creeped out.

'What a lovely day!' he repeats and crawls under the car. She notices a beam of flashlight under it.

This car will never be repaired.

In the chair, she falls asleep and dreams that Max is roaming around the parking lot with a machine gun. The lot is mottled with drops of blood. She wakes up, startled and sweaty. She turns off the heating. This was a bad decision; she should have never moved to a new country without Adil. What was she thinking? She had never lived alone. Never had to shop alone. Never even went to a conference alone—the two of them used to pitch joint abstracts and were on the same panels. She should have waited for other opportunities. What is she doing in this small town in Georgia all by herself? She wants to weep. There is a lump in her throat. Everything is quiet and slow. So quiet that she can hear the wind. She feels as if she is walking on a country road, alone for miles, lost.

The phone beeps.

She looks at her phone screen and finds a message from Adil. 'Received the documents from your university that we need for the visa. Bhal lagise.'

She is calm. She isn't walking on a lonely country road anymore. She is home. With her cup of tea, her legs on the ottoman, her body reclined in a comfortable wooden chair that has a lovely cushion. Everything will be okay when she wakes up startled, when he is lying next to her. She will ask him to switch off the air conditioner or the ceiling fan. There will be someone to take care of her.

Annie and Max are fighting, and she can hear bits and pieces.

'Fuck you.' Annie's voice.

'Oh, fuck you—you are responsible for all my misery.' Max's voice is louder.

'Ya, right, just blame it on me. I am the one who . . . right?' Annie's voice is louder now.

'All you do is complain . . . just fucking complain . . . leave me alone!'

'You fucking leave me alone.'

'You leave me alone.'

Nafisa and Annie:

The next day, Adil schedules his visa interview and books his tickets to join Nafisa in two months. Perhaps that is why she accepts Annie's suggestion to go to the Indian restaurant in town.

On the way, Nafisa wonders if she should tell her about Max repairing the car at 12 a.m. but restrains herself. She has a strange feeling about it, as if talking about it will ruin Annie's mood. Annie is often upset about her dead cat. She often cribs about her insurance. Today, she is cribbing less. Nafisa is surprised that there are no signs of last night's fight on Annie's face.

They walk downtown because it is just one and a half miles away. And the weather is good. Annie asks if Nafisa would mind if she smoked. Nafisa says she wouldn't, though she will. Annie talks about her love of Indian food, the better options available in Chicago, where she was born. Nafisa nods quietly: partly because Annie talks so much that she can't contribute at all and partly because she just wants Annie to speak. She is also tired by the walk; this is a hilly city. She just wants to think about Adil's arrival, his smooth visa process, his mother's recovery from her hysterectomy. At the restaurant, she doesn't tell Annie that, like most Indian eateries in America—even this place named 'The Taj Mahal Restaurant'—the spice levels in the buffet are really low to cater to an American taste, and it is run by a family from Pakistan's Punjab. She thinks it would burst Annie's bubble because she wants to have 'authentic' Indian food. Nafisa wants to tell her that India is such a large country that there is no singular authenticity; for everything you say about India or claim as authentic, the absolute opposite is also true in some corner of the country.

The two of them pick a table near the large window. They can see the university buildings from here. In India, Nafisa studied at a private university that never made it to national rankings. It was a small campus of just three acres. Now, the size of this campus, the massive lawns, the beautiful gothic buildings just amaze her. She still has so many things to explore: the huge botanical gardens that have many themed trails—the white trail, purple trail, yellow trail, blue trail. She wants to walk with Adil on the purple trail, wearing purple printed shorts like Annie. She will find a lonely spot. She will sit on his lap, slowly hardening him. She will rub his neck with her thumb and flick his earlobes with her tongue when no one is looking. Will she be able to do that? She wants to, but in public? The thought makes her tense. Her cheeks are warming up.

Annie and Nafisa sit down to eat after serving themselves from the buffet. Annie says that she is sorry if the noise her boyfriend makes bothers Nafisa at night.

'Oh . . .' It takes a while for it to sink in. Nafisa realises that Annie means the late-night quarrels. As if calling them 'noise' makes them less disconcerting. Nafisa lies, 'No, I have heard no noise.'

'That old man who lives alone, he complained about us to the cops, you know.'

'The one who drives a black SUV?'

'Yes, that's right,' Annie says, chewing the chicken tandoori. 'Asshole. He is horrible. I mean, if you have a problem with us, why don't you fucking talk to us?'

Then she bitches about that neighbour for the next fifteen minutes: how he called the cops on them twice, and how it is true that they fight a lot, how people should come and tell them to keep it down instead of calling the cops. Nafisa thinks it doesn't take much common sense to understand that you shouldn't fight late into the night when your neighbours are sleeping. She just says, 'That's terrible.'

Annie is agitated now. Her face is red. She says the food is spicy, even though there is only a hint of chilli powder in it.

Nafisa says, 'Yeah, it is spicy.' She finds the food here quite bland, actually. She wants to add chilli flakes, but this is not Italian or Mexican food. The chilli has to be nicely fried and mixed with the dish, not sprinkled on top at the end. She also doesn't want Annie to know that she lied.

'I get it, you know, I get that we fight a lot,' Annie continues. 'It used to happen a lot in Chicago, too, when we were living there. But we fight a lot less now. We are working hard on our relationship. Our therapist says we should get a dog, but I don't like pit bulls, and Max wants nothing but a pit bull. We were just fighting about that, and he started blaming me for everything terrible in our life. This was last night. Then that old fart complained, and the sheriff sent a cop to our house. Max was so wound up, he left the house and started to repair the car. He does that when he is stressed and during his manic phase. Did I tell you he is bipolar?'

'Oh, I see. I'm sorry.'

'It's okay. At least things are taken care of. Do you want something sweet?'

'No, I am good. How about you?'

'I would love that mango pudding.'

When Annie leaves to get the pudding, Nafisa reclines on the chair and wonders what she is doing spending time with her. She doesn't like Annie, but she is happy that someone asks her if she would like to get out during the weekend for lunch. She wants to tell Annie that they are really noisy, that Max should start wearing longer shorts, and that they shouldn't fuck outdoors, but Nafisa decides otherwise. She dislikes herself for clinging on to this semblance of a friendship with a person she would never be caught dead with if she were in India. She is confused about finding Annie and Max's dysfunctional, scattered, and morbid life strangely fascinating. Like a toxic, addictive family soap opera, she wants to continue watching them. Breaking her friendship with Annie would mean switching the TV off. She wants this train wreck of a soap opera to continue. Besides, everything will be okay when Adil is here. She won't be hanging out with weird people she doesn't like.

When Annie returns, she isn't holding a bowl of mango pudding. She is in tears. She asks Nafisa if she is done. 'We have to go, don't worry. I paid already.'

Nafisa follows her. Words such as 'wait', 'what', 'what happened' tumble out of her mouth as she tries to catch up. She has eaten a bit too much. She feels bloated. On the sidewalk, she is not able to walk as fast as Annie. The speeding cars make her nervous. The sun feels hotter.

'You go ahead, I will take a cab.'

But Annie just turns to her and weeps, 'I am sorry, I am sorry. I have to be fast, but no, I won't leave you here. Actually, we should take a cab; I forgot that we walked here.'

'What happened? Tell me what happened? Can I help?'

'No, you can't. I have feared this. You know, he has, Max . . . Max has these manic phases when he goes out in his car. Oh god, I should have never left the car home. Today, when I wanted to bring the car, he said we could just take the bus. I didn't know he was planning to go out. And it is a bit embarrassing to drive around in a car with a broken bonnet.'

Nafisa is breathing fast now. 'Is he okay? Just tell me what happened.'

'He's been arrested because he hit another car, and this is the second time he has done this. We don't have the money for a fine or higher insurance.'

Nafisa begs her to calm down, 'Annie, I got this. You just wait. I will take you home.'

The cab driver tries to chat with them but gets only monosyllabic replies. His car smells of lavender, and it is really cool inside.

Annie looks out of the window. She has calmed down now but has a forlorn, lost look, her lips pursed. She whispers, 'Nafisa, I am really sorry I panicked. But you know, with so many men getting killed by cops, you can't always be calm when Max gets into trouble. He is not a danger to society, but he drives very badly when he is in his manic phase. I don't know how many more hundreds of dollars this will cost.'

As they are about to reach their apartment complex, they see the cops. Annie starts looking for their lawyer's number. She reclines on the backseat and murmurs, 'You know, I love him, but I am not his therapist. I become his therapist when he dumps his shit on me. Sometimes, I just wish I was single.'

Nafisa feels a weight on her heart. As if someone has pressed her chest gently—that's the kind of pressure: of reassurance, of companionship. Sometimes, I just wish I was single.

She wants to ask why Annie won't get out of this relationship and seek out her independence, but she isn't sure if that is a good question. Nafisa doesn't say a word. She enjoys the reassuring weight on her chest, puts one of her hands on Annie's shoulder, and pats it. She understands.

The parking lot has three police cars. Their blue lights blink, and since the sky is cloudy, it feels like evening though it is just 2 p.m. Nafisa hurries inside and watches. Max is sitting inside one of the cars, head bowed. His hands are cuffed. She feels scared. Scenes from *Law & Order* come to mind. She has read reports of men killed by cops, especially Black men. She is worried about Max though he is not Black. Her heart starts to beat hard. He will be fine, she tells herself, patting her chest. He will be okay, he is a veteran, and she presses her chest with her hand and pulls down the blind.

Later that night, Annie texts her that he is now out. The judge ordered his release.

She texts back, 'You take care of yourself.'

'Thanks, babe. Hugs,' Annie replies.

Nafisa pauses for a few minutes, staring at her phone before writing, 'Sometimes, even I wish I was just single.'

'I fucking get it!!' Annie writes back.

Nafisa and Adil:

Nafisa wakes up late on the morning after the department conference. Even at 10.30 a.m., she is still sleepy because she attended a dinner party where she talked to other scientists. Some of her colleagues danced and asked her to join, but Nafisa isn't comfortable dancing, and she has never danced with any man but Adil. However, unlike other occasions, she stayed till late, enjoying the party.

Now, she decides to go to the lab later than usual. The day before was a good day but busy and exhausting. To meet so many people who cared about the same things she does is reassuring, and now she feels she isn't the only person spending her days overwhelmed by the sound of test tubes tinkling. She isn't the only one awake when the rest of the world is sleeping.

She is shocked to find several missed call notifications from Adil. What happened? Is his mother okay? Did her mother call him again because she was unable to reach Nafisa? Missed calls from India are bearers of anxiety. Her heart sinks, and instead of calling Adil, she calls her mother. After all these years, that is her biggest nightmare: that she will be sleeping through one of her parents' deaths, and by the time she returns, it will be too late—a garlanded photo waiting for her, with a candle burning in front of it.

Her mother sounds normal. She is watching her daily soap, and her father is reading the paper and commenting on the increasingly terrible world, 'We are all going to die due to climate change. Imagine, what will happen when two hundred million Bangladeshis move to India in search of living spaces?'

'Let's talk about it later,' she says.

Adil had called her for something specific. It must have been important—he called several times.

When she rings Adil, he is sad. 'I don't have good news. I should have travelled with you, Nafi. Now, I don't know how long I will be stuck here.'

'What are you saying? Is your mother okay?'

Yes, his mother is recovering well, and after he leaves, one of his cousins will stay with her. That cousin is responsible. She will cook and clean and talk to his mother and go shopping with her—nothing to worry about. She couldn't come earlier because she was writing her exams. 'I am surprised you don't know what is happening. Don't you read the news?' he says.

She is still groggy. 'I had a late night, and I woke up just now. What happened? You know I don't have cable. I don't like it.'

Adil sighs, 'I may have to cancel my tickets.'

'What?'

'I don't know if I will get a refund since I am cancelling just a month before my flight. I don't even have so much money to waste, that is if I have to cancel my tickets.'

'But why?' she screams and sits up on the bed, his sentence working like a shot of caffeine. The mattress bounces under her body. 'Why do you have to cancel your tickets?'

Adil pauses.

'Why do you care?' he asks. 'You were sleeping till late. You were at a party, must have been dancing with someone random. You are having fun, and here I am, roaming around in Delhi, hiring a cab, haggling with auto-rickshaw drivers, standing in line in front of the American embassy. Do you know how long the queue is?'

'Adil—have you gone mad? Why don't you tell me what's wrong?'

'Do you really care? You are having fun. You just don't care.'

This has never happened since she moved to America—Adil has thrown tantrums to get her attention, but he has never been this unreasonable. And it is not that he accuses her of having fun while he is toiling away in India to get all the paperwork done and taking care of his mother. He's accusing her of dancing at a party. It is so unexpected, so out of the blue, that she loses her mind. She wants to scream 'fuck you' like Max or Annie, but she bites her tongue. 'Adil, you are getting me panicked now. You need to tell me what happened.'

She walks to her dining table, where she rarely dines. It is her workstation. It is the same place from where she watches people hurrying towards their destinations, the parking lot, Max getting arrested, and just the road lying there like the back of a black snake when the world is asleep.

'It is Trump. You know my flight is via Saudi Arabia. I mean, I am not the citizen of a Muslim country, we are Indians, but you never know with this government—we can't forget our names, our religion, can we? He has banned travellers from some Muslim countries. I don't know what to do. Maybe divert the flight via Frankfurt?'

Nafisa tries to sound calm as she reads the headlines on Google News. 'We don't even go to the masjid, Adil. I mean, we are both atheists. I inject chemo into fat rats in the laboratory.' She tries to sound funny, but he isn't reassured. 'You still have forty days, Adil. You are going to Delhi next week for your visa interview.' But she realises that she doesn't believe her own words. For the first time in her life, she feels very Muslim. She wishes her name were Katy or Catherine or Bipasha.

'Well, what if they reject my visa at the interview?'

She ignores the fears. 'By then, something will happen. All these countries that run luxury airlines are not going to just sit and take this when
people start to cancel their bookings, you know?' Nafisa says he will be fine,
that she will book him a ticket via Frankfurt or Amsterdam or a direct flight
from Bombay to New York, but she disconnects the phone as soon as possible. Her laptop is covered with drops of tears. She feels alone again. That
feeling of being the only one awake when the world is sleeping wraps her
like a dark shawl over her face. She knows that even if she books him a new
flight, it would be such a dent on the little savings she has made since coming here that they will need to shop from cheap stores and eat lousy food for
a long while. She has never lived like that before, from paycheque to
paycheque.

Nafisa and Ian:

'Come to the house party,' Annie tells her that afternoon. 'We have sausages, sandwiches, pulled pork.'

'I am not sure,' Nafisa replies. 'I will let you know.'

She is sure she will not go to the party. She doesn't want to meet Annie
and Max's friends. She is worried they will be noisy and crazy and public
fuckers.

But in the evening, there is no peace at home. She sits with a glass of
water on the loveseat and tries to clear her mind because Adil's messages
and calls are driving her crazy. She can hear the music from the party.
Come anytime, if you change your mind, Annie had told her. She is still
upset with Adil. How could he accuse her of dancing with 'someone random'? Of course, he meant 'some random man', not 'someone random'. He
has a dirty mind. Something has changed in a single night between them.

She wants to shout at him, but she hasn't because he is going through a hard time now.

Adil has been sending her every news item he can find about the Muslim ban. She wants to think about something other than the Muslim ban. She wants him to stop, but she knows if she says that, he will be hurt. She doesn't want to respond to his political commentary, which is now veering towards alarmism. Back in India, he hasn't slept all night, which means she hasn't been able to sleep after lunch, or watch *Law & Order*, or relax and have some me-time. Is this the drama and excitement she has been waiting for to disrupt her boring life in America?

'Adil, what would be the worst case?' she asked him an hour ago. 'I might have to go back. Find a job at the Indian Institute of Sciences. Don't panic. Go to sleep.'

But he doesn't go to sleep. After about half an hour, he starts sending her conspiracy theories: they are now going to eject people with green cards from the country, people with green cards won't be allowed to enter, new Muslim citizens will be disenfranchised, Chinese Americans will be sent to internment camps, and naturalised Indians will lose their citizenship. This is followed by a barrage of misinformed advice: take your passport with you every day, keep copies, don't go outside the city without your passport, reach out to your department head, and ask for help.

She starts to get a headache. Nafisa tells him, 'I am going to take a nap now; you, also get some sleep.' She turns her phone to silent mode. As she sits on the chair, sipping some water, she makes a decision.

Annie told her that she had invited a lot of people to the party. But there are only three other faces there: a handsome man who says this is his last month in the city, a red-haired woman, and her younger boyfriend with a long beard reaching his chest. They look happy together. He gets her beer after beer as she talks to Annie, spends most of his time with Max, and occasionally checks if the red-haired woman needs more beer. They are smoking outside on the portico full of trash and dried leaves and pots that perhaps had herbs in them once upon a time. They are getting quite drunk. Max is tipsy, and when Annie asks him to be careful, he screams at her, 'Shut up, you don't get to tell me . . .'

'Hahaha, he always shouts at me when he gets drunk,' Annie laughs loudly, cutting off his sentence. He leaves, in search of more beer.

But Nafisa notices that Annie's eyes are misty. She forces a smile and asks everyone to eat more before adding, 'I get so anxious when he drinks. My anxiety . . .'

Annie is taking out mugs and plates from the dishwasher. Nafisa walks up to her and asks, 'Do you need help?'

'No, babe,' she says. The word 'babe' makes her uncomfortable. She doesn't understand if only lovers use it for lovers or friends also use it for each other in America. 'I'm fine, are you having fun?'

'Yes, it is great. I am so happy to be here,' she says, though she doesn't mean it. She wants to get out as soon as possible. Did she make a mistake by not bringing her phone? What if Adil is having a panic attack? Should she run and get her phone? But she had told him that she would be napping. She is worried that if he finds out she's at a party, he will get offended: I am frightened to death here, and you are dancing at another party? As she has been recently reminded, he is very capable of saying horrible things when he is stressed. Once, when they were working in Chennai, he found out that his mother had taken ill. He rushed to her house at the other end of the city, rushed her to Apollo Hospital, and returned late. Nafisa's parents were visiting from Assam at the time. Her mother suggested that, since he would be late, they should cook a proper meal and set it aside for him. She cooked fish tenga and chicken korma, but he returned earlier. With a smile on her face, her mother laid the table for him. He was in a bad mood, Nafisa noticed, and she followed him to the bathroom where he broke a bottle of perfume. 'My mother is in the emergency room, and you guys have cooked up a feast! Is this for her funeral?'

No, no, she can't tell Adil that she is at a party. But she decides to stay for a while, be a good neighbour. Her presence is perhaps perfunctory, but she wants some distractions.

'I hope things have settled down now, I mean, with Max.' She hesitates to say that, but she has been thinking about the arrest and wants to check.

'Oh, thank you for asking.' Annie shuts the dishwasher and heaves a sigh of relief. 'It is just a matter of time, you know. We will get our settlement and then move out of this place. This city is too small actually, and it stresses him out. He needs a lawn to work on, a tree's shade, some space to plant stuff—get busy, you know? We will be fine after that. We won't have to live from cheque to cheque.'

'I didn't know about this settlement, but it sounds good.' Nafisa isn't sure if she should probe further, but she has already pressed the button.

Annie loves talking about her life and her problems. 'I told you that we had an accident in Chicago, remember? It was a drunk teenage girl who just rammed her large SUV into our car. I have severe cervical pain because of that. It is unbearable, and I can't work for long hours at a desk. I can't accept any job or go to school. I do hope I will complete my coursework someday, but I am not sure if I will be able to meet all the challenges. So, we are really looking forward to this settlement.'

'I am so sorry. This sounds like a lot!' Nafisa gasps. 'So, when will this settlement reach you?'

'Oh, in a couple years.' She shrugs. 'Maybe more. But our lawyer is trying his best to get it done soon. He will get a cut, so it is also in his best interest. So, if we get this settlement, we will put in part of the money for a house in the suburbs. The houses are cheap there, not so expensive like in Atlanta. You will have to come to the housewarming.'

'That would be so nice.' Nafisa is genuinely excited for the two of them. 'There is much to look forward to.' The music is loud. People are talking. The little apartment is noisy, and she feels warm.

Annie lowers her voice. 'And until the settlement money reaches us, I have to live with him in this house. I can't even break up with him. It is one of the terms, because we filed the lawsuit together as one party, as a couple.'

Nafisa scans the table for food. Annie has now laid the plates and cutlery. There is only meat: chicken burgers, sausages, pork chops, and some mac and cheese. She doesn't like any of this. She grabs more corn chips and salsa, sits in a corner, and debates if she should eat the chicken burger. She likes pork, but only when it is cooked with garam masala.

Ian, the handsome guy, says it is a pity they have never spoken to each other despite living in the same building. She has never noticed him before. She agrees, but honestly, she doesn't care. He says that he has been busy 'mending a relationship'. He has found an excellent job in Oklahoma, and his boyfriend works as a waiter in a local restaurant but is not willing to move. It is such a good job that his boyfriend will not have to work; he could go back to school and concentrate on writing more poetry; he wants to be a poet. But his boyfriend doesn't want to live in Oklahoma. Nafisa asks why, and Ian pauses at her question. He is surprised. He says, he doesn't want to go; there is no reason. There is no reason—Nafisa is astonished. Her surprise seems to rub Ian the wrong way. He just doesn't want to go, he repeats. Then he gets defensive, saying that his boyfriend—who is now his ex-boyfriend— does not have to have the right reason for not wanting to go.

'So, you guys just broke up?' Nafisa asks, sipping more pink lemonade. She can't believe she is drinking pink lemonade—she used to make fun of it.

'Yeah, he was just not willing, and he wouldn't do long-distance. I haven't even moved yet. The last few months have been horrible, but soon I will be in Oklahoma, and maybe all this will be behind me.'

She is quiet. Nafisa feels sad for him and then realises it is rude in this country to not explicitly say that she is sorry. 'I am sorry,' she says and finds it funny that there is a nasal sound in her tone. She is becoming American, or, as Adil would joke in Hindi, Umrican. Umrican indeed: nasal sounds, pink lemonade that tastes just like regular greenish lemonade, drinking coffee in the morning, and watching *Law & Order*.

'Thank you, I really appreciate it,' Ian says.

At home, she thinks about the word 'mend'. Ian used that phrase, 'mending a relationship'. She sits with her cup of tea, watches the world outside, and thinks, what an apt word: 'mending'. Everyone is mending something. Max is mending his car, Annie is mending their relationship until the money comes, Oklahoma-bound Ian has spent the last few months mending his relationship only to fail, and Trump has ensured that a lot of mending would be required once he steps down from the throne—the throne itself would need mending. She is surprised to find herself thinking about Trump. Everyone seems to have an opinion about him. Even if she wants to avoid him, she can't.

And what about herself? Will Adil turn up? How will his visa interview go? What if his visa is rejected? Will he come here and mend the boring life that forces her to have strange friends? What if the money never reaches Annie and Max or takes too long to reach them? Will they go on living together? What kind of living is this—to sail a ship with holes and continually drain out excess water with a mug to stop it from sinking?

She thinks about the Muslim travel ban again. She doesn't want to read the news. It is stressing her out. Her iMessage and WhatsApp is already full of updates from Adil, all about the travel ban. She is annoyed with him for staying up and unburdening his stress on her. She is the one who is alone here. She is the one who has failed her learner's permit test. She is the one who is stranded after dinner. She is the one who is at a house party with people she has nothing in common with. She is going to become an old lady who has done nothing extraordinary or adventurous in her life. She sees herself with Adil when she is fifty: with grown-up kids and lots of test tubes.

It is late.

She paces her balcony and thinks about Ian. She admires how quickly he can move from mending to moving on. She wants to be like him, but she also knows that she would immediately fail; she is convinced she's just not built that way. Ian is so handsome. Great thighs, amazing shiny hair, taut neck, broad chest. She feels sad that he is gay, as if she would have plans for him if he were straight.

The thought makes her laugh. She is surprised. She says aloud, 'I didn't even drink at Annie's home, why am I laughing like this?' There is some peppy music coming from Annie's. Perhaps everyone is dancing. Annie had asked her to stay. 'We will have some girl time, it will be fun. The boys are going to be so sloshed,' a slightly drunk Annie had told her, holding her hand firmly.

Nafisa steps out of her house and pushes Annie and Max's main door open. Everyone is dancing. Max has taken off his shirt and is shaking his ass. He is wearing those shorts that reveal his butt when he bends—and he is bending a lot. Annie repeatedly slaps his ass and shouts, shake that, and he shakes it harder, aiming it at Annie like a dog wiggling its butt to get attention.

'Oh my god, is the music too loud?' Annie asks when she notices Nafisa, slightly worried. She is slurring her speech. The red-haired lady with the younger boyfriend continues to dance. Max is completely oblivious.

'No, I like the music so much that I thought I should come back. Am I weird?' Nafisa screams at the top of her voice, giggling.

'You are being fab, babe!'

'Come on, wohoooo,' Ian says.

Annie slaps Max's ass. He shakes it harder.

'I thought you wanted some girl time!' Nafisa steps in, a bit hesitant. Annie drags her to the middle of the room—the dance floor for the night. Max follows them, shaking, and says something to Ian.

'You don't like me here?' Ian is screaming. 'Don't worry, I am a straight woman. Who said I am a man?'

'I love it that you are here! You are my new best friend!'

Nafisa takes some tequila and starts laughing. 'Shake it, Max,' she screams. 'Shake it!'

'Max,' Ian screams.

Max inches up to Ian and starts to twerk, rubbing himself against Ian's crotch.

'Are you getting aroused?' Annie asks Ian. 'My boyfriend is hot.'

'You are so sloshed,' Ian says, placing his hands on his crotch. 'And Max is naughty today.'

Nafisa starts to shake her body a little and click her fingers—like she sees in the movies. She looks at Annie and grins, throws a flying kiss to Ian, and walks up to Max and slaps his ass. Annie cheers her on.

'The world is asleep, and we are dancing,' Nafisa screams and then bursts out laughing. She has always wanted to have fun like this, but after meeting Adil, those opportunities never came.

'We are fucking dancing,' Annie says, shaking her body vigorously. And suddenly, Nafisa likes her. She feels an ache in her heart and wants to be Annie's good friend. She holds Ian by the waist, faces him, still dancing, brings her mouth closer to his face, and screams: DO NOT GO TO FUCKING OKLAHOMA.

ABOUT THE AUTHOR

ARUNI KASHYAP is a writer and translator. He is the author of the novels *The House with a Thousand Stories* (Viking, 2013, English) and *Noikhon Etiya Duroit* (Panchajanya Prakashan, 2019, Assamese). He won the Charles Wallace India Trust Scholarship for Creative Writing, University of Edinburgh, in 2009, and his poetry collection, *There Is No Good Time for Bad News*, was a finalist for the 2018 Marsh Hawk Press Poetry Prize and the Four Way Books Levis Prize 2018. His short stories, poems, and essays have appeared or are forthcoming in various journals and anthologies, including *The Oxford Anthology of Writings from North-East India*, *The Kenyon Review*, *The New York Times*, *The Guardian*, *The Hindu*, *Evergreen Review*, and other publications. He is an associate professor of English and creative writing and the director of the Creative Writing Program at the University of Georgia, Athens.

From the Latin *gaudium*, meaning "joy," Gaudy Boy publishes books that delight readers with the various powers of art. The name is taken from the poem "Gaudy Turnout," by Singaporean poet Arthur Yap, about his time abroad in Leeds, the United Kingdom. Similarly inspired by such diasporic wanderings and migrations, Gaudy Boy brings literary works by authors of Asian heritage to the attention of an American audience and beyond. Established in 2018 as the imprint of the New York City–based literary nonprofit Singapore Unbound, we publish poetry, fiction, and literary nonfiction.

Visit our website at www.singaporeunbound.org/gaudyboy.

Winners of the Gaudy Boy Poetry Book Prize

Interrogation Records: Poems
by Jeddie Sophronius

Waking Up to the Pattern Left by a Snail Overnight: Poems
by Jim Pascual Agustin

Time Regime: Poems
by Jhani Randhawa

Object Permanence: Poems
by Nica Bengzon

Play for Time: Poems
by Paula Mendoza

Autobiography of Horse: A Poem
by Jenifer Sang Eun Park

The Experiment of the Tropics: Poems
by Lawrence Lacambra Ypil

Fiction and Nonfiction

Lovelier, Lonelier: A Novel
by Daryl Qilin Yam

Bengal Hound: A Novel
by Rahad Abir

The Infinite Library and Other Stories
by Victor Fernando R. Ocampo

The Sweetest Fruits: A Novel
by Monique Truong

And the Walls Come Crumbling Down
by Tania De Rozario

The Foley Artist: Stories
by Ricco Villanueva Siasoco

Malay Sketches: Stories
by Alfian Sa'at

Other Series

New Singapore Poetries
edited by Marylyn Tan and Jee Leong Koh

Suspect: Volume 1, Year 1
edited by Jee Leong Koh

From Gaudy Boy Translates

Picking off new shoots will not stop the spring:
Witness Poems and Essays from Burma/Myanmar 1988–2021
edited by Ko Ko Thett and Brian Haman

Amanat: Women's Writing from Kazakhstan
edited by Zaure Batayeva and Shelley Fairweather-Vega

Ulirát: Best Contemporary Stories in Translation from the Philippines
edited by Tilde Acuña, John Bengan, Daryll Delgado, Amado Anthony G.
Mendoza III, and Kristine Ong Muslim

Books by our other imprint, Bench Press

Sample and Loop: A Simple History of Singaporeans in America
by Jee Leong Koh

Snow at 5 PM: Translations of an Insignificant Japanese Poet
by Jee Leong Koh

Seven Studies for a Self-Portrait: Poems
by Jee Leong Koh

Equal to the Earth: Poems
by Jee Leong Koh

Lightly in the Good of Day: Poems
by Bob Hart

Try to Have Your Writing Make Sense:
The Quintessential PFFA Anthology: Poems
edited by Donna Smith and Howard Miller